ATTACK: THE BEST FORM OF DEFENCE

G. F. CUSACK

Attack: The Best Form of Defence

By

G. F. Cusack

First published in the US 2020

ISBN: 978-0-473-53814-9

Cover Design by Sarah Oliver
www.saraoliverdesign.com

CONTENTS

1
———

UNDER ATTACK

14 February 2206

B arry was out of his comfort zone. He had served the Kompaniya for seven years now, but this was the first time he had left his homeland.

Ever since the Kompaniya had gained its new leader, Barry and his comrades had been preparing for this mission. On their previous missions, they had always held the upper hand with superior firepower when they faced the masses.

Of course, there had been a minor chance of injury given most of their previous missions had involved facing down lightly armed civilians. Sometimes the enemy was unarmed but, either way, the result was more of a massacre than a battle.

When Barry had got off the boat in this strange land, he'd felt wary, almost scared. Having mind-readers as his comrades didn't help. They were supposed to be there to protect him, to mask his thoughts of destruction. In reality, their presence made him feel that he was continually being second-guessed.

The security people at the docks had their own telepaths. He imagined them searching his mind and learning what he intended. He tried not to focus on being a bomb technician whose sole reason for visiting this sanctuary was to dismember and kill people.

Barry didn't have a conscience when it came to killing; he remembered his first kill like it was yesterday. At the age of only sixteen, he had shot a rebel in the distance. The boy had been running away from their raid and Barry took him down at a distance of 800 metres. The rest of the squad had shouted and screamed and called him "Hotshot". That nickname had stuck with him for several years, even after he became a bomb technician.

After the vehicle crash had damaged his shoulder, he could still kill someone over a short distance, but his days of taking out a long-range target were over. Their society had little use for damaged soldiers, but he was fortunate that his bosses respected him for his previous shooting successes. His comrades in the truck had not been as lucky – all but one had died in the crash.

Malik, the driver, had survived but lost his leg and had supposedly been given a medical discharge to spend time with his family. The fact that since then Malik had never contacted Barry or any other members of the squad fuelled suspicions that injured soldiers also ended up in the liquidation plants.

If news spread that they cast injured soldiers off like everybody else, that could ruin discipline in the military. The illusion of wounded soldiers being cared for was part of the story that the Kompaniya fostered and keeping someone like Barry on helped perpetuate that story.

On this mission, Barry's task was simple. He had four bombs to place around the capital of this sanctuary. One each for the power and water plants, while the second two devices were destined for the political infrastructure. The goal was to kill or maim as many of the leaders as possible and cause maximum disruption.

It had been a challenge to smuggle the devices into the sanctuary without detection. This sanctuary was littered with as many spies as there were back home. When life was worthless and resources were scarce, loyalties were easily bought. People would inform on their own family members for even a small reward.

The smallest of suspicions could inspire people to raise the alarm to either the authorities or criminals. The returns from black marketers or local hoods were higher than from anybody in any form of government, hence they were usually informed first. This made smuggling difficult, whatever the size of the cargo.

Conventional wisdom would dictate that transporting explosives in parts would be safer than smuggling in fully assembled ones. Barry had decided that shipping components separately increased the chances of a component being discovered, resulting in no bombs at all. He chose instead to ship each bomb separately, but with all the ingredients for each bomb together. Of the ten bombs that they had started with, only four had made it. Barry had calculated that he needed a minimum of three bombs for the mission and felt lucky that four of the ten had survived.

Shortly after getting off the boat, Barry had recovered the four bombs, and in only a brief time they were ready to go. Other team members had placed the two bombs at the utility plants with no problems. As expected, the security here at the government buildings was a lot tighter.

Anya and Gabe were with him to stop anyone from scanning his mind and also to act as lookouts. He had already placed one of the bombs in the capital buildings. Now, with only one left, he was ecstatic – he was achieving the impossible. Just this last bomb and he would succeed.

Barry had always included some escape strategy as part of his planning, but no matter what the odds, he had no choice but to attempt the assignment. Deploying on this mission had guaranteed that his family would receive extra rations and supplies. Failing to deploy would leave his family to the same fate as any other criminals or traitors to the realm. They would end up in the gel plants.

If he could just set the timer of this last bomb, he had a chance to escape, clear and free.

As he walked towards the broad set of stairs, something seemed off. They'd been briefed that security would be heightened upstairs, but it shouldn't have been this strong downstairs in the open area. More security people were around here than he'd expected; they were checking bags. You even had to pass a security barrier before you could reach the stairs.

Looking at Anya and Gabe, he saw something strained about both their faces. These were not two people who were always smiling, but they generally seemed happy with their lot and usually acted with a superiority that came with their powers. At this moment, though, they didn't look superior at all.

They appeared to be in pain, each holding their hands to the sides of their head. This reaction was drawing attention: several men in grey overalls were heading towards them.

Suddenly Barry had his own problems. A young man and a woman had joined a hand with each other and each was pointing their free hand at him. More armed men in grey overalls were moving, but this time towards Barry. They reminded him of the security guards in his sanctuary, but these people had different triangle emblems on their shoulders.

Barry was unsure what to do. Should he abort the mission? He noticed grey-clad men were now positioned at every door, stopping anyone from exiting. He had a decision to make. There was a good chance that one of the many armed men would shoot him. If they took him alive, they would no doubt torture him.

Everyone gave in to torture eventually, and if they considered him a traitor, his family would likely suffer. Barry wasn't a coward, but he wanted to get out of this alive if he could, and he had lots of thoughts running through his mind all at once.

With his hand on the timer in his pocket, he had to make a quick decision. The timer had a button that automatically set it to go off after twenty seconds. This was a fail-safe for bombers who thought they were likely to be captured.

Barry decided that he had no choice; he placed the parcel on the floor and pressed the timer as he walked away with the rest of the crowd. He intended to get as far away from the bomb as possible before it went off.

"Oy you, pick up that parcel!" someone called out to him.

Deciding that his priority was to get away from the bomb, Barry continued to walk away, without turning around.

"Stop, stop," he heard. Barry didn't slow his pace. He hoped that he would be far enough away to be safe. Perhaps the blast would be enough of a distraction to allow him to escape.

"Stop, stop, or I'll shoot." Perhaps the voice was talking to Gabe or Anya? He knew in his heart that it wasn't.

Suddenly there was a loud bang, and Barry felt a searing pain in his left shoulder. The impact made his body spin around. As he crumpled to the ground, he could see someone holding a pistol in both hands and pointing it at him. The man had a startled expression on his face, and it was evident that he was the shooter.

Before Barry had time to hit the ground, there was a blinding flash, and the ear-shattering bang was the last sound that he heard before an explosion engulfed him.

2

———

SOMETHING IS COMING

13 January 2206

It had been three years since Zap and Flo had discovered that they were siblings. Since she had grown her hair back to its natural blonde colour, they looked even more alike. They were always busy, but they still scheduled to meet up at least once a week for breakfast.

Zap now had a key role in maintaining the infrastructure, and his technical skills were used continuously to support the sanctuary.

Flo was becoming an influential young woman. The skills she had developed in the last few years and her blossoming friendship with her mentor Frank had made her a key asset in the new government.

Hubert had initially seemed the obvious choice to lead the council and had been the interim leader for the first few months after the rebellion. Frank had succeeded him and was now the leader in this new regime.

There was no animosity between Frank and Hubert.

Like the rest of the council, Hubert had other responsibilities. As Frank was an outsider without those responsibilities, it was decided he was the better option.

He was ideally suited to deal with the influx of immigrants from the rest of the sanctuary, drawing on his knowledge of the outside world and his experience of managing a resistance stronghold. His logistics experience also allowed him to control the distribution of resources in all parts of the country.

The initial goal was to wean people off the gel packs. Here he could use what he had learnt from building an infrastructure with the farm that had supported his stronghold, which was invaluable in organising supply and distribution of resource assets and workforces for these assets.

Although the twins only talked in person once a week, they spoke in their heads all the time. Over the last few weeks, it had become increasingly clear to them that something was coming. Their mind talks had felt strange; it was as though something was mentally blocking them.

For the last two years, the twins had developed a programme to identify other telepaths and to collect them into a centre for education and training. That the school was some distance from the capital had provided valuable thinking space. It had reaped some promising results. They were creating a haven for these scared, inexperienced people with strange abilities. Although Zap and Flo were only twenty-one, most of the other students were in their teens or younger and just developing their skills. This support helped to develop their skills far more than they would if they had continued to be treated as freaks. Older students such as

Iris and Foster (who were both older than the twins) were more advanced with their abilities and able to support them.

Starting the day with a communal breakfast was a way of helping the students bond and providing some company for the younger, quieter students. With Zap often absent to deal with his other duties, Flo made a point of being there for every breakfast.

The students sat on the benches with food in front of them. Flo waited until the last one had finished chewing. A hush fell over the crowd as though she had waved a magic wand.

When Flo first came to the sanctuary, she had been a quiet, reserved, inexperienced girl, but over the last three years, she had grown into a young woman who was confident and prepared to address sizeable groups.

"I want us all to try an experiment," she said, projecting her voice to the back of the hall.

"Over the last year, we've been practising sending our thoughts out to look for other people with skills like us. Recently we've all sensed some blockages; this seems to be affecting everybody, some more than others. What I want us to do is to combine all of our forces."

She looked around the room of over forty young people. Although they might not seem much to an outsider, Flo knew that their combined powers, once developed, could be formidable.

"You'll see in front of the room an apple on a pillar. For those of you that can't see the apple clearly, I have projected the image onto the screens around the room. We will focus our energy to see if the interference is natural or if we can break through it."

Looking around the room, she could see that they

were all listening carefully. Even the children who sometimes fidgeted were hanging off her every word.

"I want you to focus on the apple. Think of nothing else but the apple. Look at the image and burn that image into your minds. Now continue to think of the apple while you close your eyes. Focus on this apple; it's delicious and crispy. Imagine biting into it and hearing the crunch in your mind. Now I want you to imagine offering that apple to a hungry person. It doesn't matter who you are giving it to, keep focusing on the apple. I will count to three, and I want you all to think of the words *have an apple*. Keep this in your mind; don't say it out loud.

"Here we go: one, two, three, *have an apple*. One, two, three, *have an apple*. One, two, three, *have an apple*. Keep thinking this same thought, send it out to the world. One, two, three, *have an apple*. One, two, three, *have an apple*. One, two, three, *have an apple*."

It didn't take long for Flo to feel *have an apple* in her head, with all of those people together sending out that same simple message. She hadn't known if it would work, but the concentrated thoughts seemed to produce results. The previous fuzziness was clearing as the message seemed to go out like a beacon.

Everybody was thinking in unison here. The mental message could be going out to anyone who had the ability to receive it – she didn't know who. Remembering how scared she'd been when she discovered she had powers, she had chosen this simple message as the safest option. Being offered some food would hopefully not seem threatening to any new telepaths out there.

Her only concern had been that if somebody living

in a less-developed part of the sanctuary received the message, they might not know what an apple was. She hoped that even if they didn't know what an apple was, they'd pick up on the positive vibrations the students were sending out.

Once they had repeated the words fifty times, it became laser-focused, going out as one single message. Recently the interference had been stopping clear communications and she could feel the interference disappearing.

Suddenly the voices of her students weren't the only voices she could hear. Some strange unfamiliar voices were coming back, with no mention of the word *apple*.

She'd heard the thoughts of people who spoke in unfamiliar languages before. Although thoughts don't have an accent or a language, she felt there was something different about these.

She heard only one message: *stop, stop, stop*. Not sure if she and the other students were hurting anyone, she told everyone to stop.

"Clear your minds now, just think of what you want for lunch. Don't try to coordinate your thoughts and stop sending messages. Everyone relax – start talking between each other with your mouths, not your minds."

Flo was unsure where the messages had come from, but she had felt several voices, as though they were concentrated in groups but not as focused as her students.

"I want you all to take a pencil and paper out of your bags and, if you heard or felt anything, write it on the piece of paper. Even if you only heard the word *apple*, write it down. If you heard the same voice or unfamiliar voices, I need to know what they were saying.

Try to describe how it felt – was the sound like a soft piece of paper falling to the ground, or was it heavy like a stone? Write as much as you want. Just think of what you heard. Don't worry about sending out any more messages today. I want to make your lives as comfortable as possible, which is why I waited until after breakfast to carry out this exercise. Lately something has been making our conversations harder, so I want you to write for at least ten minutes before we wrap up the exercise."

The room suddenly became a mass of activity. Some people were talking between themselves, while others were sitting quietly alone, but everyone was scribbling frantically with a pencil and paper.

Flo wished Zap had been here, but they needed him at the drone farm. She waited until she had gathered all the pieces of paper before contacting him.

"How did the exercise go? I heard them offering me an apple even here."

"Yes," Flo said. "And isn't it great how I can hear your thoughts clearly? It appears we have been listening to a radio with static for the last few months and someone has just removed the static. It feels like how we used to talk in our heads."

"What did you hear?" Zap asked.

"Aside from the voices of our students and us, offering apples, I heard other voices, but I couldn't understand what they were saying. They seemed strange. It was like when someone talks with a thick accent. I couldn't work it out exactly, but it felt like the voices were saying *stop* or something similar. As though they were trying to block us."

Zap's brain was naturally wired for problem-solving. "It sounds like those voices have been the thing blocking us and our combined signal overcame their message by brute strength. We had so much concentrated power that they weren't able to block us."

Flo was becoming concerned. "I don't think they were just asking us to stop offering them apples. There was no desperation in their tone. It didn't feel to me like it was hurting them. I felt like they were somehow bad."

"Yes," said Zap, "and they have been doing this for some time. Why would someone want to stop us communicating?"

He tried to keep his thoughts in his conversation with his sister between them so they wouldn't worry the students. While he and Flo blocked their minds, they could not be sure that no student was strong enough to read them. All they could hope was that these students were too young to have the full mature strength.

Some older students with more developed skills had been helping at the ports. They'd been reading the minds of people entering the sanctuary and scanning for anyone whose thoughts showed ill intent.

Over the last couple of weeks, these students had reported issues. At sporadic times of the day, they found themselves unable to read almost everyone's minds.

"Do you think somebody else is working with telepaths?" Flo asked.

"Well, our peace with the two other kingdoms is very tentative," Zap said rather off-handedly. "And of course the leaders of the three kingdoms almost destroyed the world in the first place – no doubt some descendants of the ruling classes have inherited their greed and competitiveness."

Zap paused for a moment and then had a lightbulb moment. "We need to report this now."

"Calm down."

"You don't understand; they could smuggle anything in or out of the sanctuary! Resources are so precious, and we are only just starting to get beyond survival mode. We have only recently weaned most of our people off the gel packs."

"There is no reason to attack us," Flo protested. "We aren't a risk to the other sanctuaries."

"That's because you don't think like them. As far as you're concerned, the fundamental thing is for our people and the people around us to be happy, to have shelter and enough to eat. You don't see everybody as a threat."

"Not everyone is a threat!" Flo retorted.

"Unfortunately, some people out there, no matter how much they have, always want more. When we first came to the sanctuary, you saw that the elite had everything that they needed but still tried to extort money from people who were starving."

"Why are people like this?"

"Some people see themselves as better than everybody else, and they think everyone else is just there to serve them. To cater to their every whim."

"So, you think we could be in danger?"

"I'm not sure, but we can't chance it," Zap said. "We need to speak to Pepper and Frank and some of the others. We need to warn the council."

"I've still got to read all the notes from the students, but lots of them heard other people and there was some mention of weapons."

"Although we've learnt so much in the last three years, the council trump our experience with all the years they've seen between them. We need to present the problem to them as soon as possible because, whatever is happening, somebody's doing something wrong."

"When will you be back here?"

"I'm due there tomorrow, but I can call in on Pepper at the capital first. I think this is something we need to discuss in person."

"Okay, I'll put together all the students' notes and call you tonight." Talking through thoughts over a distance for a long time was draining, so they used radios and telephones for more extended conversations.

"I'll call Pepper in a minute and arrange a meeting for tomorrow."

It made sense to tell Pepper first, so he could inform Frank and the other members of the council that something strange was happening. They trusted his instincts and knew that he'd take whatever actions he deemed necessary.

"Be careful, Zap, I can feel something is coming, and it feels dangerous."

"I'll be fine. Do your best to keep the students calm and remember that you have people like Foster and Iris to share some of the load."

"I will do. Speak later."

3

FLO WARNS THE COUNCIL

15 January 2206

Flo was fortunate that, as someone without an official government position, she still had ready access to council members. Pepper usually acted as an intermediary, although for an issue this important, she'd been tempted to go straight to Frank.

Ever since they had overthrown Brand, Flo had spent a lot of time with both of them. Frank called on her regularly, but they had no current meeting scheduled. Flo had thought this information was time-sensitive and couldn't wait for Frank's call. Zap had made the initial contact, but now it was left to her to attend this meeting.

When Flo approached Pepper, she wasn't surprised to see Eric, but she was glad that things between them weren't as awkward nowadays.

After Pepper had freed her from her kidnappers and returned her to the Farm, Eric had fostered feelings for her that she couldn't reciprocate. She saw him as a brother while he saw her as a potential girlfriend.

In reality, it wasn't that she'd given him mixed signals but that he did not understand about relationships. With no family to show him acceptable behaviour, he had hooked onto Flo and it was hard for him to understand boundaries. Luckily Pepper had taken him under his wing, which was surprising given that on their first meeting, it had seemed like Eric would kill Pepper.

Pepper had liaised with Frank to convene a full council meeting. Getting all the council members together at short notice wasn't so easy. Each council member had their own schedule. Eleven o'clock at night was the only time that they could all get together and, for some, this meant giving up not just free time but sleep.

On a regular night, the council chambers were silent, but tonight the sound of boots clicking on the tiles echoed around the halls. The combined number of all the council members' security details made more people than you would find in the entire government buildings at this hour. Pepper had scheduled more security personnel tonight than on a regular day shift. The times and days of full council meetings were a closely guarded secret as they created an opportunity for anyone to take out the governing body in one fell swoop. Pepper was taking no chances.

He had reason to be worried. Although the overthrow of the previous regime had been relatively popular within this sanctuary, some seeds of unrest remained. People had been brainwashed for most of their lives that Brand and his cronies had been their benefactors, supposedly the only people who could feed them.

Added to that, the expected attacks from the other sanctuaries hadn't happened yet, but that was no guarantee that they wouldn't.

Once everyone had taken their seats around the table, Frank entered and took his position at its head. "I appreciate that you all have busy schedules. I have convened this meeting urgently because I think this is a pressing issue that can't wait." After checking that everyone was paying attention, he continued. "Flo, you are the principal reason that we have convened this meeting, so tell the council of your concerns."

For a moment, Flo was hesitant. On the one hand, over the last three years, she had proved her worth and gained the respect of these important elders. Yet she was still relatively young and felt nervous standing in front of them.

"I also want to thank everyone for making the time for this meeting," she began. "I wouldn't be asking for your time if I didn't think this was important. Our Telepath School has been making significant progress. We have a steady flow of recruits and are providing a safe place for young people who suddenly discover their abilities. In return, the students are contributing to the security within the capital and even helping Mr Hook to stop the smuggling before goods leave the ports."

Hook nodded his agreement and smiled at Flo.

Acknowledging Hook's smile, Flo felt her confidence growing. "I don't know the exact nature of the threat, so I'm just going to lay out what I do know. Over the last few months, Zap and I have been gathering reports from the other telepaths. They have reported times and places where they have felt their abilities are fuzzy. At times when they could normally monitor others' thoughts, they had blank spots. This inability to read minds was not limited to particular telepaths and was primarily focused around the ports. Both Zap and I visited the ports and also experienced these phenomena, and they have been increasing in intensity lately."

"Have you brought us here just because some children are having headaches?" Hubert blurted out.

"No." Flo immediately cut him off. She had expected some pushback and had checked with Zap for a more technical explanation she could use as a rebuttal. "This is not just headaches. Think of telepathic waves like radio waves. When you get static while you're talking on a radio, it is usually something wrong with the radio device or the signal. In the same way, a disruption in telepathic waves means nothing is wrong with me or other the telepaths – something is wrong with the signal. These disruptions occurred at different times and locations, but always in the ports after a boat had arrived."

Flo took a breath in case more interruptions followed, but it seemed they would now allow her to finish. "Two days ago we conducted a trial at the school. The combined force of all of our telepaths broke through the fuzziness. We identified that a telepathic force is being transmitted to block our signals. Although we're unsure of its source, the signal stopped for a while when we all transmitted together. As the council has years more experience in the world than me, I welcome your questions or guidance on this matter."

Pepper spoke up. "When Flo brought this matter to me, I had lots of questions, and I doubt if I could have described the situation as eloquently as she just has. The crux of the matter is we have someone that doesn't want us to know what they're doing, and they're using telepaths to cover their activities. The reports from the school show this is happening in several areas of the capital. As the issue has also occurred at the port, we have to assume that they don't want us to know what they're bringing in. If this were just a case of criminal activity, I would hope that someone around this table could set our minds at rest. Before the uprising, together you controlled most of the crime in the capital."

Hook joined in. "We are still stopping things being smuggled in; there has been no noticeable increase or decrease in the number of shipments we have intercepted. If someone is trying to use this technique to smuggle, it is either ineffective, or they're smuggling something out of the ordinary. If it's something out of the ordinary, they are doing it successfully."

"What would you class as out of the ordinary?" Frank asked.

Hook paused pensively before replying. "Most of the things that are smuggled in are luxuries or items that can be quickly turned into a profit. One thing that I'd class as out of the ordinary is weapons. People have had little cause for weapons since we took over the capital. As Pepper said, those of us who are gathered around this table used to be responsible for most of the criminal activity, so if we don't know what's entering the sanctuary, should that concern us?"

"Spider, you've got the biggest network of spies in the capital. Have they heard anything?" Frank asked.

Spider was hesitant. "Even though people have more food than they had before we took over, most of them would turn on their own family if they thought it would benefit them. This makes it difficult for anyone to carry out covert activities. There have been rumours of unknown people being seen in the capital. Most areas are tribal, so outsiders stand out; however, nothing has been substantiated. My sources are not aware of an enormous amount of resources suddenly appearing in the capital. If something valuable is being smuggled, I would expect it to be either personnel or weapons. If I am right, those resources would be primarily used for an attack on the infrastructure or an attack on us. That would only benefit someone outside the sanctuary."

"I agree that this sounds like an external threat," Frank said. "When I attended the last joint sanctuary summit, everything seemed peaceful, but that means nothing. Just like Brand, the leaders of the other two sanctuaries have reached their position through murder and power grabs – they are psychopaths. If they're mounting an attack on us, it might not be for rational reasons. These kinds of people tend to be paranoid, and fear can make people do strange things."

"Have there been any issues with the food supplies?" Pepper suddenly asked.

"No," Hubert said. "No issues, in fact if anything it's been quieter than normal. A feeling of unrest continues in certain quarters, but food theft seems to have declined since we took over. The last couple of years have been peaceful."

"CT," Frank said, "now that your supply chain is focused less on luxury items than on everyday types of supplies, have you heard anything?"

"You'd be surprised," CT replied. "Even though we don't still have the elites screaming for luxuries, there is always somebody who wants a drink or some other delicacy for a special occasion, or just to make them feel special. Trade has been good, but sadly I have had no one new buying enormous quantities of luxuries that they could use as rewards or bribes."

Listening to the conversation so far, Karla had been thinking of her experience from the last few years of enhancing security and helping train personnel. Her practices had led to better choices of new soldiers, in place of the psychopaths who had been sought for the old training techniques. She spoke up now. "It worries me that with all our networks of spies and contacts, something seems to have slipped under the radar. Someone has created an invisible mental shield to transport something into the capital. From what Flo has said, this smuggling could have been going on for some time. If the intensity of the signal is increasing, we need to assume an attack is imminent."

"If they wait a couple of months, they can attack while I'm away at the summit," Frank said. "Perhaps that's what they're waiting for. We've always felt that the summits were safe because there's no point taking out a sanctuary leader if the infrastructure at home will just replace them. Perhaps they intend to take out our council leaders at the same time that they kill me at the summit. So how can we combat this psychic blocking? I am open to suggestions."

The room was quiet as everyone mulled over their options. Then Pepper said, "I've been discussing this with Flo today. In the time since the discovery experiment, she has been working on some psychic countermeasures. Flo, you can explain better."

"As far as I can gather, the prime task is that we need

to come up with techniques to overcome the psychic block. We have started training and have managed some successes that will hopefully improve in the coming weeks," Flo said.

"That's fine," Karla snapped. "But we don't know if we've got a few weeks. We need to do something now. How about we get every psychic out of the school and send each of them out to investigate what's going on?"

"No! We can't do that." Coming from a small woman, Flo's voice suddenly sounded a lot louder. "A lot of our telepaths are young and untrained – they've come a long way, but if we disperse them too widely, they will not be effective. Even if we deploy them now, we need to keep them in pairs. That will mean we can't send them to so many places but, if our current techniques are being blocked, there is no point in sending them out untrained."

"What do you suggest then?" Karla asked in a calmer tone.

"We need to train them as fast as possible. Zap and I already have trainees working on the techniques. As soon as we have more trained telepaths, I will let you have them. We will work around the clock, but this mental work is very tiring. There is no point in deploying someone untrained if they are ineffective. It's different from having an armed deterrent who is visible but may not need to do anything; our telepaths must be able to actively scan with their brains and then break through blocks when they find them. They are not machines; they're vulnerable, inexperienced people."

"We accept your expertise here," said Karla, "but how many people can you spare now?"

Flo felt a bit disheartened as she made her next

statement. "In reality, we have only six people ready to go. They have only been training for twenty-four hours, but they are our strongest telepaths and so they have picked it up faster. Ideally, I would like them to sharpen their skills so they can train the rest. If you need someone ready now, we could deploy four of them, while the other two stay at the school training other recruits."

"Four people in a city this size?" Spider said. "What use is that?"

"Hold on," Frank said. "I agree that the number is not ideal, but before this meeting, we were facing an unknown threat with no means of addressing it. Actually, before this meeting, we didn't even know we were under attack and now we are working on a deterrent. In this situation, the question is, where do we deploy the first two pairs of telepaths?"

"The gel plants," Hubert said. "If the enemy takes out the gel plants, we'll have rioting in the streets. We've weaned many people off of the human gel packs, but we are still close to a tipping point. If we lose the plant production and we can't feed the masses, this council will be in control of nothing."

Before Frank could reply, Karla cut in, "Infrastructure can be rebuilt, but without leaders, this sanctuary would descend into chaos. A true target would be the government buildings. If they cut off the head of the snake (I mean us), the sanctuary would be easy pickings for an outside force. It would only have to wait for most of our people to kill each other, and then it could swoop in and take whatever it wanted. I suggest that we make this the last council meeting for a while and post one pair of telepaths in this building. At the same time, we create a rotation so that only two council members at a time are in session here."

"I agree with having two telepaths in this building at a time, but I think the water plant and power plant are more critical than the gel plants," Frank replied. "The reason we are weaning people off gel packs is that we now have larger supplies of fresh water thanks to the desalination plant and with a ready supply of water we don't need gel packs to keep people hydrated. We need a strategy, but until we train more telepaths, I'm going to rule that we base two of them in this building and two at the water plant."

"I took the liberty of bringing the first team of telepaths with me tonight and they're downstairs, providing security," Flo said. "Pepper agreed that this meeting could be the target the attackers were hoping for, so it made sense to put them in place immediately."

Although a few eyebrows were raised around the room, no one in the council complained about Flo making their safety a priority.

"I had to make the call for the security tonight," Pepper said. "I apologise that I couldn't brief you all before, but time was of the essence."

"Time is of the essence," Frank said. "Before we leave here tonight, I want a list of priority targets in the sanctuary so that we can decide on the right places to deploy more telepaths as they become available."

"Although I'd normally be fighting for resources for the ports," Hook said, "I think it's safe to say that anything being smuggled in through the ports is already here. We might be too late to block further shipments, but I'll increase my patrols and speak to my contacts at the ports to see if we can identify anybody who has been acting suspiciously lately."

Spider responded, "As soon as we leave this meeting, I will wake up every spy in the city. Nobody will sleep until I get some information." It was clear that Spider was not happy. As the council member responsible for intelligence gathering, he saw this breach as a slight on him. Whether or not someone had sneaked something past him, this situation placed suspicion on him.

It was a matter of personal pride for him now that he had become a valued member of the council. This was a marked change from the past when the other council members had been wary of him, knowing that his allegiances were always with himself first. Since the council had come to power, the actions that he divulged to it had always served the greater good, and the suspicions of his fellow council members had largely disappeared. Spider wanted to keep it that way.

"We are all now agreed that there is a threat," Frank said, bringing everyone back to the task. "We must assume that it involves weapons and personnel in some form. I suggest we approach this matter on two fronts. First, Flo will train up the telepaths as fast as possible and liaise with Karla on that. Second, each council member will reach out to their contacts to glean any information they can. I want you all to keep me up to speed but also to talk to each other and get things done fast.

"As Pepper is not a full council member, he will be the liaison between council members and will report to me at least once a day. The council's security is paramount, so don't take unnecessary risks and try not to meet up in person too often. If something is urgent, you can pick up the radio or the phone, but work under the assumption that any attack may target our communications as well."

Ever practical, Pepper asked, "Can you ensure that they fuel the backup power supplies at the fighting pits? As that's the secondary capital command post, we'd better be prepared if we are under threat."

After Karla motioned across the room to Miyamoto, her bodyguard nodded back in agreement. "I will sort it," she said.

"Hubert," Frank said, "I want you to treat your compound as a third rallying point. If things go badly here, you might be hosting the remnants of the council."

"Agreed," Hubert said.

"Before everyone leaves this room, have all the conversations you need to take action tonight. We have no idea how big the threat is, but let's prepare for the worst and hopefully avoid chaos. Unless anyone still has anything to say to all of us together, split off into your groups and let's get this done."

As Frank looked at each council member in turn, they nodded their support.

"One last thing," Frank said. "I was put in this leadership position by you. That doesn't mean that I am better than you. You are all highly capable, so unless you need me to help out with any particular task, work together to get this done."

With the council breaking off into smaller groups, Hook headed straight to Karla. "I need some extra security to escort the generators and other emergency supplies." Not one for small talk, he went immediately into his requirements.

Karla nodded. While listening to Hook, she was

walking towards Flo, who was already talking with Pepper.

In another part of the room, CT was deep in conversation with Spider and Hubert.

Frank felt like he was at a loose end. He wanted to circulate and be seen as available, but he was not critical to what was currently happening.

Thinking about why Zap hadn't accompanied Flo, he realised Zap was no doubt already working with the telepaths to advance their training. Another reason for Zap's absence would be that there were enough targets here without adding one more of the capital's critical assets.

When Karla reached Flo and Pepper, she addressed Flo directly. "I want to send you some more security for the school. You have just become our number one weapon and hence a high-value target."

Flo recognised the need to protect the school when their focus needed to be on building telepath skills in scanning for threats. She was, however, cautious. "Please advise your people that a lot of the students are young. They've had frightening experiences with security forces in the past."

"I know just who to send. Before you leave this meeting, they'll be here and will escort you back to the school," Karla replied. "How soon will you have more trained telepaths for me?"

"I can leave you Iris and Foster right now. They're waiting downstairs, and I briefed them to pack a bag and be prepared not to return to the school for the foreseeable future. They're two of my best students, so they were quick to train."

"What about the others you've got trained?" Karla asked.

Flo turned to Hook. "I have the two telepaths you need for the water plant security, and that leaves me two final students to train the rest. It may take a couple of days to get everyone else close to the same level with using the same techniques. Our main focus is a technique to break through the mental blocks. When the telepaths are deployed, they'll still be scanning thoughts, but once they detect a fuzzy area, they will concentrate solely on sending mind spikes. To do that, they will have their eyes closed, making them vulnerable, so they do need to have armed guards escorting them."

"That's what we're here for," Karla replied. "My people will protect your people as our own. Without them, we have no idea what the threat is or how to defend against it."

"Can I have somebody for the convoys?" Hook asked.

"We can supply some armed guards, but assuming that the attackers have limited assets, it would make sense for them to go for static targets. I'd suggest you use your two trained telepaths for the plants and leave the convoys without telepath cover," said Karla.

"Yes," said Flo. "I intend to withdraw all the other telepaths back to the school for training. The sooner we get them trained, the better protection we can provide."

Hook and Karla exchanged glances at this revelation but, before either of them could speak, Pepper cut in, "That's non-negotiable. Tomorrow morning the telepaths currently deployed will return to the school, but not before Hook receives two telepaths trained in the new techniques. Where do you want the two to report?"

"Send them to the water plant and I'll meet them there at nine," Hook answered.

"Please look after them. They're still young, and they're not soldiers," Flo added.

"That's okay," Hook replied. "I'll make sure they have warm beds and armed protection, and they'll be fed and watered."

Smiling, Flo whispered, "Thank you."

In another corner of the room, Hubert was holding court. "We all know that some of our contacts are also spies for Spider." Before Spider could object, Hubert raised his hand. "Don't worry, I'm not going to ask you to divulge who they are. It just seems to make more sense to avoid overlaps. I propose that you tell CT and me what areas you want to focus on, and we'll cover the rest."

Although he nodded, as always Spider was wary of divulging any of his sources. Like the others, he had sources in the ports and other areas of the supply chains, but he was the only person with sources in the Badlands.

"Leave the Badlands to me," Spider said. "You deal with everywhere else but leave the Badlands to me."

He got no argument from Hubert or CT. The Badlands – the roughest areas of the capital – were inhabited by the lowest of the low, and neither of them had any resources or interest there.

"Do you need any help with security escorts?" Hubert asked.

"No," Spider replied. "I have my own resources, and if I take any outsiders in, they will only make it more dangerous for everyone."

Like most of the other council members, Hubert

had heard the rumours that Spider had been born in the Badlands.

The rumours made no mention of his father, but it was said that his mother had been brutally raped and Spider was the outcome of the rape.

Spider wasn't as tall or muscle-bound as some of the others, such as Pepper. He had survived all of these years on his wits. He'd got where he was in his own way and, if he said he didn't need any support, Hubert knew this wasn't just vanity speaking.

As Frank completed one last circuit of the room, he caught the eye of each of the council members in turn and gave a brief wave but didn't interrupt anyone. He'd decided to leave as there was no point in sticking around and getting in people's way.

Although they all still served their own aims, one of the reasons they had taken part in the uprising was that they cared about other people. While everybody in his council could work autonomously, they also knew that working together was the best way to serve their own needs.

Frank motioned for Pepper before he left the room. "I want you to provide me with daily updates of what is going on. You are my eyes and ears in this group. Whatever time of day or night it is, if you need to contact me, wake me."

"If you ever leave your office, I'll wake you up in our hovel," Pepper said, smiling.

"Our hovel!" Frank retorted. They'd been flatmates for over a year, initially as an all-boys' club, and they had grown as close as brothers. Recently, with Pepper dating Debs, it sometimes included a female visit, but it was still primarily just the two of them.

By nominating Pepper as the liaison, Frank had filled the post with someone he could trust. This also provided Pepper with an excuse to come home once a day as a sounding board for Frank.

With no guarantees in life, Frank felt that as he and Pepper had survived so many perils, they should make the most of every day.

Frank had just one more meeting tonight in his residence. Debs and some of his other close advisors needed to be aware of the threat so they could prepare for the changes in the capital.

His security detail accompanied him out of the chamber. Cenk had been one of his chief bodyguards for over twelve months. He'd come a long way since the convoys north and had grown into this position.

4
______

THE SCHOOL VISIT

02 February 2206

Frank had tasked Pepper with getting an update on the twins' progress. While Pepper had wanted to avoid taking Zap and Flo away from their primary tasks, he had also jumped at the opportunity to get away from the capital. A trip to the countryside was always a welcome reprieve from the dirt and noise of the city.

Zap was dividing his time between the Telepath School and the drone farm. This added to the pressure on Flo, who also was using her skills in dual roles of training at the school and advising Frank in the capital.

Bringing Debs and Eric along with him gave them a well-needed break from the capital too, but Pepper had other reasons for their presence.

Debs was his right hand, and a lot had changed since he had met her. Back then, she was supporting Frank in running a small compound and now she helped Pepper run the security for the whole capital. They rarely travelled together as if anything happened to him she was needed to take over his duties.

Pepper had had very few romantic relationships over the years, so he'd been blindsided when Debs had asked him out on a date. He wasn't sure what the protocol was for approaching your boss romantically, but overthrowing the elite was meant to reduce bureaucracy, so he had accepted.

They had been out for dinner a few times, and she had even visited the quarters he shared with Frank. He knew that the hours Frank worked weren't healthy, but he was sometimes glad of the privacy on those evenings.

So they were dating, and it was nice to have her along, but she was really here because the threat out there made him determined to bring her entirely up to speed with it. The twins' activities were crucial to the defence of the sanctuary, and he wanted Debs to see first-hand how they were progressing.

Pepper was happy to have Eric along as he had effectively become his protégé. Eric was a quick learner, and his education was very similar to Pepper's own early life: he was not book smart but a more intuitive learner. Whenever Pepper gave him a task, he did whatever was needed to complete it both quickly and efficiently.

When they pulled up at the security gate, Pepper was glad to see that the armed sentry looked alert. There was a youthful girl by the guard's side who Pepper knew would be a telepath. It seemed odd having a telepath guarding a school full of telepaths, but Flo had impressed on him the need for someone to be focused on security so they could be at their most efficient. The school was too prestigious a target not to be adequately protected, and the intense training that they were undertaking was mentally draining for even the most accomplished students.

With the large pool of telepaths on site, they could rotate the students through in short shifts to reduce the stress on anyone at the barrier.

Even with the increased security, Pepper didn't need to show identification: everyone knew the tall, dark-skinned security chief and his assistant Debs. The sight of Eric, with his bald scalp and its distinctive scars, provided a secondary point of identification, but Pepper still insisted on following protocol.

"Where are Zap and Flo?" he said, handing his papers to the sentry.

"They're in the school building, sir. Do you know where that is?" came a rather wooden reply.

Pepper had initially hated the term "sir", but over time he had learnt that it was easier to accept it as the sign of respect it was meant to be. "Yes, I know where that is."

The sentry returned his papers and lifted the barrier.

It didn't surprise Pepper that the twins would be in the school complex, as he knew that part of the school's daily routine was a shared breakfast there. His party had set off before breakfast, so he hoped that some food would be left over when they arrived.

As they exited the vehicle, Pepper noted Flo and Angus waiting in the doorway. He smiled, thinking there was no need to broadcast your arrival when you visited a telepath.

Pepper glanced momentarily at Eric. He no longer had to keep him apart from Flo as he had while Eric was intensely infatuated with her. The distance from Flo had helped and, as Eric had matured emotionally, he had broadened his interests. Angus had helped by training him to fight, as this had given Eric a practical focus for his anger.

Pepper had never had a son, and he had lost his father before becoming a man, but he assumed the subtle differences between men and women were a subject for a father and son talk. As Eric grew to trust Pepper, he'd tried to share his limited wisdom on this matter. Eric had progressed so well that Pepper now felt comfortable using Eric as the primary message carrier between Flo and Frank.

Pepper himself knew more about cutting off emotions as a survival technique than about experiencing them, but even he was learning to open up. He sometimes wondered if Eric's lack of a surname made him feel more distant from his roots, and he'd discussed this with Flo. She pointed out that when Eric first came to the farm, he'd been almost feral, so getting just one name out of him had been a struggle.

Flo and Eric smiled at each other as he approached, before proceeding to a giant hug.

The hug had helped solidify one of the decisions Pepper had come to discuss. He turned his attention to Angus. "How are you doing, you old rascal?"

"I think I've got this place locked down as well as I can, but I'm sure I could be of more use elsewhere."

Angus had been Zap's primary security since the rebellion, but until recently he could train fighters as well, something he couldn't do while stationed at the school. "I have an idea about that, but we can discuss it after breakfast. You have got some breakfast for us?"

"We can feed you, but I'm not sure if we have enough for Eric as well," Angus joked. In all the time that Pepper had known Eric, he had maintained a healthy appetite, but since he had started training with Angus and as he was coming into manhood, he had become so muscle-bound that now he was almost as broad as he was tall.

"Remember what we've talked about, Eric – stop eating when you reach your fingers," Pepper added.

"You're looking a bit tired, old man," Flo broke in.

She was the closest thing he had to a daughter, and their bond had continued to grow since he rescued her from the rebel compound.

Debs giggled. "You look like you could do with more sleep yourself, young lady."

"I know, Zap keeps telling me I need to rest more, but I've got lots to do and anyway he can't talk as he gets less sleep than me."

"If you can't sleep, let's make sure you're eating. Lead the way to breakfast," Eric said.

Everyone was laughing as Angus led the way inside.

Debs appreciated the levity here. Even with an unknown threat looming, she felt that being away from the capital somehow lightened the mood.

As they walked down the corridors, it was apparent to Debs that the layout of the school was more about grass and nature than the drab grey buildings that she inhabited. She assumed that the natural environment relaxed the brain, allowing the telepaths to remain calm and focus more.

When they entered the dining hall, most of the students seemed to have left. It didn't take the visitors long to fill their plates or for those same plates to become empty.

As soon as they'd all finished eating, Angus escorted them to the office where Zap sat working at a computer.

Flo went immediately to her brother's side. And Pepper was taken aback at the contrast between now and when he'd first met her. Back then she had jet-black hair as a disguise courtesy of her captors. Now Flo's hair was back to its natural blonde colour, her resemblance to Zap was remarkable. Comparing them side by side with their blonde hair and blue eyes, anyone could see that they were related.

The dark hair had made her look to be under a dark cloud. But now, even though she was under immense pressure, she looked somehow lighter and more carefree.

They weren't identical twins, but they were definitely of the same ilk.

The next thing Pepper noticed were the bags under Zap's eyes. "Are you getting any rest at all?"

"I'm fine; statistically, I'll get all the sleep I need when I'm dead. And if I don't figure out how to combat an unknown threat, that could occur sooner than I'd like," Zap smirked.

"Enough of the heroics, give me a proper update," Pepper said.

"Flo's taken on the bulk of the telepath training, which has freed me up to focus on using the drones as a potential defence. Do you want to update them on the training?" he asked Flo.

"I've already given Pepper the numbers of trained personnel and the potential numbers for a month's time. We're still getting a steady flow of raw recruits that have only just discovered their powers. I haven't included them in the totals as their talents are unknown. This doesn't mean we have a never-ending resource of telepaths. When inexperienced people discover their talents, they can be more of a danger to themselves than a resource for anyone else. Eventually, we should have enough people to guard all the major sites, but not yet."

"I'm afraid we are more reactive than proactive at the moment," Zap added. "For small-scale attacks from within, we can mount the drones with some limited heavy weapons, but our limited fuel supplies put restrictions on the payloads. I think having drones hovering over the capital would create more fear and chaos, especially as we don't know what the threat is."

"That sounds good in theory," Pepper countered, "but I hope that we have enough troops just to combat a small-scale attack from within. If someone mounts a full-scale attack from without, then we might struggle."

"I've been working with Professor Hawkins on improving the drones' efficiency so that they can carry explosives – in effect, turning them into missiles. Ideally, if we're assaulted by sea, we could then use them to assault ships. Plus, I've looked through the computer archives and I have another potential option."

"Don't wait for me to beg – what have you come up with?" Pepper frowned.

Zap turned the computer screen around so that Pepper could see the information listed on it.

"I've come across some long-range missiles. The type that was designed to carry nuclear warheads. They are unstable and weren't decommissioned properly."

"Hold on!" Pepper said. "Is your plan to blow up the planet? Some people have already tried that."

Before Zap could reply, Pepper continued, "To summarise our current firepower options: for a small-scale attack, we attach some large machine guns to drones that have a limited fuel supply. For a large-scale attack, we sacrifice our limited supply of drones by filling them with explosives and firing them at any attacking ships or, worst-case scenario, we fire nuclear warheads." He had lost his temper, more in frustration at the situation than in response to Zap's suggestions, and he felt guilty as soon as he'd stopped talking.

"Please let me finish before you pass judgement," Zap said calmly. "Professor Hawkins and I have visited a few remote sites, and we have found missiles that have had their nuclear warheads removed but are stable as missiles. We need to work on the fuel, but potentially they could be filled with conventional explosives and fired over longer distances."

Now he'd piqued Pepper's interest. "What kind of missiles and distances are we talking about?"

"Everyone has heard stories and rumours of these weapons of mass destruction that they used to end the Water Wars. Missiles that flew thousands of miles and killed most of the environment. Think of a huge drone, but without the wings, that has the potential for devastation. But for now, we are focused on the weapon and not the payload."

"Why didn't you lead your briefing with these weapons?"

"The stable missiles, the ones not attached to warheads that could destroy the planet, are quite advanced technology that hasn't been tested for some time. Professor Hawkins has been working on those at the same time as the drones. I've told him to prioritise the drones, but the missiles are a long-term project. We assumed when we took over that the threat of the missiles was keeping the peace, but in reality, they have to be maintained mainly to stop the sanctuary from self-destructing."

"I suppose that makes sense," said Pepper. "I thought it was just because it didn't seem profitable to them."

"I think, given time, we can get the missiles up and running as a proper deterrent."

"Hold on. Remember what happened in the past, when the power of such weapons was entrusted to people like Brand? I don't think we're ready for that kind of power any time soon."

"Let's shelve the discussion on the missile possibilities for the moment. I've prepared printouts of our current progress for you to take back to Frank and the others so you can bring them up to speed. Don't worry. I've broken the information down, so it's as simple as possible. It's just a basic inventory with projections of timeframes for our progress."

"Break it down – how prepared are we? What could we do if we're attacked today?"

"It would depend on who attacked us, what weapons they used, and where. I'm afraid I have supplied you with the tools, but you and the others need to figure out where you want to use them."

Pepper's shoulders seemed to sink a little. "I appreciate all you've done, and I'm sorry that we don't have more of an idea of the threat. If it weren't for you and Flo, we wouldn't know there was a threat, so don't think I'm ungrateful. I'm just trying to make us as prepared as we can be."

"I can only prepare to a certain extent, but not knowing what the specific threat is means I will have to remain reactive. I will maximise the resources we have available, and that's all I can do."

"You've achieved a great deal in such a short time," Pepper said. "I'll brief the council with the info you've provided, and I'm sure they'll be impressed too."

Pepper was more concerned about how tired Zap looked. One of the principal reasons for the visit was to see how well the twins were holding up.

The two of them had matured at an accelerated rate. Over the past few years, they'd been under a lot of pressure.

"How's your security holding up?" Pepper enquired.

"Whenever I travel to the drone farm, I have an armed guard, and I'm accompanied by at least one other telepath so that I can rest on the journey. Angus is in charge of the security here at all times, especially when I'm away."

Pepper was glad to hear this as he knew that even a powerful telepath like Zap couldn't focus on all his tasks and remain vigilant for his own security. He would require rest at some stage, and that is when he'd be most vulnerable. An enemy didn't keep shop hours, so Pepper approved of this precaution.

"What about you, Flo? I was serious earlier. You look almost as worn out as Zap."

"Telepaths surround me and we don't all train at the same time. This is probably one of the safest places for me to be. If someone can approach the school without us knowing, I don't hold out much hope for the other places we're guarding. It's when I travel to brief Frank that I'm most at risk."

Pepper was aware of similar issues with Flo's travel security. "One reason I've brought Eric here is to take some pressure off. Soon this place may be under even more pressure, and you all have enough to be going on with. Angus, Eric is going to assist you and, if necessary, he can double as an escort when one of the twins leaves the school. I'd like to reduce the trips Flo has to make so, where possible, Eric will also act as a courier."

Because Eric had little academic training, he'd developed a fantastic memory over the years. If given a spoken message, he could repeat it verbatim, which made him an excellent courier as he carried nothing in writing that could be stolen. Pepper had used him to ferry messages to Frank, and even he was amazed at how much information Eric could retain.

As he'd discussed with Pepper the idea of him staying here before they'd left home, Eric had brought a packed bag with him.

"I appreciate that you all know what you're doing here. Eric's not here to take over, but to learn from you, Angus, is that okay?"

"We can always use a powerful pair of hands like Eric around here. I'm just unsure if we can feed him long term," Angus said, winking at Pepper.

Pepper turned to the twins. "Everyone on the council appreciates the amazing job that you are doing, but we can't afford to overload either of you. Working twenty-four hours a day is not sustainable.

"With Eric here, Flo can spend less time travelling, Angus can focus more on Zap's security and hopefully Zap can rest a little more. I've instructed Eric to sit on you, Zap, if you don't take regular rests." Although Pepper was trying to keep things light, it was true he had ordered Eric to keep an eye on Zap and report if he was doing too much.

"I'll listen to my big brother," Zap said. Eric was shorter than Zap, but twice the size in muscle mass, and ever since Zap had met Eric, they had hit it off better than most brothers.

Pepper nodded before continuing, "I've also brought you another troop of men. Eric's been working with them, so he will primarily command them. They can bolster the escorts for the twins, but if you need them for anything else, you're in charge, Angus. We will stay for a while as I want Zap to take Debs and me through the information in the briefing notes. If anyone can think of any ways that we can improve things, let me know before we leave."

"Flo, can you go with Eric to grab his stuff and show him where he'll be staying? I'll go sort out where the other troops will stay and meet you back here in thirty minutes," Angus said.

"Okay, Eric, come with me. Angus, Zap and I have a few rooms in the main house, and we don't use some of them so you can stay with us."

Pepper and Debs sat down opposite Zap with copies of the reports as the other three left the office. "Take us through this page by page," said Pepper. "I know you think you've made it simple, but I want to know this information inside out before we leave."

"I'll grab a jug of coffee then," Zap said. "This could take some time."

5

IRIS AND FOSTER PROTECT AND SERVE

14 February 2206

Iris and Foster were two of the most talented telepaths trained at the school. Since the revelation that someone had been using telepathy as a weapon, they'd been training incessantly. Their primary defence involved linking their minds to increase the strength of their powers.

This made them an ideal addition to the security force that was guarding the capital buildings. They could scan people's minds to check for ill intentions and also scan for other telepaths trying to block this scanning.

They'd developed a technique they called the "thought bomb". This involved focusing on the word *now* together, over and over. They'd trained and trained until they'd perfected this technique so it only affected telepaths.

As they were the only known telepaths on the ground floor of the capital building, they felt safe in using this technique. If they affected someone on this floor, that person could only be either a telepath that had not disclosed themselves or an enemy telepath from another sanctuary. The double benefit of the "thought bomb" was that it offered a way of both finding fresh recruits and exposing potential threats.

After being on duty for several hours, Iris suddenly looked at Foster. "Can you hear that?"

"Yes, I hear *stop, stop, stop*," Foster said.

"It sounds like it comes from two people; there is a slight gap between the two words," Iris suggested. Their practice of patrolling side by side meant that they could quickly join hands to help focus their brains on the same target. And she reached out with her left hand now, weaving her fingers with Foster's on his right hand.

This was what they had trained for since this signal was identified at the school, and it was working surprisingly well.

"On three: one, two, three." *Now, now, now*, they repeated in unison. As they continued to transmit the word, they scanned the room for any reactions. Suddenly Iris noted a man and a woman whose faces were twisted in pain. Next, they'd raised their hands to the sides of their heads. Iris and Foster's concentrated transmission was causing them discomfort.

Iris pointed to the couple but didn't say a word, still focusing on *now*.

One guard who was walking beside them immediately noticed and grabbed his radio. "Hello all stations, this is Ground Floor six. We have unknown telepaths and, therefore, an unknown threat down here."

"Hello, this is Upstairs one. We are sending reinforcements," came the quick response.

"Grab those two over there," the guard said, pointing to the couple holding their heads. In no time at all, armed security was restraining them.

Once Iris and Foster had identified the enemy telepaths, they focused on scanning for anyone who the telepaths might have been shielding. Reaching out their minds into the crowd, they searched for fear and tension.

Tied up and disorientated, the telepaths were no longer shielding their ward's thoughts, so Foster soon picked up on the bomber's intentions.

"That man over there," Foster said to the nearest guard. "He's thinking about bombs and explosions." As Foster and Iris pointed towards him, the guard motioned for two nearby guards to converge on him.

The man dropped his parcel and walked away from it.

"Oy you, pick up that parcel!" one of the guards shouted.

The man continued to walk away from the parcel.

"Stop, stop," the guard shouted to no effect. "Stop, stop, or I'll shoot."

In the next few seconds, it seemed to Foster as though everything happened at once.

One guard fired his pistol into the man's shoulder, and the impact from the bullet spun him around.

As the injured man crumpled, there was a bright flash accompanied by an enormous bang and a blast wave that washed over everyone nearby.

Iris and Foster were close enough to the bomb blast to be thrown to the ground. Iris screamed as the shrapnel hit her. Foster, though winded, felt he like he was pretty much okay.

He crawled towards Iris as she was trying to sit up. "Wait there and I'll get us some help."

Looking at the devastation around them, he wasn't sure how he was even going to get out of here, let alone come back with help. "On second thoughts, do you think you can walk if I support you?"

"Yes, I think it's just a few cuts and bruises."

After using the wall to pull himself to his feet, Foster discovered his leg was covered in dry blood and the trouser material was sticking to it. As he tried to walk, it seemed that his leg was dragging a little, but he could stay upright.

Iris struggled to her feet with Foster's help, but it seemed she was more injured than she'd first thought. She slumped on him and let out an audible "Arrgh."

"Are you okay?"

"I think my leg is broken," Iris said.

"I don't know if it's safe to stay here; there could be more bombs. I'm going to try support you and get us out of this building. Is that okay?"

"I'll try not to hold you back," she murmured.

As they headed towards the doors, a new danger emerged. Others around them were breaking into a run, so they had to avoid being trampled.

"We need to stay close to the walls," Iris said. "I don't know how many people survived, but anyone trying to get out of here is not slowing down. We need to stay out of their way."

It took them a few minutes to reach the exit doors. It was then that they heard the shooting outside.

6

RICKY'S ATTACK

14 February 2206

Ricky and his three comrades were waiting outside the capital buildings. Barry, the bomber, had taken the two telepaths inside with him, and that was fine with Ricky.

He was suspicious of people who could read his mind, whichever side they were supposedly on.

Having no telepaths to provide mental cover for his team didn't faze him as it was doubtful this sanctuary had enough telepaths to waste covering an external location.

The plan had been to wait for Barry and the two telepaths to exit the building. Once the bombs exploded, they would take shots at the first security or medical personnel to respond.

If, for some reason, either Barry's team didn't emerge or there was no explosion, Ricky and his team would shoot random passers-by and then leave. This wasn't a suicide mission; they'd been deployed to sow the seeds of unrest and confusion to make these people feel unsafe.

The bombs were not scheduled to explode for at least thirty minutes, so his team had plenty of time to take up their positions and to confirm their escape routes.

Of course, Brand didn't care if they escaped or not, but Ricky viewed Brand like any boss, only as a means to an end. Brand was someone who would get him things that others couldn't.

Ricky had briefed the others to be in position ten minutes before the bombs were due to explode, and he could see them all evenly spread around the open square. They were trying not to look suspicious while monitoring the main doors. Their secondary role was to lay down covering fire if Barry and his team were pursued on their exit. Ricky was more concerned about his own survival than that of Barry's team.

Scanning his own team, he scratched his nose, and they all discreetly replied by raising their eyebrows. This was the agreed signal that they were ready to move into position.

Suddenly from inside the building came an ear-shattering boom. The windows shattered and smoke began billowing through the gaps.

They were caught off guard and out of position. Despite the ringing in his ears, Ricky quickly gathered his thoughts. Something had gone wrong; the explosion was not only early but was smaller than expected. Both bombs were supposed to go off together. Having seen the results in their practices, he knew there should have been more carnage.

Through his dulled senses, he surveyed his team.

They all seemed a bit taken aback, and their eyes were darting around rapidly. Two of them looked uninjured, but Maeve had blood coming from her head. It was only a flesh wound though, perhaps she'd caught a bit of flying glass.

Making a snap decision, he took out his pistol and motioned to his team to do the same. As the doors burst open to the capital building, people ran out and Ricky began shooting.

The first people to exit were a woman and a young child. Without any hesitation, Ricky fired two shots into each of them, and they crumpled to the ground. Their prone forms landed in front of the doors, which created a bottleneck, funnelling more victims into the gunfire.

As other doors opened further, Ricky's team mowed down anyone who tried to leave. These victims were doubly stunned as they fled from a bombsite and were blinded by bright sunlight. Even the armed security guard's coveralls were quickly stained red as two bullets impacted his chest, leaving him dead in the doorway.

In a short time, a dozen bodies were strewn in front of the doors, creating a barricade that made it harder for others to get out.

Ricky had to decide: Was this enough? Had his team created enough mayhem to merit them making their escape? By now, the people inside would be cautious about escaping from the building, which increased their risk of injuries from smoke or other hazards created by the bomb blasts.

It was clear that Barry and the two telepaths had been either killed or compromised, so there seemed little point in waiting for them. He motioned with his fist to his team, pointing in the direction of the escape vehicle.

By leaving now, they would live to fight another day and cause more confusion then.

Although they had lost a bomber and two telepaths, Ricky felt that they'd served their purpose. With all the bombs used up, in effect Barry would just have been a liability going forward. Whereas, apart from Maeve's minor injury, his team looked in pretty good shape.

Another loud explosion rang out from inside. Although it was followed by more flames and a few broken windows, it seemed as though the first bomb had already done the most damage.

Suddenly Dave's head exploded. Before Ricky could react, blood burst from the side of Maeve's body and she too collapsed. The round of bullets that had caused this obviously hadn't come from the building in front of them.

Pivoting, Ricky saw eight armed men in grey coveralls, all aiming their weapons in his direction. Most of the guns were pistols, but two were rifles. It was clear that the rifles had taken out his teammates. Before he could use his pistol, Ricky heard two more shots. He thought he saw the bullet coming towards him – that part might have been an illusion but he certainly felt a searing pain in his shoulder. He had been shot before, but that had only seemed like a flesh wound compared with this hit. The rifle bullet felt like somebody had struck him with a sledgehammer.

Immediately Ricky fell to the ground, carried forwards by the momentum of the bullet. Before he could move any further, he looked up to see two of the men in grey coveralls pointing their guns down at him.

Ricky thought this was it. Sure that they were going to finish him off, he decided that he was ready to die.

Then one spoke. "Remember the brief: a live prisoner is more valuable than a corpse."

"What about his shoulder wound?"

"We can patch him up and take him away. If he dies, he dies; if he survives, we get the kudos."

"Sounds good to me. I'm sure Debs will be glad to have someone to interrogate."

Ricky wondered if any of his team had survived, but his main focus was his own survival.

His initial pain was subsiding, but he was still losing blood. The last thing that Ricky felt before he succumbed to the darkness was someone lifting him and placing him on a board of some kind.

7
———

FRANK AND FLO'S ESCAPE

14 February 2206

Frank, Pepper and Flo were upstairs in the capital building when the bomb went off. Since Flo had warned them of a threat, full council meetings had been prohibited – they just created too much of a target.

All the same, the heightened security and anticipation didn't stop the explosion taking Frank and Flo by surprise.

One of the advantages of inheriting Brand's office was that it was reinforced, with its own private exit. Using the secret staircase, they could leave the building without having to navigate the carnage in the foyer downstairs.

Flo could feel the pain of the people below. Although she couldn't actually hear them from this far away, she could pick up their thoughts and the screams inside their heads. Both she and Frank had felt the building shake when the bomb went off, and they could now hear the shooting coming from outside.

"Stay away from those windows," Pepper said. "They're supposed to be bulletproof, but we don't know what else is happening."

Frank crouched low, and Cenk placed himself between his leader and the windows.

Pepper scooped an arm around Flo and almost dragged her for the door to the hidden staircase.

As they ran down to the waiting vehicles, Pepper was quickly but calmly speaking into the radio, "This is Alpha team leader to all stations. What's happening outside the capital building? Over."

The response was quick. "Alpha team leader, this is Rover one. There was an explosion on the ground floor of the capital building. Our team inside was in the process of apprehending the bomber before the bomb went off. Immediately after the explosion, we encountered four armed personnel firing at the people exiting the building, over."

"What is the status of the four shooters now?" Pepper said.

"We have neutralised the threat. Two are dead and two are wounded, one critically. The wounded are both in custody, over."

"This is Alpha team leader. I am taking the primary to location two. Any roving teams are advised that we may need backup," Pepper replied.

"This is Rover one. Do you need immediate assistance?"

"Alpha one, not at present. The primary is unharmed, but we'll advise if the situation changes. Contain the situation but get those prisoners to interrogation as soon as possible. Have you had any communication with the Bravo teams downstairs?"

"Rover one, the radios are down and Bravo one has suffered a lot of injuries, but most of Bravo two is intact and clearing up inside. They will give a sitrep in six zero minutes."

Frank turned to Flo. "It seems your concerns were correct. Something was coming, and it appears it's arrived. I fear this is just the beginning."

Grabbing the radio, he keyed the mike on the handset. "Hello, all stations, this is Frank the primary." He hated the code word but it was practical rather than just a hangover from the previous regime. His use of both the code word and his name wasn't lost on him.

"Be on hypervigilance. It seems we're under attack, and as yet we do not know the scale of the threat. We are initiating a thirty-minute protocol. All stations are to check in every thirty minutes with their base locations. Commanders are to initiate a wide sweep of their sectors and all major infrastructure. I will issue more orders as this situation unfurls, but this is my initial order. All leaders, respond and confirm."

"Charlie one, message received, will comply."

"Delta one, message received, will comply."

The replies continued as if on an automatic loop – Echo one, Foxtrot one, Golf one.

Frank was glad to hear his commanders' voices. At least they were all currently alive. "Thank you all for your rapid response. You know what needs doing, so go do it."

He hoped that his security could stop any further explosions, such as at the water or power plants. The gel plants were another possible target. Although Frank wanted to shut down the plants and wean the population off the packs, the sanctuary did not yet have the facilities to dispose of dead bodies. The previously enforced euthanasia had left behind a relatively young population, but the healthcare system had been sorely lacking so they still had no shortage of corpses. The mortality rate from even minor ailments was still comparatively high.

Karla's fighting pits were the ideal location for the secondary capital command post. Since the overthrow of the previous regime, the pits had been refurbished and fortified. They still hosted fights but not to the death – the events were more to do with boxing or mixed martial arts and happened on a smaller, more regular scale.

A lot of the fighters training at the pits were now members of the security forces. As a result, the pits were far safer and a ready supply of off-duty personnel was available to mobilise for a rapid response force.

Karla maintained her office in the pits as she was now responsible for training the security forces. As a resident council member, the extra security measures provided for her safety, as well as offering meeting rooms and a fall-back command post.

With the renovations and fewer fighting events, some entrances to the pits had been closed off, making it easier to secure the command post.

It was only fifteen minutes' drive from the capital buildings to the pits, but while the Alpha team were in transit, they heard two massive explosions in the distance.

"Hello, Alpha team leader, this is the power plant over."

"This is Alpha team, go ahead."

"Power plant, we have just had a large explosion in the main transformer. We can still supply power but only a limited amount. We have several injured personnel and three dead."

"This is Alpha team leader. Put the plant in lockdown, increase security patrols, and call command post two with a sitrep in thirty minutes. We already have a team staffing the communications desk there."

Before Pepper had time to discuss the latest event with Frank, another call came over the radio.

"Hello, Alpha team leader, this is the gel plant, over."

"This is Alpha team, go ahead."

"We've had an explosion that has taken out our backup power supply. We have no power from the main power grid and have no backup supply. The radio shed has a small generator, but that is our only source of power."

"This is Alpha team. Do what you can to preserve food stocks. Increase security patrols and call command post two with a sitrep in thirty minutes."

"Message received and understood."

Frank said to Pepper, "They've taken out the power and gel plants. Check on the water plant."

Pepper responded promptly. "Water plant, this is Alpha team. Do you read? Over."

"This is the water plant. Everything is fine here, although we are on backup power."

Frank grabbed the radio. "This is the primary. I want a sweep of the whole location and increased security at the gates, and no one gets in there. Get the engineers to check that nothing has been tampered with.

Check for obvious devices but also check for anything out of the ordinary. No one gets any downtime for now; we will send reinforcements later. Do you understand?"

"Yes," came the stunned reply.

Frank realised he was making people nervous and handed the radio back to Pepper.

"Call in a sitrep to command post two every thirty minutes," Pepper said over the radio.

"Understood, will do."

The radio operators at the plants were more used to communicating via phone. Their radio procedure was erratic, but the general message was getting through. That was all that Pepper cared about at the moment.

Frank said to no one in particular, "Why take out the gel plants and the power plant but not the water plant?"

"Perhaps they had limited explosives, and they think that food is more important?" Pepper suggested.

"Which would make sense if they came from another sanctuary," Frank said. "They might assume we are as reliant on gel plants as them, not realising how valuable the water plant is to us in helping us wean people off them."

Arriving at the pits, they were quickly recognised by the sentries, who waved all three vehicles immediately through the barrier.

As they drove through the arches and pulled into the enclosed car park, the lights were dim. Frank was grateful for the backup generators, installed as part of the refurbishments.

Miyamoto was ready for them as the cars stopped. "Karla's waiting for you upstairs," he said.

Frank thought it unusual to see Miyamoto anywhere other than at Karla's side. For as long as Frank had known Miyamoto, he'd been her bodyguard. That hadn't changed, even with her increased security detail.

Karla had taken Flo's warnings seriously, and sending Miyamoto was a signal that she was well prepared.

"Follow me," Miyamoto said.

Watching Flo walking ahead of him, Frank reflected she had spent more time with him recently, perhaps more than necessary. As one of the strongest telepaths, she would have been a valuable supplement to his security detail, but she also had her duties at the school. Frank felt guilty about taking her away from the school, but her briefings were more useful in person. Previously she had communicated a lot through Pepper, but he was also now stretched to the limit.

She had come a long way, too, in the last three years. Frank appreciated her as one of his regular confidants. Although somewhat reserved, as a sounding board she brought a different perspective to some of his plans. Her views reflected a maturity beyond her years but were less cynical than those of the council members and allowed him to formulate unorthodox solutions. It had been because of her that they now took more water through desalination plants, as a much more principled way of hydrating the masses than gel packs.

8

RICKY'S INTERROGATION

15 February 2206

In the past, Frank would have carried out the interrogation himself. Now that he was an essential member of the council, the task fell to Debs.

Over the years, she had learnt a lot from Frank yet her small stature led some to make the mistake of assuming she was not a force to be reckoned with.

This prisoner's shoulder wound from the assault on the capital had gone straight through, so it wasn't life-threatening yet. But, if it was left untreated, it could prove fatal.

Debs had instructed the guards to leave the prisoner naked and shackled in the interrogation room. From past experience, she knew that the interrogation process was about steering the prisoner through a routine. Breaking down his resistance would begin even before she stepped into the room.

Historically torture wasn't believed to give reliable information; however, as Debs had seen first-hand the results of the attack on the capital, she was determined to get the information by whatever means necessary.

When she entered the room, she wasted no time. "We're going to start with a few simple questions. Who are you? Where did you come from? Why did you attack the capital?"

The smile on the man's face was more of a grin. If he'd been stood upright, he would have been a full head taller than Debs. Currently, he was hunched over and shackled to a chair, which was bolted to the floor.

He had quite a muscly physique, which pleased Debs, if only because she thought he would survive a lot of punishment without dying on her. She picked up a flat steel bar and brought one end down on the knuckles of Ricky's left hand.

Ricky winced as the bar crushed two of his knuckles.

"Are you ready to talk yet?" she asked, not expecting anything useful at this early stage of the routine.

"Never, little girl. Are you going to keep tickling me?" he replied defiantly.

"Look, you've already been captured. If your mission was to cause chaos in the capital, you have done that. You and your friends killed a lot of people; surely, you want people to know about your success. Don't you want us to know why you did it?" She paused for a couple of seconds, not expecting an answer yet, but to provide pace and allow him to think.

"Are you terrorists here on some crusade to fight a war we don't know about? You have a choice; if you survive the interrogation, you are going to be our prisoner for the foreseeable future. You have to justify to me if it's worth us spending resources to keep you alive. Food and medicine are valuable assets at the moment.

Many people suffered in today's attack, people who either lost someone or were injured themselves. They would not be willing to spare anything to keep you alive. If I left you on the street in your current state, I doubt if you would last more than an hour."

"Let me try," he said. "I doubt if those weaklings out there could take me out."

"So, you're a fighter," Debs countered. "That's great because I hate it when people make it easy and give me the answers too quickly. It's so much more fun for me to play." She eyed the steel table in the corner of the room. It was stacked with instruments designed to inflict injury and pain.

"They say that during the Water Wars and in the years that followed, there was a great deal of brutality. In the three years since we took over the sanctuary, we've tried to be more civilised than the elites. Unfortunately, when things like your assault happen, it reminds us that it's still a cruel world. If we're determined to ensure the masses survive, there have to be some sacrifices. We have to sacrifice our civility, which is why I have been sent to you today."

"I thought that you had been sent to me as a gift. I've always wanted a pet!"

"Whatever happens to you today, I will leave here with a clear conscience, knowing that what I am doing to you is justified. Just as you may have believed that what you were doing in killing and maiming citizens was for the greater good, I believe that extracting information from you is for the greater good. Although I won't take much pleasure in inflicting pain on you, if necessary, that's what I'll do.

"Here's how it's going to go. I'm going to ask you

some questions. If you answer the questions to my satisfaction, this will be over fast, and you will have a comfortable cell, medical treatment, and more rations than you probably deserve. If you aren't prepared to answer my questions, I will start inflicting pain on you until you decide to change your mind," Debs said in something of a monotone.

His next words flowed like bile. "You think you're better than us because you are ruled by the 'so-called' people? You're no better than us! You're minions playing at being the bosses when you don't know what you're doing!"

Debs analysed his words carefully. The man seemed to be indicating that he wasn't from this area of the world. If he was from here, perhaps he just wanted things to go back to the way they were before the elites were overthrown. Some people still found it hard not to be told when to eat and what to do. It was like breaking a wild animal and then trying to give it back its freedom.

"Okay, question number one. Have you got a name? I can continue to call you scum, but I'd like to try to keep this more cordial."

The prisoner spat in her direction.

"There is no need for this unpleasantness. I can see this is going to take a while, but don't worry, I've got as long as it takes. I want you to consider your options while I go and get a drink for myself." Debs knew that the anticipation of interrogation was sometimes as effective as the interrogation itself.

Within five minutes of Debs leaving, Flo entered the room. She'd brought a jug of cold water and used it to fill a plastic beaker for the prisoner. "Here, have a drink. There's no reason for this to be unpleasant."

Flo planned to be the nice one. She had no reason to torture this man and, more than that, she was hoping that by being kind to him, it would open up his mind. "I have to tell you that my friend is going to hurt you. There's nothing I can do about that. But I'm not the same as her. I'd like you to at least have some water as it's sweltering in here. That bullet wound in your shoulder means you have already lost fluids and I don't want you getting any worse."

Suddenly in her mind, she heard, *You dumb bitch. This good guy, bad guy shit isn't going to work on me.*

It seemed like he didn't know that she could read his mind. "Drink the water, it's okay," she said, taking a sip herself to show it wasn't drugged. "Do you want some food? I can get you some food if you want. My friend wants some answers and she'll get some answers. The only factor you can control about those answers is whether she gives you pain or not. It doesn't make a difference to her, but it makes a difference to me."

Again, he didn't say anything out loud. *You don't understand, do you? If I did say anything, I'd be dead quickly afterwards. He has spies everywhere in this place. I will never be safe. I'll take my chances with the torturer.*

Flo wondered who this "he" was. Now they knew somebody had spies here – either in the capital or elsewhere in the sanctuary. She tried to get more. "Can you at least tell me your name?"

What does it matter, are you going to write Ricky on my tombstone?

Flo didn't react outwardly to this information, keen to conceal her skills for as long as possible. For the time being, she'd just store this information, and if they divulged it later, they'd pretend that it had come from another source.

"What have we done to wrong you so that you and your friends want to kill and maim us?"

Yes, that's right. I don't give a shit about you and your people. I'm a soldier; I do what I have to do and your people are just in my way.

"We can't help you if you don't help us."

Ricky spat in her face and began speaking out loud, "I don't need your help, and you people are weak. You haven't got the stomach to get information out of me. I'd rather die than help you." He knocked the water off the table with the back of his hand, causing the water to spill onto the floor.

"I was going to bring you some food, but I assume that you'll just use it to redecorate this room?"

In her mind, she heard, *Of course I want food and water, I'm not stupid, but we've been trained for this stuff. As soon as I start accepting things from you, you'll think you've broken down the barriers. If I'm going to give you any information, I have to make it look realistic and I have to make you feel like you've dragged it out of me.*

"I want to help you, I do," Flo said. "But if you won't accept warm food or water, would you like a blanket to cover yourself up?"

Even though she'd said the food was warm, it wasn't really. And the water was only to stop Ricky from becoming dehydrated after he had lost bodily fluids as a result of the bullet wound.

"Would a blanket help you?" she offered again.

Stop trying to humanise yourself; you're the enemy. Then Ricky said out loud, "Go away. You're boring me."

"Okay," Flo said. "Just remember that when my

friend comes back in, she isn't going to be as polite as me. You had the option to do things the nice way." She walked across the room, picked up the discarded beaker and left.

Debs was waiting in the soundproofed the room next door, on the other side of a two-way mirror.

"That went well," Debs said. "Did you get anything useful?"

"He wasn't trying to guard his thoughts so he can't be one of the telepaths. I could be wrong, but he didn't seem to be trying to block his mind. His thoughts were transmitting loud and clear whenever he became emotional. He's called Ricky and is more concerned about being killed by spies working for some man than he is about the pain of torture. It seems that the man he's afraid of has a network of spies. I'm not sure if they're here in the capital or somewhere else in the sanctuary. Ricky referred to that man as 'he' and was clearly scared of him."

"Anything else?" Debs asked.

"He seems to have had some resistance training. He was constantly thinking strategically, like when he refused any food or water or the blanket. He didn't want to seem weak, but he was also preparing to give the impression that any information that he offers us is genuine by making us work harder to get it."

"Are you ready for me to go back in there?" Debs asked. "You know it could get nasty."

"Yes, I know – I don't agree with torture, but I understand the threat is huge. I will monitor your interrogation from here and write down any thoughts I pick up, including any thoughts that contradict the answers he gives you."

"Okay," Debs said. "Clearly, it would have been nicer if he'd accepted all that you offered and pretended to cooperate. In reality, he's behaving just as I expected. Make yourself comfortable; this could be a long night."

As Debs re-entered the interrogation room, Ricky looked up. "Glad you came back. You're much more my type than your girlfriend. She's a bit soft whereas you're rougher around the edges."

Debs accepted his bravado. His denigrating attitude would make her feel less uncomfortable about what she was about to do to him.

"Let's start again. I'm going to ask you a few questions. We have captured some of your companions and they've provided us with some useful information. I need you to confirm what your friends are telling us is true. As we are comparing your answers with theirs, if the answers don't match, it will be obvious someone is lying." She paused in the knowledge that silence encouraged prisoners to talk.

"If you provide honest, truthful answers, you will leave this room and continue with a reasonably comfortable life. Should you choose not to answer the questions in a satisfactory way, I cannot guarantee that you will leave this room alive."

"Do you think I'm scared of a little girl like you? Are you going to hurt me, little girl?" Ricky taunted her.

One thing that Debs had learnt from Frank was that when you tortured a prisoner, they might decide they'd nothing to lose and attack the torturer. For this reason, Ricky was securely restrained.

It never got any easier for Debs. She had come from an abusive home, regularly beaten by her father. After that, already scared and vulnerable, she was about to be attacked by two feral men when Frank had rescued her. Taking her under his wing, for the next few years Frank had brought out a strength in her that she hadn't known was there.

Frank had got the most out of her by pushing her a little at a time. The first interrogation he had made her observe had made her vomit. Frank never tortured just for the sake of brutality. The purpose was always to get information to protect them and theirs. Early on, the thought that it was all for the greater good was what kept her going.

As the years had gone by, she had learnt more about her own strengths and weaknesses. This increased her understanding of how her prisoners thought. Inside she always hoped that they would cooperate, but on the outside she had to appear strong.

The pain from Ricky's shoulder wound had subsided, and she needed to provide him with some motivation to talk. The plan was to inflict pain but keep him alive long enough to provide information.

With one hand, she picked up a long piece of shiny steel, with a sharp spike on one end and a flat face on the other. In the other hand, she wielded a medium-sized hammer.

"I want to be clear that this is on you. I tried to be helpful, but you didn't want that. You want us to come down to your level, a barbarian. You and your friends killed men, women and children yesterday. You decided that their lives were worthless and, at the moment, so is yours. For you to be of any value to me, you're going to have to give me information. Now I'd like to keep you alive, but that doesn't mean that I have to keep you all in one piece. I'm sure that the families of the dead and wounded want me to hurt you, on their behalf. Remember, it's not up to them how much pain you endure. We can stop any time you want. It's up to you."

"Just get on with it!" Ricky shouted. "Is your idea of torture just to keep talking? Listening to your whiny voice is so painful. Please just shoot me and put me out of my misery."

"Let's start with an easy question. Give me the names of your team." She was placing pictures of the dead attackers on the table in front of him. "One of your teammates told us your name is Ricky."

For a split second, Ricky deliberated. *Is Maeve or one of the others alive? No, they wouldn't give any information away. Then how did they get my name? There must be a telepath nearby. What have they heard?*

He stared at her with disdain and anger. He stayed silent, deciding that was the best way to control things.

"Perhaps you've already forgotten your teammates? Let's try a simpler question. Why did you attack the capital?"

Pushing the flat end of the steel into his bullet wound, she kept going until he squealed in agony. Leaving it there for ten seconds, she began to wiggle it, watching the bright-red blood flowing out as she ripped apart muscles and tendons that had only just started melding back together.

Pausing for a few seconds to see his response, she grasped the steel tight and quickly pulled it out. Blood and tissue followed the steel and splattered on her top. As Ricky had no clothes, she used his hair to wipe the end of the steel clean.

"How does that feel? Is the little girl hurting or just tickling you?"

His eyes were watering with the first sign of tears, but through gritted teeth, he managed to mutter, "Go to hell."

Rotating the steel in her hand so that the spike was now facing his good shoulder, she plunged the spike into his flesh while at the same time hitting the flat end with the hammer.

Although he wasn't making a noise, he was now writhing in agony.

She could have asked another question, but her routine involved inflicting pain and then leaving the prisoner to contemplate.

Kneeling in front of Ricky's feet, she swung the hammer with all of her strength, and the flat face of the hammer came down, smashing the two middle toes of his left foot. She could hear the bones crunching and splintering. It looked like his toes were now the leftovers from some bizarre banquet.

Ricky was groaning in pain. In the next room, Flo heard the pain in his thoughts too.

"I'll leave you some time to think. When I come back, I'd appreciate some answers," Debs said.

Entering the room next door, Debs saw Flo shaking her head and asked, "Nothing – he's thinking nothing?"

"He's thinking something, but he seems to be using a blocking technique."

"What can you hear?"

"He's repeating a mantra to block his thoughts, and it seems like something a child would sing."

"What is he thinking?"

"I know a song that'll get on your nerves, get on your nerves, get on your nerves, I know a song that'll get on your nerves, get on your nerves, get on your nerves."

"I don't get it." Debs was smiling slightly.

"It's effective, simple enough for him to focus on and quite irritating." Flo was also smiling. "I'll tend to his wounds."

Flo had lots of practice in dressing wounds from when she had been a hostage with the rebel clans. They had wanted her for her telepathic skills, but as there were always armed scuffles between the clans, they needed someone to bandage the wounded more than they needed her telepathy.

For the next few hours, Flo and Debs went through a rotation of Debs inflicting wounds on Ricky and Flo bandaging and tending to those wounds.

Debs staggered the interrogation intervals to keep Ricky off guard, but he didn't give out any useful information. On more than one occasion, he collapsed from the pain.

9

ARRIVAL AT THE KOMPANIYA

29 September 2202

On arrival at Sanctuary Two, Brand surveyed the contents of his helicopter. He hadn't been able to bring much in the way of resources with him.

He was met on the helipad by Risslo Deripask. A couple of inches taller than Brand, and well-built with piercing green eyes, Risslo reminded Brand of a younger version of himself.

When he'd first met Risslo at a previous summit, Risslo had only been a low-level diplomat in the entourage of Orlov. A good judge of character, Brand had fostered relationships with people like Risslo so he had options to escape from his own sanctuary in an emergency.

Risslo was a political animal, and Brand recognised that his ambition would make him easy to manipulate. Brand saw that Risslo wanted power but doubted that he possessed the brutality to succeed with this ambition.

Brand had previously supplied Risslo manpower from his Company men, in the form of untraceable assassins, leaving Risslo in his debt.

Of course, the assassins were never allowed to return home. Even though they'd killed his political opponents or just general enemies, Risslo was able to claim responsibility for their capture.

Their public executions reinforced his claims to be keeping their kingdom safe.

This was a win-win situation for Risslo: he'd been supplied with untraceable killers to do his bidding, and he got to dispose of them so they couldn't expose his hand in any assassinations. Risslo's position in state security made it unlikely he would ever be investigated, and he did like to play the hero.

While willing to sacrifice his assassins to get what he wanted, Brand had hoped to never need this escape plan, but he always believed in planning for the worst. Once he'd seen that the greed of the elite in his sanctuary had the potential to create an uprising, Brand had put more effort into this endeavour.

Risslo wasn't aware that whenever Brand sent assassins, the boats also carried extra personnel as sleeper agents should they be needed. If they weren't required, it was of no concern to Brand, but they would be available if he had to play this last-ditch card.

Because of the distance between the two sanctuaries, fuel was a critical factor in Brand's payload. By piloting the aircraft himself, he'd avoided the potential weight of extra personnel. The secret flying lessons had definitely paid off.

With a limited choice, he'd decided that the best weight-to-value ratio for cargo would be diamonds and other gems that he'd accrued over time. These took a lot less space than other valuable resources, and they had both aesthetic value and potential industrial uses.

Despite the advantages these gems offered, he realised that he was heading into an unknown future without the security of his previous home.

He would be like a homeless person arriving at the elite compound in his own sanctuary with a bucket full of valuables. There was no guarantee that Risslo wouldn't just kill him and take the gems.

Brand was gambling that his intimate knowledge of his sanctuary made him a valuable resource, supplementing the gift of the gems. All he needed was some time to do what he'd always done – build alliances and a power base.

As he readied the helicopter to land, he was on high alert. Risslo was waiting on the pad with half a dozen armed men. Brand waited for the rotors to stop before opening the door, quipping to himself that the armed men seemed to provide enough of a hazard so he didn't need to kill himself by walking into a rotor blade first.

"Well, hello traveller," Risslo said a little too energetically in Brand's native tongue.

Brand wasn't much for small talk, but he managed to reply, "Hello Risslo, good to see you again."

"I'll have my men unload the cargo into one of the trucks. Did you bring any weapons?"

Understanding this meant 'Give me your gun' and that he was outnumbered, Brand said, "I brought a pistol in case I needed it on the journey, but as I am now under your protection, I guess I won't need it anymore."

He slowly handed Risslo his gun, butt first.

"That's right, you're here as my guest and are as safe as if you were in your own sanctuary."

Brand noticed a slight smirk from Risslo. If he'd been safe in his previous home, he wouldn't need to throw himself on this imbecile's mercy. "That's good to know."

For a split second, he thought back to the men he'd left on the roof in his homeland. He felt no regrets about leaving Will and the others to die. They'd served their purpose by helping him survive. That was all that mattered.

After they climbed into the nearest vehicle, things seemed initially cordial.

"I have told the other council members of your impending arrival, and they are keen to meet you," Risslo said.

Brand analysed his situation. So Risslo wanted to show him off straight away. This meant that not only would the other council members be judging Brand's worth, but he would have the chance to look for allies and immediate threats.

Not wanting to give too much away, he just nodded.

"We'll let you get settled for a couple of days before we expose you to the finery of our high society," Risslo continued.

Although Brand and Risslo had similar traits, Risslo had never had the killer instinct to be a sanctuary leader. But his lack of killer instinct helped Brand. He'd managed to convince Risslo that the council would value Brand as a resource and would reward Risslo with power for introducing him. It was true that Brand could be a useful resource for the council, but it was he who sought the power.

When they arrived at Risslo's house, Brand followed Risslo into the huge sprawling mansion.

"You must be tired after your flight. I'll have Olga show you to your room. She will tend to your needs while you're here – whatever you desire," Risslo winked. "I'll see you for breakfast in the morning."

"Thank you," Brand said as he followed the young woman up the stairs. Olga was almost as tall as Brand, perhaps in her mid-twenties, and her short red dress showed off a well-toned body.

They were flanked up the stairs by two of the armed guards, and when they entered the bedroom, the guards took up a post outside. It was going to take some time for him to earn some trust here but he had accepted this on the flight. So far his long-term plan was on track.

Olga opened the wardrobe to display a selection of clothes in his size. All of the windows, even the ones in the ensuite bathroom, had sturdy bars attached on the outside.

"These clothes are for you. But if you require anything different, please let me know, and they will be supplied. Would you like me to run you a bath?" Olga offered.

"There is no need just now. I want a shower and then sleep."

"Would you like me to join you in the shower?"

Brand considered this for a minute but decided that he was probably being judged at the moment. "That's fine. I can wash myself."

"I'm expected to share your bed. There is a selection of lingerie in the wardrobe – have you any preferences?"

If he were back home, he would have used this woman for his pleasure, but he decided to wait and see what was ahead of him. And he could be persuasive, even with a spy. "Wear what you feel comfortable with. You might have been told to serve me but I won't disrespect you."

Olga was taken aback. Perhaps people in other sanctuaries weren't as brutal as the masters here. She'd been told to keep an eye on this man and report on his activities, but if he were true to his word and treated her well, she would weigh up her options going forward.

Over the following days, Risslo paraded Brand around with him at functions as the (ex) leader of another sanctuary who would do his bidding. He thought of Brand as an ornament like some kind of jewellery or fine clothing that would give him gravitas in the court.

What Brand realised, but Risslo didn't, was that the politics of the sanctuary meant that Risslo's rivals saw what Brand really had to offer.

Risslo had accepted a wolf in sheep's clothing into his flock and he could live to regret that.

10
___

UNREST IN THE CAPITAL

02 March 2206

In the weeks that followed the power cuts, unrest had grown around the capital. The crews were working to fix the damage, but the power infrastructure for the general population had always been sparse on maintenance.

Although life had improved for the general population since the uprising, people always wanted more. In most areas of the capital, it was still a case of surviving more than thriving.

One of the results of the power shortages was reduced street lighting. As has happened throughout the ages, the cloak of darkness brought out the predators. The most vulnerable were a ripe target.

Before the uprising, the members of this council had controlled most of the capital's criminal activities. Now in their more respectable positions, although they kept their fingers on the pulse of the underworld, they were mainly out of touch with daily street crime.

After considering all other options, the council decided to impose a curfew. It felt like a throwback to the old regime, where curfew breakers could be shot on sight.

This new curfew was not enforced as rigidly. The rule was that anybody found outside after 10 pm was liable to be stopped and searched – but it was more of a warning than an edict.

This peacekeeping strategy wouldn't make people who were stopped feel any better about it, but they were less likely to run if they had done nothing wrong. It was supposed to give the defenceless a reason not to work late.

Although the one percent no longer ruled the sanctuary, human society abhors a vacuum. A hierarchy remained in which the lower-level workers were still subjugated and downtrodden.

Debs accompanied a random night patrol, not because she was needed for security, but because she liked to keep her ear to the ground. No matter how well-crafted others' reports were, there was no replacement for personal experience.

Tonight she was out with one of the patrols covering the West sector of the capital. It had been an uneventful night so far; they had found no reason to stop ordinary people going about their business. The trucks' headlights were the primary source of light as only every third street light was illuminated.

This left a lot of areas in shadow and darkness, for bad people to do bad things.

Even with the three sets of high-intensity lights on each patrol vehicle, pockets of darkness remained.

"Stop!" Debs suddenly shouted. Out of the corner

of her eye, she had sensed something out of place down an alleyway. "Pull in over there," she instructed the driver.

Grabbing the radio mike, she pressed the switch. "Hello Golf two, this is Golf one, I saw something in the alley and we're going to investigate it. Leave a sentry with your driver and the other four of you, come with us."

"Golf two, message understood. Wilco, out."

Debs got out of her vehicle, accompanied by three of her crew. On a regular patrol, each vehicle would be crewed by a team of four, but because of Debs's presence, each of them held six people. No commander wanted to field the patrol that lost Debs and, with the current state of unrest, it made sense to bolster the crews.

With their weapons drawn, they approached the alley. The beams from the strong torches fitted to each of their rifles merged to show five figures. Three were standing, and two seemed to be on the ground. Something did not look right here. As they got closer to the group, it was clear that the two prone figures were a man straddled on top of a woman.

As they edged down the alley, the three men standing ran off. "Go get them," Debs ordered the crew from the other vehicle.

The hunted had not realised it was a blind alley. As the pursuing soldiers closed the gap, their torches illuminated a solid brick wall.

Meanwhile, Debs and her team were focused on the figures on the ground. The man was trying to get up while pulling up his pants. "Grab him!" Debs shouted and two of her team quickly pounced on him.

On the floor, the woman lay motionless, battered and bleeding. Her clothes had been ripped, and she was crying.

Debs stooped down and wrapped her jacket around the woman's shoulders. Helping the woman to her feet, she gently asked, "Do you know what time it is?" Debs was careful to keep her tone gentle, with no hint of blaming the victim. "Where are you going, dear?"

The woman said nothing; she looked to be in her early twenties. It was hard to tell as her face was severely bruised and covered in dirt from the ground. She was still crying and shaking.

"You're going to be okay," Debs tried to sound convincing. "You just have to come with me to the vehicle and we'll keep you safe."

Looking over her shoulder, Debs saw three men facing the soldiers at the end of the alleyway. Before, when they were attacking a lone woman, they may have felt brave, but now they were facing armed soldiers.

Clearly not knowing how dire their circumstances were, the largest of the three rushed at the soldiers, knife in hand. But before he got within six feet of them, two of the soldiers fired their weapons. Both shots impacted simultaneously, drilling two rounds into his head. One bullet entered his forehead and the other went through his eye socket. At this close range, two explosions from the back of his head were visible. Instantaneously the body crumpled to the ground.

Fred, the leader of vehicle Golf two, shouted to the other two prisoners, "Right you two, pick up his body now. He's your friend, and I'm not getting his brains all over my clothes! All you're going to do is pick him up and throw him in the back of the vehicle. Don't try anything stupid or you'll end up just like him. Do you understand?"

The two men nodded and slowly bent down, gingerly picking up their comrade. By the time this group got back to the vehicles, the fourth prisoner had his hands bound behind his back and was lying prone on the floor of the back vehicle.

Debs had not allowed him to finish securing his trousers, so they were now somewhere close to his ankles. This made it harder for him to run away while providing her with the bonus of degrading him.

"Put the body on the roof rack," Debs said. "It's cold tonight, but there is no point having him smelling up the inside of the truck with the rest of you. The other two can sit in the back with him."

The inside of the vehicles was already a little cramped with the extra troops in this patrol, and they were about to add more people to the truck's payloads.

"Golf two, you take the prisoners and I'll take the victim," Debs ordered. "We are going to head back to base, drop them off for processing and then head out again. I have a feeling that this is not going to be the last incident tonight."

Over the last week or two, this patrol had seen a lot of unrest, from break-ins to rapes and murders. The number of crimes per night seemed endless. It had got to the stage where each of the vehicles was fitted with a special scoop on top of its roof rack. The scoops were designed to store dead bodies, and it was becoming a standard occurrence to pick up one or two bodies a night.

Investigations were limited so unless they came across a body with both a knife protruding from it and the wielder of the knife still attached, most crimes went unsolved.

Unfortunately, this was just the nature of the beast at the moment. It was hard to keep the peace in a world where food was short and life was cheap. They did the best they could with the limited resources on hand.

The loss of good men during the assaults on the capital had left their armed forces stretched thinly just in protecting the key installations while the workers repaired the damage from the attacks.

It had been a busy few weeks clearing up. The initial search for extra shooters in the capital had not turned up any positive results. The only outsider they had managed to detain was the one capital attacker that had not died in the assault.

They had also apprehended some local people who had assisted the attack for their own financial gain.

These locals were not masterminds; they were just corrupt or trying to get a little extra for their families, partly for survival but also for greed.

As a way of dissuading anyone else from helping similar ventures, the locals had been given summary executions. That may have seemed harsh to some, but people needed to know that the penalty for treason against the state was death.

It was the only real deterrent that they could impose.

Of course, the possibility remained that one or more of the people that they'd executed would later be proved innocent. The council had decided that this was acceptable, collateral damage.

Unfortunately, in this post-apocalyptic world, people only understood the fundamentals of right and wrong. If you did something wrong, you were punished.

Over two hundred years ago, a guilty person with lots of resources may have been able to put up a good defence and be found innocent. At the same time, an innocent person without those resources may have been found guilty for something they didn't do.

The current justice system was more basic. The chances of someone getting away with a crime if they were tried were limited. Justice erred on the side of caution. If there was more than a fifty percent chance that you were guilty, it was assumed that you were guilty.

As a result, innocent people were sometimes put to death, but these were harsh times. The survival of the capital, the sanctuary and, in effect, the whole of their people in the kingdom was precariously balanced on a knife-edge. At times, people got caught in the judicial crossfire.

For all that, where possible, Debs – like Frank, Pepper, Flo and the other members of this new regime – tried to be fair and just. She wondered if there would ever be a time when society could provide regular fair trials, but for today she would work within the parameters available.

11

PLANNING A RESPONSE

05 March 2206

The other council members had voted Frank as the leader, but they still recognised Spider for his strategies and his cunning.

So it was little surprise that in a meeting that had been convened to find a response to the attacks, Spider would be the first to speak.

"The main problem with trying to plan a response is that we don't know who attacked us. If it had been Sanctuary Two, surely they would have used drones filled with explosives. But then again that would have tipped their hands. Sanctuary Three isn't close enough to use drones, so that would make them the more likely attacker. Have we gained any further information from the prisoner?"

Pepper – along with Zap and Eric, as others highly involved in the sanctuary's security – attended most of the meetings as a matter of course. "Unfortunately not. The prisoner has taken his own life."

"What? How did that happen?" Hubert protested.

Before Pepper had a chance to answer, Karla interrupted. "Are you telling us that the only prisoner that might have given us any information is now dead? Who was in charge of his safety and security?"

Pepper knew that Debs was in charge of the prisoner's security, but he wasn't prepared to sacrifice his team for something they couldn't predict. "Flo and Debs spent time interrogating him and managed to get some information. But while he was being transported between locations, he suddenly threw himself at a steel shelf bracket in a corridor. He impaled his throat on the steel, severing his main artery. There was nothing we could do. If someone is determined to die, it's hard to keep them alive."

"You should have taken better precautions!" CT chimed in.

"And what would you have done?" Pepper said in disgust. "It wasn't like someone gave him a gun or a rope. No one could have predicted that he would hurl himself at the first sharp object that came into view. How would you expect a sane guard to prepare for someone's insane act?"

"Why would someone do anything that insane?" CT tried being more conciliatory this time.

Flo, who had been standing by the wall, spoke up. "During the interrogation, it became apparent that the prisoner was scared of a man, a man so frightening that even after capture, the prisoner would rather die than betray him."

"Do we know who this man is?" Spider asked.

"While Debs was interrogating him, I was reading

his mind. He never divulged a name, and he never gave away where he was from."

"If it's a leader of one of our enemy sanctuaries, it's not hard to decide between Radka and Chang. I know I'd be more scared of Chang," Frank said.

"That's assuming he was referring to a sanctuary leader; it could have been the head of some secret unit from either sanctuary," Spider said.

"Surely the main question isn't who attacked us, but why wait till now?" Frank responded. "It's been three years since we overthrew the old guard. It would have made more sense to hit us back then before we had the chance to organise."

Ever the fighter, Karla wasn't backward in adding her opinion. "Yes, it's important to know why we were attacked, but until we know where the threat came from, we need to be prepared for them to hit us again. Zap, what defences have you prepared?"

"We are increasing the shifts for the trained telepaths and accelerating training of the new trainees."

"The telepaths didn't do us much good in stopping the last attack," CT said.

"If you'd let me finish," Zap cut him off. "We started to prepare our telepathic defences as soon as we identified there was a threat. At that time, we didn't know what the threat was, but even in their semi-trained state, Iris and Foster still saved many lives with their warning. Since we've learnt more about the threats, we have become better trained and more prepared."

"What about technical support for our protection?" Hook asked.

With Zap's computer expertise, he was even more

stretched between his duties at the Telepath School and supervising the drone site. "We are still working on our stocks of drone fuel and are not yet ready to arm the drones with anything more than heavy machine guns. At a push, we could fill one with explosives and hit an enemy vessel leading a sea attack, but we are still working on our other assets. I am working on a system to block the frequency that allows drones to remain in the sky, just in case that's where the next attack comes from."

"There's an old saying that attack is the best form of defence," Hook said. "I have a suggestion that will need limited resources but may prove effective. The summit is only a month away and, whether we experience another attack or not, the summit may prove useful."

"What are you proposing?" Frank asked.

"I suggest we send a boat ahead of time. Load it with a team and set them off to get close to the summit location. If Frank can determine who attacked us while he's at the summit, the boat will be positioned closer to the other sanctuaries. If we don't get any further information, they can turn round and they haven't risked much."

"But if they do find a target, there is every chance that you are sending them on a suicide mission," Spider noted.

"What kind of resources are you suggesting for this magical boat of yours?" Hubert asked suspiciously.

"I can produce a full breakdown of our requirements given a few days," Hook answered.

"I guess I'm leading that boat then," Pepper said.

"Hold on," Frank said, startled. "Why is it you that has to go?"

"I am the obvious choice. I am the one who has

spent most of his adult life surviving against the odds. If anyone can survive a suicide mission, it's me," Pepper said with some resignation.

"You may lead the assault team, but if this boat has a chance of even surviving the journey, I need to be in charge of the boat," Hook said.

"Hold on a minute," Frank said. "Our head of security and one of our council members deploying on a suicide mission. Have you both gone mad?"

"We have other people we can send," Hook said, "but their chances of success will diminish exponentially without us two. And we'll need a couple of telepaths."

"Is there anything else you'd like, perhaps Karla or myself?" Hubert asked in a mocking tone.

"If we assume that whoever attacked us has more telepaths, we need some way to combat that threat to gain even a slim chance of success," Pepper said.

"I'll see who we can spare," Zap said.

"I want you two to go away and refine the plan and present us with our options at the next meeting," Frank said to Hook and Pepper. "Has anyone got anything else to contribute that will be for the good of the people?"

One of the reasons the council members had chosen Frank as their leader was for his empathy, which differentiated him from the previous elite rulers. They appreciated him now for his concern for the people in the streets.

"For your little trip, I think everyone should be volunteers. They should know what they are getting themselves into," Karla said. "I am pretty sure that some of my fighters will be willing to volunteer. Ever since we stopped them fighting to the death, some of them have been bored. There's bound to be a few within their ranks who are keen for a mission where the odds are stacked against them." She looked across at Angus. "Well?"

"If it pleases the council, I'd like to tag along. After all, the chances of success may increase with two teams, and they'll each need a leader."

"Welcome aboard." Pepper smiled, looking around the room to see that there were no objections.

Hook was the only one to speak. "You know this isn't a pleasure cruise?"

"You might be the captain of the boat, but I'm the officer in charge of morale," Pepper said, and Hook just shook his head, smiling.

Frank could feel the impatience building around the room, but he had one more item to address. "Before we dissolve this meeting, I've got one more issue to raise."

This caught everyone's attention.

"We need to do something to break the tension in the capital. Sending our people away to fight our enemies is a good tactical move but it won't appease the masses right now. The attack on us has created confusion and anxiety and has made us look weak. We need to do something to distract them."

"What have you got in mind?" asked Spider.

By way of an answer, Frank asked in turn, "Karla, how fast could you put on a fight night?"

"It would depend on how big a show you want and how many fighters. Perhaps two weeks for something on a small scale. These events take a lot of coordination, you know?"

"I understand, but we need to do something fast before there is anarchy on the streets," Frank replied.

"That makes sense," Karla said. "Ending the ageing

ceremonies has been great for reducing anxiety – it helps people to know that they and their loved ones may live past their mid-forties! But I think many are missing the fights that went with the ceremonies and helped them release their aggression. I could organise a smaller fight in a couple of weeks and larger ones later if we can get more volunteers."

Frank was looking at the schedule in front of him. "How does Friday, March 28th suit? Can we get everything in place in time?"

"CT and Hubert, I'm going to need food and drink?" Karla asked in turn.

After getting a nod from Hubert, CT replied, "We'll make it happen."

"Debs, can you help Hook maintain the smooth passage of anything coming into the capital? I'm sure you'll have plenty to do prepping the boat for deployment, so do you need anything else?" Frank asked them both.

"Whatever it takes," Debs said.

"Whatever it takes," Hook agreed.

"If there is nothing else for today?" Frank asked. As everyone shook their heads, he continued, "We've got a lot to do so let's get on with it."

As people started to file out of the room, Pepper looked across at Eric. He'd brought him along today to give him a break from the school, but also to continue with his education in matters of state – what he was missing while away from the capital.

While Eric had been living at the Telepath School, Angus had taken the opportunity to train Zap and him together.

Under Angus, Zap had become technically skilled at

fighting, but Eric had an advantage when it came to natural strength and aggression. Now that this strength had been channelled, he was a fighting force to be reckoned with.

Pepper had seen the look on Eric's face when the 'fight night' had been mentioned; he had been part of Eric's journey to becoming a skilled fighter, as he had given him most of his training before Angus had taken over.

"Okay, what are you thinking?"

"I think I should be part of that fight night," Eric answered.

"And how do you propose to do that?"

"With all he has to do now, surely Angus will bring his team of fighters to the Telepath School to train so I could train with them and Zap. That way I can keep an eye on Zap and train for the fights at the same time."

"You sound like you've got it all figured out?" Although Pepper tried to phrase it as a question, he realised that Eric had thought ahead. The school was the ideal place to train, and it also provided the teams with the opportunity to get used to working with telepaths. For Eric in particular, it was a chance to sharpen his skills and discipline his impulsiveness while providing additional support for the teams that were deploying.

"If Angus and Karla agree, I'll allow it." Pepper was still finishing the sentence when Eric ran off to ask for their permission.

12

THE NIGHT BEFORE THE DEPLOYMENT

15 March 2206

Frank had wanted to spend some time with Pepper on his last night in the sanctuary, but Pepper had brought things forward a night. His excuse was that he'd too much preparation to do on the night before sailing. Frank knew that the real reason was that Pepper planned to spend his last night with Debs and Frank didn't blame him. When they did get together, Frank and Pepper drank heavily and talked into the night like only soldiers could do.

So today Pepper was a bit tired, but he didn't mind – he had now freed up plenty of time to spend with Debs.

They used most of this time to go over security details for the sanctuary and confirm her duties while he was away. The handover did not require too many details as she had been his deputy for so long that she knew this stuff off by heart.

By five o'clock, they had gone their separate ways for

a couple of hours, he to take his final load to the boat and she to get ready for dinner.

Pepper was glad that Hook was in charge of the boat, not just because Hook was the more skilled sailor but also because it allowed him time to tie up loose ends around the capital before departure.

Dumping off the rest of his equipment, he did a quick check of the vehicles and weapons. They had been checked many times already and would be inspected a lot more once they left, but while they were still on land, the mission was Pepper's domain.

When he reached the armoury, he found Angus was already there. Angus wouldn't be joining the boat until later in its journey, so he wanted to ensure everything was prepped before departure.

"How's everything shaping up?" Pepper asked.

"All the main stores are loaded. I'll stay with the boat until tomorrow's tides when you push off. Have you said your farewells and tied up any loose ends?"

"I've got a few people to speak to, but I've said most of my farewells. Who will you leave behind when the time comes?"

"I'll say goodbye to Karla and Zap, but I doubt anyone will miss me," Angus said with a sigh.

Like most of the volunteers on this crew, Angus would leave very few people behind to mourn him.

Pepper pondered this himself. If someone had asked him a few years ago who would mourn his death, he would've been hard pushed to name one person. Now he had several people close to his heart: Frank, Eric and Flo were like family and of course there was Debs.

He did question why he was volunteering now that he had people in his life that made staying behind worthwhile. He told himself that the reason he had volunteered was to protect them.

During his company training, he had been told to repeat, "There is no greater love for a man than to lay down his life for another." At the time he thought this was just propaganda, but something seemed to have sunk in as he was now putting himself on the line for the people he loved. Perhaps this sacrifice would make up for the terrible things he had done in the past.

Turning his attention back to the moment, he asked Angus, "I've loaded everything apart from the few things I'll bring in the morning. Can I leave you to oversee the rest?"

"Yes, the others in my team who are joining you from the plane have loaded and checked their stuff. Any of the crew sailing with you that aren't here yet will be here in the next few hours. By nine o'clock tonight, everything and everyone will be loaded and ready to leave – except you."

"I'll be here by first light tomorrow." Pepper knew that Angus wasn't criticising him, but he felt a little guilty and was determined not to hold up the boat's departure.

"I hear that you have a hot date," Angus grinned.

"Are there no secrets in this place?"

"You've hardly tried to hide your friendship when you are together. Allow an old man some excitement. My life of solitude is such that I have to live through others."

"It's your choice. I'm sure many women would want to share the bed of such an esteemed warrior."

"You missed out the word 'old'. Most women like their men a little younger. And of course if I did have someone to come home to, you might have one less volunteer to come on this suicide mission." His infectious laughter had Pepper chuckling loudly too.

"Fair enough, I'll see you in the morning." Pepper joined his escort and headed back to the government buildings.

The drive passed quickly as Pepper was again lost in his thoughts. His pride wouldn't let him drop out of the mission, yet it was at odds with his survival instincts.

At the government buildings, he walked past the door guards and took the elevator to his top-floor accommodation. It still amused him that he and Frank lived in Brand's former home.

He knew that Frank would be down below in his office attending to important matters, as he had agreed to give Pepper some privacy for the night.

As a true friend, Frank had not only made himself scarce for the night but also prepped the food earlier. Pepper could cook to survive, but Frank was able to produce something that you could share with civilised company. With so much on his mind, Pepper was grateful for having one less thing to focus on.

After a long hot shower, he was finishing off the cooking when there was a knock at the door.

Seven o'clock on the dot. Debs was always on time. "Come in," he said, knowing that the security guards wouldn't have let anyone else close enough to the door.

When Debs walked through the door, he was stunned. Her dark hair trailed loosely over her shoulders, her blue eyes were sparkling and she was wearing a tight-fitting red dress. In her daily work, she rarely wore anything other than loose-fitting fatigues and he liked that, but tonight she looked incredible.

"What have you done to Debs?"

"Very funny," she said.

"I'm impressed."

"I'm glad that you appreciate the effort."

"Clearly in the time I was at the ship, you've been busy?"

"I don't do this for everyone, but I figured it might be our last night for a while," she said as she walked over to him. Although she was a few inches shorter than him, with the heels she was wearing he didn't have to stoop down as far as he usually did to kiss her.

Wrapping her arms around his neck, she looked into his eyes and asked, "Remind me why you volunteered to leave me and go on a suicide mission?"

He pulled away, releasing her to grab two glasses of red wine from the counter. After handing one to her, he took a large gulp from the other.

"Answer me. Why are you going?" she persisted.

"I told you before. I've done things in my life that I'm not proud of. If this mission does nothing else, it may make up for some of the bad stuff in my past."

"I don't understand – if it's redemption you're after, who's it from? Surely it's better for the people who care for you today to have you around, rather than to sacrifice yourself for someone in your past."

"If I were after redemption, it would be from myself, not anyone else. I told the council that I was the best man to assure the success of this mission. Of course, the chances of success are low anyway, but some chance is better than none."

She shook her head sadly. "I don't want you to go."

"I know – and you know this is tearing me apart too.

But it can't change the fact that I am leaving tomorrow so let's just enjoy tonight."

Debs looked away, appearing to gather her thoughts, before saying, "Okay" with some resignation.

"The food's almost ready. Take a seat."

She sat on a stool to watch him stirring one pot and then running around feverishly to taste from the various pans on the stove.

"I didn't realise you were such an accomplished chef," she giggled.

"I think that you know that Frank did most of the prep work?"

Having known Frank for a lot longer than she'd known Pepper, yes she believed he'd had a hand in tonight. This was just the kind of thing she assumed these close friends would do for each other. "Well, I hope you're good at the finishing touches. He's cooked me plenty of nice meals over the years."

"He might have prepared the food, but I bet he didn't include the extra ingredient that I use."

"Go on, I'll humour you – what ingredient?"

"My love, of course." Although he was laughing, it could not hide his real feelings.

"I don't know what the food is going to taste like, but I could be sick if you keep talking like this," she joked uncomfortably.

As fighters for most of their lives, neither of them had much practice at being in a relationship. But they were practising now. For the next few hours, they ate and drank and talked about everything and nothing.

Checking her watch, Debs found it was one in the morning. "Is Frank not coming back tonight?"

"He's busy. He'll be back at breakfast time," Pepper

said with a wry smile. "I need to leave in about four hours. I know this isn't the most romantic invite but would you like to take this into the other room?"

"I didn't squeeze myself into this tight dress to leave now."

"Let's see if it's easier to take off than to put on."

Taking her hand, Pepper led Debs into his bedroom. As it was one of Brand's old rooms, it was more lavish than Debs' accommodation.

The few hours they had passed quickly and, before they had a moment to steal any sleep, it was time for Pepper to prepare to leave.

"Would you like me to come to the docks and see you off?" Debs asked.

"Thanks but you have a lot to do now that you're in charge of the security." Noticing her frown, Pepper realised he needed to do better. "It's not that I don't want to take one last look at you as we pull away from the docks, but it's supposed to be low key. Let me make you some coffee." With that, he kissed her on the cheek and threw a towel around himself as he headed to the kitchen.

Once he'd set the coffee up, he grabbed a quick shower before returning to the bedroom with a large mug.

Debs was sitting up waiting for him. "I don't want you to go."

"I thought we discussed this earlier?"

"You told me to enjoy the night, and I did – but now it's morning. I just want you to know that I'll be here when you get back."

No one had ever said anything like that to Pepper before. A long pause went by before he could think of anything to say. He looked into her eyes and put his arms around her. "I know it's going to be dangerous where we're going, but I'll do everything I can to come back to you."

They kissed, and he was just thinking regretfully that they didn't have time for more sex when he heard the front door to the apartment close.

"Good morning!" he heard Frank shouting through the house.

Debs tried to stifle a laugh as Pepper dropped his towel. "There's coffee on the counter. I'll be out in a minute," Pepper shouted back.

"Take your time. It's not like there's a boat waiting for you before it can leave."

Although Frank was obviously joking, Pepper knew that he was running out of time. He quickly climbed into his clothes. "Do you want to grab a shower?" he asked Debs.

"I'll grab one at my place," she said as she picked up her dress from the floor.

Pepper was first out of the bedroom, to find Frank was already drinking a cup of coffee.

"You ready to go?"

"My bag's packed and the escorts will be outside in ten minutes. Thanks for giving me some space last night," Pepper said as he poured his own coffee.

"Nothing that you wouldn't have done for me."

Just then Debs came out, holding her coffee mug in one hand and her shoes in the other.

"Morning," she said to Frank.

"You're a bit overdressed for breakfast."

She had known Frank for too long to even bother replying other than to shake her head at him.

"I'll drop you off on the way," Pepper said to Debs. "Do you want to meet me downstairs?"

Kissing Pepper on the cheek, she headed for the door, leaving the men to say their farewells. "I'll see you around eleven," she said to Frank. "Don't make him late for the boat."

"Yes, mother," Frank said as she left before turning to Pepper. "Looks like you two had some fun?"

"I think it could have grown into something more than that."

"Stop being so melodramatic. You'll be back in a few months." Frank wasn't sure if he believed it himself, but when fellow soldiers deploy, it's not good manners to suggest that they won't return.

Pepper tapped the pistol on his hip and then hefted his go-bag onto his left shoulder, offering Frank his right hand. "I know Debs can look after herself, but keep an eye on her. She's taking on a lot more responsibility."

Frank understood that this wasn't just a professional request. "She'll be fine, and we'll have another drinking session when you get back."

"Judging by the state of my head yesterday morning, I think it might be safer not coming back."

They both laughed as they shook hands and then Pepper walked away and out of the apartment.

13

FIGHT NIGHT

28 March 2206

Angus had been giving Eric intensive training while getting the rest of his team ready for their mission, and he was impressed by the young man's progress.

On the day of the fights, Zap and Flo were visiting Frank. As Frank's security was then protecting the twins, Angus could accompany Eric to the pits where they could focus on the fight night ahead.

Waiting in the dressing rooms, Angus was giving Eric a final briefing. "You've come a long way, but that's partly due to your natural ability."

"I'd say it's because I had a great trainer," Eric said awkwardly.

"I'm too long in the tooth to be manipulated with hollow flattery. Focus on the fight ahead!"

Eric knew that Angus wasn't really scolding him and he was genuinely grateful to his trainer, but the harsh words brought him back to the task at hand. To help

Karla, Angus had offered Eric and Smith to compete on tonight's fight card.

"The man you are going to fight is a few years older than you and has more experience. He's one of my team, but as soon as you get in that ring, it's every man for himself."

Listening intently, Eric was hoping for some good news.

"He might have more experience, but you have natural strength and the energy of youth on your side. How many training runs have we been on where you've been standing upright at the end, while the rest of the team has been gasping for breath? You need to make the most of your stamina."

Angus remembered his youth when he'd also felt such energy. It had been a long time since he'd felt like that and sometimes he yearned for the past. His training of these fighters had been different from his own experience of being trained in the past. These combatants weren't required to fight to the death so, even though the fight would be aggressive, they could still share the same coach.

In truth, he wanted both fighters to succeed. To give them an even chance, he'd given Smith and Eric thirty minutes of individual training each day.

"Remember, Eric, he's taller than you. You need to minimise his limbs, perhaps take him to the ground. Don't allow him to use leverage to escape. You need to be decisive and focus on the core moves I've taught you."

The fight styles in the pits had changed since the rebels had taken over. Previously the winner was the person left alive, but now a scoring system dictated the results. The fighting still involved a mixed form of fighting styles, including punches and kicking but also various types of holds and blocks.

For tonight's bout, Angus couldn't be in both of the fighters' corners, so he was seconding for Eric while Smith would have the new head trainer at the pits, Jason, in his corner. Jason had taken the job when Angus had needed to spend more time with Zap and, with Angus preparing for a deployment, he'd made the position his own.

Angus spoke calmly but loud enough for Eric to hear him over the noise of the crowd. "Remember you have three rounds of five minutes each. That doesn't sound long, but you're going to be fighting for every second of that time and it can feel a lot longer. Many of the death matches of the past lasted less than five minutes. You need to keep the momentum up for the whole fight, do you understand me?"

Eric nodded and quickly threw some punches in the air to loosen up.

As Smith joined Eric in the ring, Zap and Flo were watching from one of the boxes. To them, Eric was family, and they were ready to shout for him once the fight began.

To Flo, the time when Eric had followed her around like a lovesick boy seemed so far away now. A couple of years on, now that she had straightened things out and he wasn't pursuing her, things had changed.

Lately, she had started to notice him more. Looking at him now, topless and muscly, she had to remind herself that he was like a brother. She felt a little confused. Whereas before she had ignored the scars on his body, she was starting to think those scars just made him look more rugged.

The fighters were the star attraction, but it was hard for Flo to ignore Karla up on the balcony. She stood there with Miyamoto by her side, but she wasn't some weak politician needing a bodyguard. She was very much in control of everything.

The stories told about Karla were always about her brutality, but over time Flo had come to learn that there was more to Karla than the rough exterior she showed to strangers.

Karla had been in charge of the fighting pits, a masculine ecosystem that was dripping with testosterone. For a woman to survive in this environment was one thing but for Karla to thrive and maintain control of these warriors required an iron will – and, yes, some brutality.

Since the rebellion, Flo had felt Karla soften. She still ruled the pits with an iron fist, but she no longer had to prove anything to anyone. Without a psycho like Brand looking over her shoulder, she had complete autonomy, and this had helped her switch her focus.

She still drove the instructors to get the best out of the fighters and she wanted them to put on a good show. But, as she was now also responsible for training the security forces, her goals were different. With this symbiotic relationship in which the security forces supplied pit fighters and the pits provided them with training, Karla's focus was on giving them the skills they needed to stay alive in a crisis.

She could have given the job of master of ceremonies to someone else, but announcing the fighters was just another demonstration of Karla's control. The pitch and level of her voice both boosted the energy in the fighters and whipped up the passion in the crowd. Standing there waving a large handgun in her right hand, Karla addressed them all.

"In the red corner, we have a member of the sanctuary's brave security forces, a man who risks his life daily so that you can all sleep safely in your beds, Alexander Smith."

Smith stood there in loose combat pants, and a green vest stretched tight over his well-conditioned body. He raised both arms to a loud cheer, prompted in particular by the large contingent of security forces around the arena, but some among the crowd tried to show their loyalty to the new leadership too. A few among the crowd who didn't like authority booed. It was nothing like the displays of anger that swelled in the dying days of the previous regime though – just a reminder that the current leaders didn't have everyone's support.

"In the blue corner, I give you one of the heroes of the rebellion, responsible for driving leader Brand out of the capital – the one and only Eric." She knew she was laying it on a bit thick, but that was showmanship.

This time the crowd needed no help in starting their cheers. Eric was a scarred survivor who looked more like one of them than a soldier. His bald head and naked top above black loose-fitting trousers showed off the scars from his youth but also accentuated his muscles. The women in the crowd would have shouted for him, whoever he was.

Someone in the crowd began chanting, "Baldy, Baldy, Baldy."

Flo was confused. Why were they picking on Eric?

Seeing her puzzled face, Zap smiled and said, "Don't worry, sis. The crowd likes Eric – they're chanting for him, not against him."

Looking at the enthusiastic people around her, she realised that Zap was right. Under her breath, even she quietly repeated, "Baldy."

This chant began to ripple around the room as Karla acknowledged that the crowd had picked a favourite.

"Without any further delays, release the warriors!" Karla roared and fired a blank round into the air.

Immediately Eric barrelled towards Smith.

Smith had begun his own advance but, seeing Eric coming, he slowed and executed a side-step. This stopped him taking the full brunt of Eric's assault, but even the glancing blow to his shoulder threw him off balance.

Before Smith could recover his footing, Eric had swivelled around and they locked in a tight embrace.

Smith tried to use his long limbs to his advantage, squirming and trying leverage or anything else he could to break loose from Eric's grip. With Eric's lower centre of gravity and solid body mass, Smith knew that if they went to the ground, his opponent could quickly get the better of him.

He had more experience in hand-to-hand combat than his younger opponent, but what Eric lacked in experience he made up for in raw aggression and physical strength.

As they circled the arena floor, Smith tried to break Eric's grip by forcing his right arm down and at an angle, maximising his leverage and momentum. At the same time, he was fighting to remain upright as Eric tried to trip him and take him to the floor.

Sensing that he needed to do something drastic, Smith smashed his forehead on the bridge of Eric's nose. Although this momentarily broke Eric's grip, it set off a round of booing from the crowd.

Smith took a few steps back, giving himself a little distance, but his respite was short-lived. Eric charged and this time he was ready for the side-step. His fist connected with a stinging blow to Smith's ear.

Smith had his hands forward with his forearms forming a defensive V. This helped deflect Eric's attack but not entirely. Although the blow to his ear dazed him slightly, he had no time to rest.

For the next couple of minutes, the two of them stood toe to toe. They had both been taught in the same styles, but Eric tended to default to a more aggressive and less disciplined approach.

Smith was continually attacking with both hands and one leg at the same time while keeping the weight on his rear foot to draw his power from the ground. Eric was brawling like a street fighter.

Watching from above, Karla was pondering that in similar fights where one fighter was attacking with three points at once and the other was just using his top half, the advantage would go to the former. Yet even facing the better technique, Eric's youth, energy and aggression were keeping things very competitive.

As Eric absorbed the kicks, they both punched in a wheel, dropping the front hand while punching from the rear in a constant barrage. Each fighter found some of their punches bounced off their opponent's forearms while others got through to his torso.

It was brutal for Flo to watch. Even though Eric was holding his own, she felt worried for him.

Then Karla fired to finish the round and the two fighters separated to opposite ends of the arena.

Jason was waiting for Smith with a stool for him to sit on and a water bottle. "Try to keep your distance. You've got reach and height on your side – use it!"

As he spat blood and water into a bucket, Smith took a breath and replied, "I'd appreciate it if you told Eric I've got the advantage."

At the other end of the arena, Angus was talking to Eric. "What are you doing out there? Don't you remember anything that I taught you? This is not a wrestling match. You might have more strength and youth on your side, but I've seen technique kill many a man."

"I've got him worried."

"The techniques you learnt in training were developed for people to fight taller opponents. He's using his height to keep you at a distance. Use the three-pronged attack – two hands and a foot at the same time. Get inside his defences. Do you hear me?" Angus shouted.

Eric's adrenalin was clearly flowing, Angus had been in this position enough times himself to recognise it. Now he needed to break through.

A slap across the face got Eric's attention.

"What was that for?"

"I had to get you to listen. This might not be a death match but if you don't start listening, you'll get hurt. Think of how you normally fight against Zap."

"I only use those techniques with Zap and hold myself back so that I don't hurt him."

"I train you in those techniques for your benefit. Use the same moves but don't hold back this time."

"Okay, I'll try it your way," Eric said somewhat reluctantly.

As soon as Karla fired the next shot, the battle started again.

This time Eric advanced at a steadier pace, keeping the weight on his back foot, almost sliding his feet across the arena.

Smith was employing the same technique, and they slid towards each other until they were within arm's length.

The crowd was shouting again, "Baldy, Baldy, Baldy."

Eric could feel the noise in the arena growing, but he kept his focus.

Now the real fighting began.

Both men began throwing punches and kicks at a phenomenal rate. The initial flurries were a blur as the punches flowed round and round like a wheel. After a minute of constant blows, they settled down into a steadier pace.

As one punch was thrown, a blow met it from the opposite direction, and the two fighters' legs were kicking and scooping in unison.

These techniques had their origins in an ancient system known as Wing Chun and it was very effective.

Eric had managed to get in closer to Smith, preventing him from using his longer reach. Both men were connecting with the odd punch but the sheer power of Eric's punches started to take its toll as he brought the energy of the ground through his heels.

The primary target for this technique was the throat.

This helped Eric as it was easier for him to punch up towards Smith's throat.

One of Eric's punches connected square with Smith's jaw, sending him reeling back.

Eric didn't let up. As Smith faltered with his footing, Eric unleashed a fury of strikes, drawing blood from above Smith's right eye.

By now Smith was struggling to keep on his feet. His head was fuzzy and even keeping his fists up was difficult.

Eric connected under Smith's jaw with a punch that lifted him off his feet.

"Baldy, Baldy, Baldy," the crowd was on their feet, screaming at full volume.

Eric was still punching and kicking Smith as he collapsed to the ground.

Jason threw a towel in from the end of the arena and Karla fired a shot to end the bout.

Eric was in a blood fugue. Angus and Jason had to run in to the ring to keep him from hurting Smith further. A medic rushed up to see to Smith.

Once Eric had begun to calm down, Angus lifted his right arm.

The crowd went wild as Karla's voice came over the speakers. "It appears the hero of the rebellion has triumphed again. Let's have a big cheer for Eric."

"Baldy, Baldy, Baldy." The chant seemed to go on for ages. Even Flo found herself drawn into the excitement of the crowd.

Walking around the arena with both arms in the air, Eric was growling to the crowd, making them chant all the louder.

As he reached Smith's prone figure on the floor, he looked at Angus.

"Show some respect," Angus scowled.

Eric's face changed immediately, and he crouched down to help Smith up. "I'm sorry, I got a bit carried away with the occasion."

Still a little stunned but now able to talk, Smith replied, half smiling and half grimacing, "You fought well, boy. The best man won and wow can you throw a punch."

"You didn't fight so bad yourself, old man." Eric grasped Smith's right hand with his own and helped him to his feet.

Eric allowed Smith to lean on him as he lifted his arm in the air. As a sign of respect, he then helped Smith to complete another lap of the arena.

As Angus watched, he was relieved that this was not one of the fights of the past. He wouldn't want to see either of them die in the arena.

The chants of "Baldy" continued, joined by the odd shout of "Smith".

They left the arena to make space for the next bout. After a quick clean-up, they proceeded to the refreshment area where Eric found Flo waiting with Zap.

"Well done, well done, Eric," she said, with a big beaming smile. He was now fully clothed, but she wouldn't quickly forget the sight of his taut physique.

Seeing Eric now brought on strange feelings in Flo. It was hard to imagine him as the scared child that she had first met in the barn. Back then, it had taken a long time to gain the feral boy's trust and build the bond they now had.

What she had just witnessed reminded her that Eric had an aggressive side but the beast he had released also stirred feelings in her that she hadn't felt before.

Although Pepper had said on several occasions that she was maturing into an impressive young woman, she hadn't known what he meant at the time.

The pressure from her captivity had suppressed her female desires for a long time. Then her deep commitment to the rebellion and its aftermath only kept that side of her hidden for longer.

Flo had lost her biological mother at such an early age that she could barely remember her. Kath had raised her like a daughter for most of her life but after she had lost Kath, she had had no real female role models in her life.

Although she had some stability from Pepper and Frank, who both treated her like a daughter, she couldn't discuss female issues with them.

Her recent focus on training for the coming threat continued to leave her with little time for anything else. Yet the emotions that Eric stirred within her gave her a glimpse of a normal life, a life that still seemed so far away.

THE SUMMIT – DAY ONE

20 April 2206

Although it was clear to Frank that other telepaths were trying to block his telepaths, he didn't know who was controlling them yet.

Distrust had always been part of these summits, so this could just be a new precaution.

Following the attack on their sanctuary, however, it seemed too much of a coincidence that this tactic was being used for the first time at the summit. He considered the other leaders suspiciously, wondering whether this was verification that the assault was from one of them.

He hoped to find out more over the next three days that would justify deploying the assault team's boat. It was a heavy enough burden to bear that the ship was full of people he could be sending to their deaths. But with Pepper on the boat, it was personal. He missed Pepper's company at night the most as someone he could confide in with total trust even in these dangerous times.

As usual, the summit was an ostentatious affair. Over the years it had become a formal occasion with set formats and procedures. Each of the three days of meetings between the three summit leaders was followed by an evening of entertainment.

The whole venue was erected specifically for the summit and stripped out afterwards. The large tents had been shipped in by the advance teams to construct something that resembled luxury buildings more than a temporary structure.

The summits had traditionally been held approximately once a year, but this was only the second that Frank had attended after missing one during his first year as a sanctuary head.

The initial period after the overthrow of Brand had been a challenging time. Because it was not a completely smooth transition, the new council had decided that they needed to solidify their position internally, before opening themselves up to external attacks.

There had been some discussion about how much attending the summit cost in terms of resources. Eventually, the council decided that isolationism was not beneficial to their sanctuary. Frank had attended last year's summit, and the lack of any open antagonism between the three sanctuaries seemed to justify the expense.

Each sanctuary took a turn at hosting a day, supposedly as an opportunity to display its affluence. As each leader had typically seen it, they had reached the pinnacle of power in their kingdom, and this was a way of showing their prowess on a global scale.

Although Frank hated wasting resources, he had to play the part of a sanctuary leader. Having to wear lavish clothes and display grooming was only the half of it. Luckily his turn as host was scheduled first so if the others outshone his offerings he could claim they had taken advantage of knowing what they had to compete against.

Chang was the first to take his seat. Even sitting down it was clear he was a big man – when standing he was over six foot six inches tall – and his shoulders ballooned out of the top of the large luxurious seat. He was bald apart from a tail of plaited hair, anchored at the top of his head. What really made Chang stand out to Frank, though, was the disconcerting difference in the colour of his eyes: one blue and one brown.

Chang was flanked by two of his female bodyguards and a tall oriental-looking woman known as Gee King. Gee was the head of Chang's security team also doubling as his translator. She was a few inches shorter than Chang but like him she was made up of taut muscle. Like Chang, she was also bald apart from a plaited braid of hair down her back.

The next to take a seat was Radka. At six feet tall, he was short relative to the other leaders. Complementing his long dark-brown hair and blue eyes were freshly manicured nails and luxurious clothes but none of this disguised his overweight frame and flabby physique.

Radka was also flanked by members of his security detail but added to that were two scantily clad females draped over the armrests of his chair. As Radka pawed the women, it was clear to Frank that, even if one of them was there to translate, the other was clearly present for Radka's pleasure.

Frank opened the meeting. Each word he spoke was repeated by his translator Enya, once in the language of

Chang's kingdom and the other in the language of Radka's. As with all the formalities of these summits, even the order of translations was rotated. Tomorrow Radka would host and everything he said would be translated into Chang's language and then Frank's.

"I'm glad that we've all survived another year in an uncertain world, but I need to open this summit with some disconcerting news. Unknown forces recently attacked our kingdom. They detonated bombs in our capital, and many were killed or injured." As Enya relayed the message, Frank looked closely at the faces of his counterparts. Obviously, even if neither of them had instigated the attacks, they would know about them already.

For the next few moments, the translators worked doubly hard to keep up with the rapid conversations between the leaders.

Frank had never liked subterfuge, but he reminded himself that he was a politician and this was part of the job. "The peace between our sanctuaries has held for decades now, so I see no benefit in either of you sanctioning an attack on our homeland."

"Are you accusing us of something?" Chang asked, as Gee rapidly translated his words. "Perhaps you should look closer to home. You have recently had issues with the disgruntled masses. If it weren't for rebellion, you wouldn't even be here yourself now."

"On the contrary, I am asking for your help to investigate who did this. No one knows your people as well as you do and I would ask that you use your resources to look into this. It may be that whoever attacked us has one of you in their sights next."

"Our people love us," Radka protested. "Just

because your sanctuary got out of hand doesn't mean that we all have issues."

Thinking that Radka was protesting a little too much, Chang interrupted. "Radka, Radka, I think our host raises a good point. If no one knows the source of this attack, perhaps it makes sense for us to work together."

Radka was flustered. He hadn't expected to have to fend off arguments from both of them at the same time. Although he wasn't a stupid man, he hadn't been chosen for his hyper-intelligence either as that would have made him a threat. Instead he had been chosen because he looked like a leader, which would help to sell the story that he was the leader.

The problem with sending someone of lesser intelligence to converse with the other leaders was that there was always the chance that he would be caught out. Thinking on his feet, Radka decided the best option was to seem amenable. "How can we help you?"

"Reach out to your intelligence sources, both in your sanctuaries and in ours." Frank could see that Radka was about to object again, so he spoke first. "Before you bother protesting, I am not accusing you of spying on us. It makes sense for you to have intelligence resources in other sanctuaries. The communication drones are intermittent, and if you ever experienced an interruption in the drones, you would need to know what was happening. Such sources may know more than we do about these attacks. Please see what you can find out."

Frank had practised this story on the plane as he wanted his lies to seem natural. It was highly likely that one of the other two leaders had either ordered the attack or knew of its source.

Even the one not responsible would be aware of the charade that was being played out but such was the nature of politics.

After the contentious opening, the rest of the day was spent reading through pre-printed proposals for trading resources between the sanctuaries and the proposed timetables for these trades.

Most of this information had been exchanged via drone in the months before the summit, so no serious negotiations were involved.

Throughout the day they had a constant supply of refreshments along with musicians and other entertainment, helping the time to pass quickly and peacefully.

It was late into the night when Chancellor Chang made his excuses to leave the gathering. As was the tradition, the person hosting was not the one who could volunteer to leave first. So, as Radka's greed clearly held him back from leaving yet, the first move fell to Chang.

To save face, Frank stayed around for another thirty minutes and then offered his farewells.

Day one down and Frank was already exhausted. It wasn't so much the daily activities that had-drained him as the need to remain amicable when he was almost certain that one of the other leaders had staged the attack on his homeland.

The only saving grace of the evening was the thought that tomorrow was another day, so only two days of the summit were left to go.

15

ERIC'S DEFENCE

29 March 2206

The morning after the fight night, Eric and Zap were feeling the after-effects.

Eric had bruises and a black eye, but Zap's injuries were more related to a self-inflicted hangover.

It had been Angus who had suggested that Eric and the twins needed to let off some steam. "It's time the three of you had some fun. You have taken a lot on your shoulders this year, and if you don't release some of that pressure, it will make you ill."

That had been his speech straight after Eric's fight. Then he'd encouraged them to consume some foul-tasting but potent drink.

It was rare that they all stayed in the capital, but they were as secure as it was possible to be, so they'd tried to relax. Eric and Flo had spent most of the night talking while Angus supplied all three of them with drinks. Flo, however, had limited her intake for most of the night.

It had been late at night when they'd finally gone to

their separate rooms, and they were now meeting up for breakfast.

Eric was sitting eating when Zap approached slowly. "How are you feeling?" Eric asked him.

"I feel like you hit me with several of your special punches that sometimes sneak through in training."

"I can't help it if you don't know how to protect yourself."

"And why the heck do you look so fresh?"

It was true that although Eric was the worse for wear from the fight, he didn't seem to have any after-effects from the previous night's drinking.

"Have you seen the size of him?" Angus interjected as he sat down next to them. "He could drink ten times your body weight in alcohol, and it still wouldn't affect him."

Eric was grinning at Zap's discomfort when he noticed Flo from across the room. She was wearing a loose-fitting dark wool dress and black leather boots and her wet hair bounced off her shoulders as she walked across the room. Eric couldn't ever remember noticing Flo's appearance before. As he thought about this, he realised that it wasn't true – he remembered her wearing a blue dress at the fights last night and she had looked very nice.

"How are you feeling?" Zap asked as she sat down with a tray of fresh fruit.

"By the look of you, I'm a lot better. I'm glad I didn't drink as much as you last night." Flo thought it was funny that she could usually communicate in Zap's mind, but his head was so fuzzy today that his thoughts seemed muddled.

She smiled at Eric and he gave her a big grin back.

It always amazed everyone how much and how fast Eric ate. In the time it took Flo to eat her breakfast, he'd consumed almost six times as much.

Zap had started to feel more human after a full plate of greasy food. "Before we head back to the school, I've got to go speak to Frank and Pepper. I should only be about an hour."

"I'll escort you there. It'll be safer if we all travel back to the school together after that. What are you two going to do while you wait?" Angus asked Eric and Flo.

"It's been ages since you visited the capital without a task from the council and it's such a nice day outside. Would you like to grab some fresh air?" Eric asked Flo.

"After all the excitement last night that sounds like a great idea," she replied.

"Okay we'll meet you back here in two hours. Don't get into any trouble and stay safe," Angus said while waving a finger at Eric.

Eric tried to look innocent, but they all knew that trouble could follow Eric around like a shadow. He'd become a lot more controlled of late, but in the past, his short temper had gotten him into more than one fight. He was just lucky that he was big enough and strong enough to get himself out of any scrapes, Angus thought.

When the others left Eric alone with Flo, he felt a bit weird. Something seemed to be different since their previous night of chatting, and he wasn't quite sure what to say.

"You've spent a lot more time in the capital than me lately. Are you going to show me around?" she asked.

"Let's head out to the main square. It has lots of

places to sit and it's close enough to keep you out of trouble."

"Okay," Flo said as she offered him her hand. "Let's grab some fresh air."

It took them only fifteen minutes to get from the dining room to the square. Eric had spent almost ten minutes of that convincing the security detail that he didn't need them to come too.

Once out in the square, they could see the mess from the night before. Revellers from the fight night in the nearby pits had left food wrappers and plastic containers strewn around the ground.

It upset Flo to see the place in such a mess, but she knew that in a short while the scavengers would be out and all this refuse would be gone. In a world of scarcity, one person's rubbish was another's treasure.

Growing up on a farm, she was conscious of the quality of the air in the city. The air here wasn't as fresh as that at the school either, but the buildings made the place appealing in a different kind of way.

As a child, she'd rarely visited places like this and even now she was in awe of the tall buildings and the clean mirror windows.

"It's nice to be away from our responsibilities for once," Flo said quietly.

Holding her hand, Eric looked at her tenderly. "And away from the threats to the school too."

They walked as though they were the only people in the square and in a short while they had traversed its full length.

Even though Flo was the centre of his attention, Eric's survival instincts were still working peripherally.

As they passed an alleyway, a faint voice came from the shadows. "Help me, someone, help me!"

In the distance, a group was standing over someone's prone form.

Flo looked at Eric. "Did you hear that? What's happening?" she asked nervously.

Eric was torn; his first priority was to protect Flo. He didn't want to put her in danger, but someone seemed to be in trouble and he couldn't abandon them.

"Stay here while I go and check it out. If anything happens, run across the square to the security vehicles over there."

As Eric got closer to the group, he saw five men standing over a smaller form on the ground. "What's going on here?"

"Hey man, we're just having a bit of fun," a man in the middle of the group replied. Eric noted that he wasn't the biggest of the group, but he had the kind of swagger that came from someone who thought they were the leader.

The figure on the ground could have been a young boy or girl; it was hard to tell as their face was severely battered and bruised.

"What did they do?" Eric asked calmly, cautious not to play his hand too soon.

"The little shit robbed Zeek last night. Did a bit of the old 'bump and pocket dip'. He'd have probably got away with it if he hadn't tried to empty my pockets as well. We trailed him the whole night and caught him here."

"Don't you think he's had enough? He's only little." Eric realised that the boy had done wrong, but he'd had to survive as a child himself and knew you did what you had to.

"Hey, you're that bald guy from the fights last night."

As the others recognised Eric from the night before, they started chanting, "Baldy, Baldy, Baldy."

It was clear from the smell that they were all still under the influence of whatever they had drunk the night before. "You may be good in a one-on-one fight, but there's five of us here so walk away, Baldy. You wouldn't want us to hurt you in front of your lady. Perhaps she'd like to feel some real men for a change?" The biggest man in the group grinned through broken teeth, indicating Flo at the end of the alley.

"It's okay, kid. You are going to be okay," Eric said to the boy on the ground.

As the men realised that the new arrival wasn't heeding their warnings, the atmosphere changed abruptly.

"This is our business, not yours! Go tend to your woman before we invite her to party with us," said the leader.

In the time since Eric had approached the group, he'd assessed the situation and determined his options. He was outnumbered five to one, but he had the element of surprise on his side and he wasn't dulled by drink. The boy on the ground was in trouble and there was no time to waste.

Any further chatter would give the group more time to prepare so, instead of talking, Eric acted.

He punched the biggest man in the throat with such force that he flew backwards and collapsed. The man didn't gasp or reach for his throat, he just laid there motionless. Eric immediately headed for the leader.

Before he could get to him, out of the corner of his eye, Eric saw someone running from his left. He pivoted just in time to block the arm that was swinging a bottle at his head. Keeping hold of the arm, he used the momentum of his attacker to throw him straight into a brick wall. The second that his head impacted with the wall, Eric grabbed a handful of hair and pounded the man's head twice more into the bricks.

Eric was now growling, and even the bravado of the leader seemed to be fading. "Don't just stand there, get him," he shouted to the other two in his crew.

The next attacker was carrying a plank of wood, but he was hesitant, and that was his first and last mistake. He held the wood in both hands and swung it at Eric's head. Whether his hesitancy came from fear or the alcohol in his blood, this attacker was just too slow. Eric charged him down and grabbed the wood from out of the air. Disarming him, he held the wood in one arm and brought it down on the man's head with such force that the wood shattered as it crushed his skull.

Now only two assailants were left standing. "Get him, do I have to do this myself?" the leader asked, but it seemed his companion had lost his appetite for the fight and just stood there frozen.

The alleyway was closed at one end, so the attackers had nowhere to go. Even with Angus's training, Eric was now in a blind rage and gave them no mercy.

The leader approached passing a long blade between his hands as a way of disguising his attack, but he was clumsy and even before he began his swing, Eric was upon him. He took the knife from his hand and threw it at the remaining attacker.

The knife flew with such force that the blade buried itself in the man's chest, up to the hilt.

He still had a hold of the leader. Lifting him above his head he brought the man down hard as he screamed out and broke his opponent's back on a nearby wooden pallet.

The boy was now wailing, apparently more scared of Eric than his previous attackers.

"It's okay, come to me," came Flo's voice from behind Eric.

It was like someone had thrown a bucket of cold water over him. Eric's shoulders sank at the sound of her voice.

He turned around to find that she had approached while he was in the middle of the fight.

The look of terror on Flo's face cut into him harder than any knife blade could. She was looking at the pile of broken bodies and then back at the boy on the floor.

Bending down, Flo helped him up. "What's your name?"

"Kit," the boy stammered.

"You're safe now," Flo said and, supporting his weight, started to walk back towards the square.

Eric said nothing but just trudged behind them. He was still aware of his surroundings, but no longer sensed a threat. Rather than considering the dead bodies he was leaving behind, he was more concerned with the look that Flo had just given him.

16

THE SUMMIT – DAY TWO

21 April 2206

Day two of the summit proceeded similarly to day one. Today was Radka's turn to play host, and he provided a vast array of rich food and drink. They were in a different tent for today's activities, although its layout was very similar to the one from yesterday.

The furnishings seemed brighter and the cushions plumper, and even more food and drink were on offer than during Frank's hosting. It was almost comical to Frank that together the leaders could not consume this much in even a week of gluttony.

The pageantry of it all made even less sense as the summit was only attended by the three leaders and their small entourages. The leaders would not be easily impressed, and it was doubtful if any of their people would tell others at home of these excesses. The attendees were chosen because they were deemed loyal to their leaders. Unless they were given specific permission, they wouldn't mention the details of the summit.

Then again, perhaps the whole show was for the benefit of security details. Perhaps the leaders were supposed to be competing to make the best impression on the security people from other sanctuaries so that they would take the information back home and spread the word that others were better off than them.

If that was the plan, it made little sense. Frank assumed that all the attendees had better lives than the masses. From his perspective, if anyone got more than they needed to survive, they would see anything extra as a bonus. The extravagances of the summit were too extreme to relate to their own lives.

It also made little sense for anyone to risk what they already had for the remote chance of gaining a bit of luxury. It was doubtful that this charade would corrupt anyone to the extent that they would turn on their own sanctuary. The life of a spy provided a high-risk-reward ratio in a world where life was so cheap.

Frank had survived minimally for years. Even though his new rank of leader afforded him some luxuries, they were nothing compared with what Brand had gained in his previous years of decadent rule.

In the eyes of the select few who knew about them, the summits were just self-indulgent parties for the sanctuary leaders.

Frank had observed that, despite the hospitality, not everyone was overindulging. It seemed the only person taking full advantage of the food and drink was Radka.

Looking at Chang, Frank thought he was not really drinking. He had lots of drinks in front of him, but his aides seemed to be removing them before he had time to finish them, creating the façade that he was drinking heavily. His hands looked more like those of a boxer than someone who was waited on from dawn until dusk. His loose-fitting clothes didn't disguise his physical shape underneath. With his shaved head and broad shoulders, he looked like he would do well in the old fighting pits.

Radka was a different story; he looked like he'd always lived a life of leisure. His long wavy brown hair was perfectly groomed, his hands were manicured and his skin looked as soft as butter. The rolls of stomach fat spilled over the top of his trousers, and his nose was red from all of his drinking to excess over the years.

Radka was consuming a constant flow of drinks and delicacies. Although he had staff to wipe the food from his face, it didn't disguise how the drinks seemed to be taking effect. After long hours of drinking, his speech was slurred.

Frank felt that something was out of place with Radka. He knew that paranoia had kept Brand in power for such a long period and assumed that this same instinct was hard-wired into most of the elites in all three sanctuaries. If so, why had Radka let his guard down? Or was this an elaborate act to lower Frank's guard? He sometimes felt that he wasn't cut out for all of this intrigue.

As one way of securing an advantage, he'd made it his mission to disguise how little alcohol he was drinking so that he could observe the interplay of events more closely than his rival leaders realised. While his years of survival living had provided him with a high tolerance for alcohol, he wanted to keep his wits about him. So he had briefed his team to make his drinks look like the alcoholic drinks his host was providing but, in reality, to give him watered-down versions. So far it seemed that his ruse was working.

Watching Radka paw over the female translators from Frank's sanctuary made him angry. They had fought for their lives to liberate his sanctuary, and here they were being confronted by the same arrogance from others.

Having every word pass through translators slowed down the conversations and the subjects they covered were so trivial that being here still felt like a waste of Frank's life.

His sanctuary provided superior cigars and Radka's produced the better wines, but obviously the weights of these products created an imbalance and when drone fuel was an issue the weight of the payload mattered.

This subject alone took two hours to resolve, and that was just one of the many seemingly pointless discussions that Radka seemed to revel in turning into an argument.

It was after long after midnight when Frank made his excuses to leave the festivities. But before he had a chance to exit the main tent, Cenk took him to one side. "Chancellor Chang's head of security has approached me. She said that Chang wants a private meeting with you."

"How safe would that be?" Frank asked.

"It'd be as safe as anything while we're here. If either of the other leaders wanted to take us out, they could bring in extra planes or boats or just bomb us," Cenk replied.

"Okay, go and make the arrangements."

"They are already in place."

"The sooner, the better as I'm ready for bed," Frank

replied. He was used to working long hours, but the forced pleasantries were tiring him out and he just wanted to get this over with.

Motioning for Cenk to lead the way, he hoped that whatever Chang had to say was worth his time.

17

FRANK'S MEETING WITH CHANG

22 April 2206

Two neutral rooms were set aside at each summit for meetings just like this one. Only two rooms were required as there could only ever be two leaders at any one time waiting for another to arrive. The fact that the meetings happened was common knowledge, but as the only people attending a meeting were two of the leaders, there was little chance that the contents of the meeting would be leaked.

Frank and Cenk had just exited the main tent.

"How long do I have before the meeting?" Frank inquired.

"Thirty minutes," Cenk replied. "All of the precautions have been taken. You will enter through different doors."

"Good, I'll change my clothes then," Frank said. He returned to his rooms and had a quick shower before changing into a pair of dark trousers and a dark sweater.

There was no requirement for fancy clothes in these meetings, but it was a cold night.

Feeling somewhat refreshed, Frank entered the meeting room.

"Good morning, Francis," Chang said. "I took the liberty of supplying a bottle of whisky for us to share. In the interests of transparency, I'll let you pour the drinks for both of us."

Frank tried not to react to the fact that Chang was talking in the native tongue of Sanctuary One. He knew that the offer to let him pour the drinks was a symbolic act of faith. There were so many ways that Chang could poison him. He could taint both glasses and take the antidote himself first; or he could have the bottle coated in a toxin that Frank would ingest by touch – to name just two possible ploys.

"Don't worry, I wouldn't waste such a nice drink with poison," Chang smiled.

As he poured the drinks, Frank said, "We haven't got long, so could you please let me know what you want at this unreasonable hour?"

"I have some information that I think you'll be very grateful for," Chang said in a tantalising tone.

"Let's dispense with the intrigue so that I can get some sleep before tomorrow's enthralling summit meeting."

"The impatience of youth," Chang sneered. "I just thought you'd like to know who was responsible for the attacks on your capital."

Frank was cautious given that in the earlier meetings both Chang and Radka had denied any knowledge of the attacks. It would not be unheard of for either leader to try to deflect the guilt on to the other. "Indulge me."

"Last year Radka had supposedly succeeded Yuri Orlov as the leader of Sanctuary Two." Chang paused for effect.

"I know that I may not be as seasoned a leader as you, but even I noticed that Radka attended last year's summit."

"Very good, but what you didn't notice was that Radka isn't the leader of the sanctuary!"

Frank was a little taken aback and tried to hide his surprise. "Who is the leader? Is it still Orlov?"

"I like the way you're thinking, but unfortunately Orlov is no longer alive. My sources tell me that his successor had him executed, to ensure there was no chance of him reversing the coup. Radka is just a front, and he is the cover for someone from both of our pasts. The new leader of Sanctuary Two is none other than Harland Brand."

Frank was still trying not to show emotions, but his surprise from this news was hard to disguise. "How certain are you of this information?"

"I would not be sharing this information if I wasn't sure."

"What do you intend to do about this?" Frank asked.

"I have done exactly what I intended to do; I have shared the information. Currently, Brand is only targeting your sanctuary for his revenge. It provides no benefits to my sanctuary to engage in an offensive against him. I will remain neutral in this matter." Chang smiled.

"If you don't intend to get involved, why are you telling me this?" Frank asked in frustration.

"If Brand defeats you easily and takes your resources, he becomes a threat to me. If I can give you some warning of the threat, you may put up a reasonable fight. If you win, you're indebted to me, and if you lose, you may still weaken Brand."

This made sense, leaving Frank with little reason to doubt Chang. "How did he come to be the leader?"

"Apparently he'd laid the foundations for an escape plan in case he ever had to leave your sanctuary. His new hosts were obviously naive in believing that they could control him. When the opportunity arose, he implemented his plan and took charge. I am unsure if he'd always intended to take against you or if it was just an afterthought. Either way, it's your problem now."

"Our time is almost up. Is there anything else you can tell me?" Frank asked.

"Apparently, in public, Radka is the face of the sanctuary leadership, but Brand attends all the council meetings and makes all the decisions. He has a right-hand man called Nikolei, who is in charge of his security. I can provide some maps and other information if you wish to pursue the matter?"

"Could you put me in touch with your contacts in Brand's regime?" Frank asked, already knowing the answer.

"I know that you aren't that inexperienced. I may provide you with information, but if I did have assets in their realm, I wouldn't expose them for you. It seems our meeting time has expired. Do you wish to have my help?"

"I would appreciate any information you can provide," Frank said, trying to act reserved.

"It shall be so," Chang raised his glass and said "Ganbei" as he downed the contents.

Chang wasn't the charitable type; he'd passed the

information on to Frank purely because he wanted to increase the friction and ill feeling between the other two sanctuaries.

Following the Water Wars, the one percent had to be on constant alert for threats to their power. As they were in the minority, their control was always going to be fragile.

Since the previous leadership in Frank's sanctuary had been overthrown, Chang was considering his own survival even more. Rebellion was contagious.

He had spoken truthfully in observing that if Frank and his team were successful in ousting Brand, Frank would feel indebted to him – and it would leave Sanctuary Two in a vulnerable state. If Brand survived the assault, trouble would likely escalate between the other two sanctuaries.

Whatever the outcome, in their preoccupation with each other they would leave Chang alone to maintain control over his domain.

"Cheers" was all Frank could say in response. After he emptied his drink, they both left the room via their designated exits.

18

—————

THE RISE TO POWER

15 February 2205

It had taken Brand just over a year to build Risslo's trust enough to be allowed the freedom to travel unfettered. He'd used his new freedom to contact his sleeper agents and to develop his shadow organisation right under Risslo's nose.

When the time had come to dispose of Risslo, Brand caught him completely unaware. By then, Brand had built his power base, and Risslo did not have enough support on the council for anyone to come to his aid or seek revenge for his loss.

Some of the other council members even encouraged Brand. They saw this as a way of replacing one of their competitors with a less dangerous opponent. They mistakenly thought that as an outsider Brand would not be able to build a strong enough opposition to ever challenge them.

What the council hadn't recognised was his blind ambition for power and revenge. He'd worked a similar playbook to become the leader of Sanctuary One. Over the last eighteen months, he had used his new position to search for any talent with powers similar to those of his own children.

When he'd arrived, it seemed that no one in this sanctuary was aware of the telepaths living among them.

Seeing their potential as a resource, Brand had corralled the telepaths. Most of them were young, so they had been malleable. He'd experimented and learnt how to refine their skills.

Some of the tactics had been unsuccessful, resulting in some fatalities in the training programme. However, the deaths were of no concern as the successful surviving recruits became an excellent resource for building his web of spies.

Unlike the spies in Sanctuary One, this new talent didn't even have to be in the same room to hear what people were thinking. Their ability to read minds was a core element in Brand's meteoric rise to power in the sanctuary.

Brand didn't see his old sanctuary as a threat to his current position – he simply wanted revenge. During his time in exile, he'd been keeping an eye on them. The reports were they had spent all of their time rebuilding infrastructure and resources.

Even with the changes in infrastructure, he still knew the weak points to attack. His only real concern was that his children's powers had probably grown so that they might detect any spies that he sent into Sanctuary One. With this in mind, he had decided to deploy some of his new telepaths and use them to block the thoughts of any mind-readers.

At the same time, unaware of Brand's location, Hubert and Frank had decided to leave it as long as possible before notifying the other leaders that they were now in charge of Sanctuary One. They were concerned that the other leaders would sense weakness if they thought Sanctuary One had a power vacuum. Frank had avoided attending the first summit and then pretended to participate in Brand's stead in the second. Although Yuri Orlov or Radka was at each of these summits and knew very well where Brand was, to Frank the ploy appeared to be working as the other sanctuaries hadn't attacked during that time.

As in the kingdom surrounding Sanctuary One, the other two kingdoms had their own elite who helped themselves to resources, while the masses were kept in survival mode. They differed in some minor ways in their system of liquid gel packs. In one kingdom, for example, the age of forced euthanasia was forty, which was said to be necessary due to its larger population as it limited how fast it could grow.

All of the kingdoms had their arsenal of large, lethal weapons. However, because of the fragile state of the planet following the Water Wars, it was of no benefit to any kingdom to start an all-out war.

Brand had more success with this strategy when he sent Radka to the summit as the supposed successor to Orlov. Brand himself wasn't prepared to show his hand yet as in the three years since he left, he had not only built a power base but had planned his revenge.

At that point, Orlov was already dead. Getting close enough to Orlov to kill him was easy as he had compromised his security detail. When he attended a dinner party at Risslo's house, it was the perfect opportunity.

Brand had taken out Risslo at the same time and seized control within twenty-four hours. During the coup, he'd also removed a couple of the other council members, in theory because they were potential future threats. In reality, he had killed them in public just to keep the others in line.

He had big plans for his revenge on Sanctuary One and they were well underway.

19

THE SUMMIT – DAY THREE

22 April 2206

Arriving at the summit on day three, Frank felt a bit strange. If he was to believe Chang's information, his day in the presence of Radka would be uncomfortable. He was not looking forward to playing politics with this apparent puppet standing in for the person who had orchestrated the attack on his homeland.

Frank was glad that he had hosted day one as he wasn't interested in carrying on with the one-upmanship that the elites had practised at the past summits. He just hoped the day, with Chang as host, didn't drag on.

As usual, the host on these days would be waiting to receive the other two leaders when they arrived at the same time through adjacent entrances.

Angus entered through Sanctuary One's tent flap at the same time as Frank did with two bodyguards on either side of him. In an instant, Frank noticed Angus had a strange look on his face and also saw Radka out of the corner of his right eye. But what caught his attention most were the three lines of muscly women standing in front of them.

Once all the guests were through the tent flaps, one of the women let out a loud guttural yell. Frank could see that both his and Radka's security details were on edge, trying to decide if this was a real threat or a show.

In unison, the three rows of women advanced, and both of the security details held the handles of their pistols nervously.

Once the women had stopped advancing, they performed what Frank could only describe as a tribal warrior challenge. For the next few minutes, the lead woman continued to yell out in what he determined was her native tongue. He couldn't decide if she was shouting instructions to the other participants or if this was all part of the challenge to the visitors.

The women dropped to one knee and began beating their chests with their left fists, while they brandished large clubs in their right and opened their eyes as wide as saucers and stuck out their tongues. Next, the group began to accompany the first in her chants. In unison, their voices grew louder and louder, rising to a deep growl. They beat the ground with their left fists and swung the clubs above their heads.

After ten minutes of this performance, all the women stood up and advanced a couple more feet. The finale was a manoeuvre that looked like the participants were threatening to cut their opponents' throats and all of the women in unison let out a deep-throated yell. Frank was happy when they all retreated and took up their positions around the walls of the tent. Even with his security detail and Radka's guards nearby, the women projected a savage aura that made him feel uneasy.

For the first time since he'd entered the tent, Frank noticed Chang standing off to one side, flanked by Gee King and two other women who were similar in stature to the performers. As soon as the performance ended, Chang began, "Welcome my fellow leaders; please accept my humble hospitality."

The floor that had hosted the performance moments ago had quickly been furnished with three sumptuous chairs, with tables in front of them that were fast filling up with rich food and drinks.

As soon as the three leaders took their seats, Radka started to toss back any drink that was handed to him. With lots of servants on hand, the drinks flowed freely.

Frank tried not to show his disgust. Even if Brand was the mastermind behind the attack, Radka was the one here gorging himself. All Frank could think of was the people who had been injured or lost during the bombings.

Since day one of the summit, he'd reluctantly played the dirty game of politics, keeping his cards close to his chest and displaying only false emotions. Give nothing away but gather as much intelligence as possible was his mantra. Yet today, every time he opened his mouth to speak, it felt like he was biting his tongue.

It seemed that Chang was also good at playing the game as he displayed very little emotion.

Frank turned his attention to Gee King. Her movements were cat-like: even when she was overseeing the tasting of Chang's food, she kept her head on a swivel.

Given Chang came from a sanctuary where men

ostensibly held all the power, it seemed strange that all of his security detail were female, although Frank didn't doubt that they were up to the task.

Deciding that letting someone else talk for a while would be a welcome distraction, he quizzed Chang. "That display from your guards was impressive. Is there a story behind their performance?"

Chang began to speak in what Frank believed to be his native tongue, as if he did not know Frank's own language. In the exchange that followed, Gee translated as though it was Chang speaking.

"I'm glad that you enjoyed the little display from my Nafanua."

"Nafanua?"

"The Nafanua are a warrior race from a tropical island. After all the men went away and died during the Water Wars, the women rediscovered their warrior roots. They weren't strangers to battle – stories from hundreds of years ago tell of a war goddess known as Nafanua. The women decided to reinvent themselves and took on the name Nafanua to strike fear into their enemies."

"Judging by the display I've just seen, it's not just their name that instils fear," Frank observed. "But how did they come to work for you?"

"They don't work for me; they're my subjects. One of my predecessors conquered their island after a battle that was costly on both sides. As a sign of respect, he chose not to execute the survivors and allowed them to remain on their island in relative freedom as long as they supplied fighters to protect our leader."

Chang looked very smug as Gee translated his words.

"And what's your story?" Frank asked Gee directly.

She looked at Chang. He said a few words in his native tongue before she replied, "My master says that is a story for another time."

Frank nodded and Chang clapped, initiating the arrival of even more food and drink.

The difference between Chang and Radka was stark.

Radka spent most of the sessions strewn prone across a sumptuous couch, surrounded by men and pawing continually at one or more scantily clad women. It seemed as though Radka was trying to express his power in a way you'd expect from someone who had none.

As Frank saw it, Radka was acting like a petulant child, as though he'd inherited his position from some rich relative. This revelation seemed to support Chang's story. Any sanctuary leader could be arrogant, but it was a dangerous position, and you had to portray strength if you were to survive the role.

As if to prove the point, Chang's behaviour was more subdued, but it was clear to all of his entourage who was in control.

With his new knowledge, Frank realised that Radka was trying to hide his insecurity. He was overcompensating for his lack of power by showing off. Yet for Chang, all it took was a pointed finger or even a raised eyebrow to display his real power. His minions observed him intently all the time and catered to his every order or whim immediately.

Frank had to study Chang closely to catch his almost imperceptible movements of command. The previous claps to initiate service had just been for the benefit of his visitors. Whatever Chang desired – a fresh dish of food, another round of drinks or a sexy dancer – it seemed to appear automatically as if from nowhere.

Chang never raised his voice throughout the whole summit and at times he spoke quietly. Even when Chang was speaking in his own language before Gee's translations, Frank felt the urge to listen.

If he accepted the premise that Radka had no power, other things now made sense to Frank now too.

Whenever the leaders discussed trade between the three kingdoms and were close to an agreement, Radka would throw in an extra condition to stall progress. To a casual observer, it would look like he was fighting for the best terms, but clearly delay was the best strategy for someone unable to make the final decision.

The main focus of the discussion was on the priority items to transport through drones – issues a leader should be able to make a quick decision about and move on from.

An item that was not on the agenda at this summit nor at any of the ones before it was the idea of replacing gel packs as a food source for the masses. Trade between the kingdoms never happened by ship as the leaders traditionally kept people reliant on them through the belief that the Water Wars had decimated the planet. If it became common knowledge that people could meet their needs elsewhere, the elite's tenuous hold over them would be lost.

Disinformation and fear were the key to maintaining power, so if anyone was caught spreading rumours of the bounty in other parts of the world, they were quickly made an example of.

Somewhat regretfully, Frank thought about how

much he could pass on to the other leaders about how he was leading his people towards a different way of doing things since the rebellion.

Certainly the changes were slow as it was hard to dispel deep-centred beliefs in transitioning people from a life of fear to empowerment. Yet day by day, as more resources became available in Frank's kingdom, they had been able to substitute some of the gel packs for real food. These resources had been available before the rebellion, but it had been a well-kept secret. As in the other kingdoms, people had chosen to ignore that they were eating parts of other humans but at the same time their metabolism had adapted to what was in effect cannibalism. Getting them to change their diet was a balancing act between educating them on the benefits of a regular diet and not highlighting their cannibalistic past.

One of the successful transition strategies that Frank had initiated was to switch some of the gel plants to processing cattle and other animals. The equipment needed little modification as the original mobile gel plants had been developed to process cattle and any captured livestock for troops during the Water Wars.

Switching diets also required changing infrastructure. Supply chains designed to move gel packs around would have to be altered to move fresher, more perishable foods; they took up more volume than the condensed gel packs and were harder to transport. Frank was happy that CT was in charge of the logistics of this.

Estimates were that it might be another five years before they could shut the plants down entirely. Five years was a long time in the context of the previous compulsory euthanasia age of forty-five. But then, Frank figured, it was all a matter of perspective – a lot of indoctrination had built up in the more than one hundred years that had passed since the Water Wars had ended.

They had learnt so much in the three years since the rebellion but for now these were lessons that Frank had to keep to himself as the other leaders would see any such ideas as a threat to their power source.

20

BRIEFING ON THE PLANE

23 April 2206

Frank took a deep breath before briefing the volunteers. "I know Angus has been training you hard since the boat left. It might've seemed repetitive, but he did that to make it second nature. When you get into the heat of battle, remember what he's taught you and you may find he has just saved your life."

Glancing at Angus, he found the old warrior was blushing. Rather than embarrassing him too much, Frank moved his focus to the parachute jump.

"From what Ranger has told me," Frank said, nodding to the jumpmaster, "parachuting is not the safest method of transport, and dropping into water adds to that danger. Remember your training and if you have any questions, address them to the jumpmaster." Frank again looked over to Ranger.

"Believe it or not, I wish I were coming with you. One of the hardest tasks of being a leader is staying behind while you send your people into harm's way. I want you to know that although only a limited number of people know that you have volunteered for this mission, I hope to sing your praises in public in the not-too-distant future. I know that on these occasions you are expected to listen but before I hand you over to Ranger, has anyone got any questions for me?" He looked around at the gathered volunteers.

These people knew the risks; they'd volunteered for what they saw as the greater good. As most of them had resigned themselves to the possibility that they might not return, they had no questions.

After a suitable pause, Frank continued. "Thank you again for volunteering. Go with Ranger now and ensure that you are ready when the plane ramp opens."

The next two hours seemed to pass both fast and slowly for Frank. Flashes of activity as the team practised their drills were followed by periods of silence with minimal movement.

They reached the predetermined check-in point. Frank liked to be in control but, as he stood on the flight deck, he deferred to Ranger's expertise for the deployment.

"Hello Roundabout, this is Hawkeye, over," Ranger spoke clearly into the microphone.

"Hello Hawkeye, this is Roundabout, we are reading you loud and clear, over," came the familiar voice of Pepper, and Frank momentarily smiled.

"Roundabout, confirm your location, over."

"We are at location Sigma one and ready to receive visitors, over," Pepper replied.

"Hello Roundabout, we will be releasing them in

about three zero minutes. Please prepare lights in one five minutes over."

"Hello Hawkeye, this is Roundabout, message understood. Wilco, out."

With that, Ranger headed down to the cargo bay for final preparations.

Although Frank did not need to watch the volunteers jump, fifteen minutes later he joined Ranger for their departure.

The volunteers each had a strap with a hook leading from their parachute. By the time the cargo ramp opened, Ranger had attached each hook to a steel-wire rope running the length of the cargo bay roof. Because the volunteers already had plenty to remember in such a short time, providing a system in which the straps automatically opened the parachutes on exit gave them one less issue to master.

Frank caught the rush of air as he waited in the dimly lit space. Without a radio, he felt a bit like a bystander, unable to hear what was going on.

It'd been agreed that Frank would remain off the airwaves to avoid being a distraction during the deployment. Ranger was in charge, and he had a headset to communicate with the boat.

With nothing much to do, Frank remained more focused on the red bulkhead light than the volunteers.

It seemed to take forever, even though it was really only a few minutes before the bulkhead light turned green. Next Ranger was tapping each parachutist on their shoulder as they left the ramp in turn.

Not waiting for the hydraulics to finish closing the ramp, Frank rushed back to the bridge to monitor the progress of the next phase of the mission.

Over the following minutes he felt himself in a painful limbo. Ranger had already confirmed the deployment, and they had agreed that no chatter would go on between the plane and the boat until the boat was sure of the results of the drop.

The odd static crackle over the radio raised the tension rather than alleviating it.

Suddenly Pepper's voice came over the airwaves. "Hello Hawkeye. This is Roundabout, over."

Frank grabbed his microphone. "Hawkeye send, over."

"Roundabout, we have all eight packages safely loaded on board, no breakages, over."

"Hello, Roundabout. Please confirm no breakages, over."

Frank was pleased to hear Pepper's voice. "Yes, all safe and sound."

Frank couldn't resist one last message to the boat. "Hello Roundabout, this is Hawkeye. Wishing you all safe travels and a speedy return home. Hawkeye out."

For the rest of the flight back to the sanctuary, there was very little talking. Frank periodically wrote something in his notebook as thoughts popped into his head. He needed to check on Zap's new security protocols. Perhaps he would visit the Telepath School tomorrow; it would be nice to see Flo again. Whatever the situation, he always came away from a meeting with Flo feeling more positive than he had before. He wasn't sure if this was a by-product of her telepathic powers but, even if it were, he'd take it.

He was also frantically tidying up his briefing notes for the rest of the resistance leaders. Initially, the leaders had been installed as a caretaker council, but they had grown into their roles and the sanctuary wasn't ready for a democratic election yet.

Although the current council wasn't perfect, as their critics pointed out, the quality of life of the kingdom's citizens had improved exponentially since the rebellion.

His thoughts bounced from the sanctuary back to the boat. He was trying not to second-guess any of Pepper and Hook's decisions. He wished his plane had been able to stay above the boat for longer and give them some cover from above, but that was too risky.

The strategy rested on the assumption that this one small boat would be able to hide in the vast ocean. As planes were rare in today's post-war world, having an aircraft shadowing the boat could potentially draw attention to it.

Adding further risk to an already precarious plan was considered too dangerous. It was always hard to calculate the success of such a mission, but brighter minds than his had crunched the numbers and had estimated the chances of success at around twenty percent.

Why would anyone send their brother on a mission with an estimated success rate of twenty percent? Yet he hadn't sent Pepper, he reminded himself – Pepper had volunteered to go. When they had first met, Pepper was constantly asking for his reward for escorting Flo. Now his focus was on the greater good of the masses rather than just his successes. His freedom from the constant game of cat-and-mouse that had been his life while he was hunted by the Company had initially helped him relax, but he had come to need some other form of diversion.

Pepper's transition had helped solidify their

friendship. The possibility of losing him on this mission reminded Frank of what it had been like to lose his brother Paris.

As he nodded off to sleep, he hoped that after the mission, he would get to see Pepper again.

21

SHIP AHOY

23 April 2206

The *Roundabout* had left a month before the summit, with no telepaths on board as none could be spared at that time.

The boat was a lot slower than a plane but was less resource-intensive when transporting stores and crew. Hook had lobbied for the early departure of the ship so that it would reach a suitable location by the time of the summit.

Pepper would be in charge of the assault team if they were given a target. Although at this stage they did not know their final destination, they had plenty of supplies in the meantime.

The neutral location of the summit made the area an ideal jumping-off point for an assault on either of the other kingdoms.

The plan was for some of the security detail going with Frank to the summit to peel off afterwards and join the ship. Angus had been drafted in as an interim leader of the security detail as he had been training the team members that had been left behind and was due to join the boat too.

The payload of the plane was at its maximum as always before a summit. Having all of those people around for the summit was more for aesthetic value than for practical reasons. The number of people that returned to the sanctuary after the summit would be inconsequential after take-off. Unless the plane crashed in enemy territory, they would just be extra bodies to transport.

Each kingdom was only allowed a set number of personnel to attend each summit.

They were allowed to deploy twenty personnel a month in advance of the summit, to set up the location. They were granted a further thirty personnel to accompany the leader of the summit. In reality, only ten of the accompanying personnel where security and the other twenty would be the likes of chefs, hairdressers and, in some cases, sexual partners.

Traditionally the leaders were thought so decadent that just because they were going to an important summit, they wouldn't refrain from their hedonistic tendencies over security. They were survivors but saw themselves as so important that their pleasure was more important than the odd security measure.

Each faction could leave any number of personnel on their plane, but this was, of course, limited by the actual capacity of the planes. Frank was not the same as the other leaders; security was important to him and also how many personnel he could transport who would have dual roles.

None of his team was solely a food taster, a

hairdresser, a chef or in any other civilian role, with the exception of the two translators. Most had combatant as their primary role, with a secondary role as well where possible.

It would be easy for one sanctuary to have a larger force secreted nearby, to overpower the other attendees.

The whole setup of the summits was symbolic, and if anyone had broken these rules over the years, it would have derailed the whole process.

Everyone thus stuck to the rules and had only the correct amount of people visible.

Frank hoped that they would gain valuable information at this summit and anything they did find would be relayed to the boat by the personnel he despatched.

Each kingdom sent a security force in advance of the summit to prepare their accommodation and security. In reality, it would provide little advantage for any kingdom to take out a leader of another kingdom at one of these summits.

Because of the hierarchal structure of the kingdoms, people tended to assume that there was always some other psychopath waiting in the wings to take on the mantle of leader.

And war was historically a great way to solidify a new leader's position.

Traditionally the ruling classes of the kingdoms were all about power and greed. These elites had more resources than they would ever need but still didn't want to sacrifice any of their gains in a war that would benefit nobody financially.

Before the Water Wars, any wars around the planet had benefitted the military-industrial complex. These divisions of the three companies profited from supplying all sides of a conflict. It wasn't unheard of for a single company to supply opposing sides, with both of those forces under its control.

Since the Water Wars, the global monetary system didn't exist in the same format, so any external conflicts were just seen as a drain on valuable resources.

All three kingdoms still had to divert some of their resources to maintain their weapons of war. Primarily this was an effort to maintain the safety of weapons such as nuclear warheads. Propaganda made the public in all three kingdoms believe that the threat was from outside and that their particular government had full control of their weapons. In reality, only a fraction of the weapons had been used during the Water Wars, and the instability of current stockpiles was a concern to all the kingdom leaders.

The ruling classes were all about the profits, and there were no profits in destroying the planet further, especially as it was supposedly already teetering on the edge of sustaining life.

Long ago, the sanctuary leaders had decided that the summits would be scheduled when spring occurred in the location of the summit. Although no one followed the pre-Water Wars calendars for religious festivals any more, their observation of the four seasons had remained relatively unchanged.

Climate change could make a winter longer or shorter but the seasons still tended to rotate in the same order. The fluctuations in the seasons also meant that each summit was not exactly a year apart, but the time difference was close enough for the event to be known as "the annual summit".

As the boat continued on its journey, morale on board was surprisingly high. Although most of them had set off on this mission as green sailors, they now spent less and less time being sick over the side.

Once the others arrived, they hoped to know their final target but, until then, they could only plan vaguely and wait. Their initial plans were primarily to create as much chaos as possible to the people that had attacked their sanctuary. Ensuring that people knew that this counterattack came from Sanctuary One would be their way of deterring future acts of aggression.

Pepper turned to survey Will. Initially, he had been against bringing him. As Will was a remnant from the previous regime, his loyalties following its defeat had been suspect. Yet once Will had recovered from his bullet wounds, he had been eager to contribute to the new society.

Over the last couple of years, he'd proved himself adaptable and willing to serve the new leaders, throwing himself fully into his new roles. It still worried Pepper that Will had been prepared to switch sides so quickly, but he was a skilled operator and could be useful on this quest.

Will had planned and implemented many assaults on rebel forces over the years. As this was probably a suicide mission, it would seem fitting for Will to sacrifice himself for the people he had subjugated for so long.

Within the next twelve hours, they were expecting the plane to drop the rest of the team from above. They would then have a few days to get to work on the brief as they headed to their final destination.

It was still a fifty–fifty guess as to whether the attack

on Sanctuary One had come from the Kompaniya or the Dynasty.

"I hope it's the Kompaniya," Will said decisively.

"Why?" Pepper asked.

"Because it's closer and I'm sick of being on this boat." It was true that Will had suffered the most from seasickness. Even now, when they were standing above decks, he looked decidedly green in the face.

"Why are you in such a rush to die?" Pepper asked. "Whichever sanctuary we end up attacking, there is every chance we're not coming back."

"That's where you're wrong," Will said. "I will survive. Remember you put a bullet in me the first time we met, and that wasn't the first time I've been shot, stabbed or beaten within an inch of my life."

"Don't mistake your previous luck for being invincible. If we're captured, you may rather be dead."

"I don't intend to die or be captured. If you plan to succeed, we can make it a quick hit, create chaos and get out fast," Will countered. "We have weapons and explosives —and once the plane arrives, we'll have trained telepaths."

"Yes we will be prepared and should have the element of surprise, but so did our attackers. Their explosives certainly left a mess behind, but not many of them lived to see it," Pepper said sombrely.

The previous regime had trained its soldiers through a brutal mechanism designed to break them down and then rebuild them as violent thugs.

Karla's training methods gave soldiers confidence and self-respect, encouraging recruits to step forward who were more interested in serving the greater good rather than just themselves. It had taken a couple of years to change the ethos of the soldiers, and luckily they'd reached that point now, just at the right time. They needed volunteers for this mission, and here they were.

Hook came onto the deck of the boat. The sea air seemed to have made Hook's skin even more leathery, but he always managed a smile. Perhaps it was because he was back on the sea, where he thrived.

"Hook you old seadog, have you got any of that jet fuel you call drink left?" Pepper wasn't a heavy drinker but the clear spirit Hook had brought with him seemed to calm his stomach while on the boat.

"I think I might be able to scrounge up a few drops," Hook smirked.

The night was progressing. Although they expected the parachutists at first light, everyone was too wired to sleep.

The tension was high, fuelled by the knowledge that they were close to the summit and risked becoming a target at any time.

After what seemed an endless night, a voice came over the radio. "Hello Roundabout, this is Hawkeye, over."

Pepper had stayed within arm's length of the radio for the last couple of hours. He snatched up the handset and, without any hesitation, replied, "Hello Hawkeye, this is Roundabout, we are reading you loud and clear, over."

"Roundabout, confirm your location, over."

"We are at location Sigma one and ready to receive visitors, over," Pepper replied.

"Hello Roundabout, we will be releasing them in

about three zero minutes. Please prepare lights in one five minutes, over."

Even though it was starting to get light, the *Roundabout* was prepared with bright deck lights, and Pepper motioned for the crew to ready them for action.

"Get the launch in the water," Pepper shouted to Donald, who promptly went to lower the speed launch. Within five short minutes, the small craft was bobbing in the water, waiting to recover anyone who landed away from the boat.

Before the radio had time to squawk again, they could hear the plane in the distance.

Pepper quickly grabbed the radio handset. "Hello Little cub, this is Mamma bear, over."

Pepper always thought of Frank as a mamma bear, and as it was his mission, he got to choose the call signs.

"Hello Mamma bear, this is Little cub, awaiting your instructions," came the reply from the speedboat.

"Hello Little cub. Launch out into open water and be prepared to collect anyone who doesn't land on this boat. Use your own judgement, but if we get better information from this vantage point, we'll update you. Over."

"Little cub, message received, launching now."

And with that, Pepper saw the white wake of the boat as it left the shelter of the bigger ship. It was helpful to get the message off before the plane contacted him. By giving the speedboat some autonomy, he would find it easier to coordinate the parachute drop.

Almost immediately, the plane began transmitting again, "Hello Roundabout, this is Hawkeye. Are you ready to receive the packages?"

"This is Roundabout, ready and able," Pepper replied.

"Hello Roundabout, packages away, packages away."

Pepper moved to the rail, raised his binoculars to his eyes and started scanning the sky for parachutes. It wasn't long before his search was rewarded. In the distance, he saw eight bright parachutes opening up.

There was no need to camouflage the chutes; the plane and the boat held the only people in this area. There was no sign of any other ships or vessels as far as the eye could see, which was many miles all around them.

The parachutes seemed to Pepper to be getting larger, which meant that they were getting closer. He remembered from the mission briefings that the chutes were steerable, which should allow the parachutists to track towards the boat. Not all the jumpers were experienced, and the ones that had trained had only jumped on dry land. Trying to land on a mobile target that was bobbing in the waves was not easy for anyone.

Pepper preferred travelling by boat than aircraft. As a young company recruit, he'd been deployed via a helicopter that had ultimately crashed. He much preferred to have his feet on a solid surface, even if this one was floating. In his mind, he envisaged that if the boat engines failed, it could still float, but if an aircraft broke down, it could fall from the sky, reducing the chances of survival for anyone on board dramatically.

Six crewmen were on the deck of the boat, all with access to long, hooked steel poles. The plan was to try to snag a passing chute before it hit the water or use the hooks to snag the parachutes in the water.

Perhaps more by luck than good judgement, four of the jumpers landed on the boat itself. A few tangled lines left parachutists dangling over the edge of the rails, but the crew with the poles soon recovered them.

Two other jumpers were attached to chutes that floated reasonably close to their boat.

The remaining two chutes were off in the distance.

Pepper keyed the mike of the radio by his side. "Hello little cub, this is Mamma bear. Can you see the two chutes in the distance?"

"Hello, Mamma bear, yes heading out to them now."

"Mamma bear. Head for the furthest first and then loop back around for the other one."

"Little Cub. Message received and understood."

Although Pepper assumed that this strategy was common sense for the experienced speedboat commander, a parachute could become a deadly anchor so he would rather be cautious than lose valuable team members. This was part empathy and part selfishness; they were short-handed and losing even one of his strike force could be a significant blow.

Thanks to forward planning, the parachutists could jump with only light packs. Each of them had packed their gear to be stashed on the boat before it left so they could make a safer jump with less weight.

Once the speedboat had recovered the last two parachutists, all eight personnel stood in front of Pepper. Some were a little wet but everyone was unharmed.

Pepper addressed them. "For those of you that haven't been on a boat before, you might feel a bit sick – if you do, the best thing to do is to come up on deck. Wear a life jacket whenever you are above deck. And let someone else know where you are at all times. This mission will give you plenty of opportunities to die, so don't sacrifice yourself to a stupid boating accident. Now quickly get down below, change into some dry clothes and check out your stowed kit and equipment. Have you all eaten?"

"Yes," said Foster. "We ate before we got on the plane."

"Good. I'll need to talk with you Foster and with Iris when you're ready. The rest of you should liaise with Donald. You all know the layout of the boat from before we departed, but he can show you the changes that we have made since we deployed. I'll hold a full briefing later today but for now, if you have any questions, address them to Donald. Did everyone get that?" Pepper asked.

They all nodded.

"Okay Donald, take them below. And once they're settled, bring Foster and Iris to me."

After the newcomers had gone below deck, Pepper grabbed the radio. "Hello, Hawkeye. This is Roundabout, over."

"Hawkeye send, over."

"Roundabout, we have all eight packages safely loaded on board, no breakages, over."

"Hello, Roundabout. Please confirm no breakages, over."

Recognising Frank's voice, Pepper replied with a smile, "Yes, all safe and sound."

"Hello Roundabout, this is Hawkeye. Wishing you all safe travels and a speedy return home. Hawkeye out."

After the final message, Pepper stepped outside of the bridge to take in the fresh morning air.

22

—————

BRIEFING ON THE BOAT

24 April 2206

Iris and Foster hadn't worked since the capital bombings.

During their physical recovery, however, they'd stayed together in the same hospital ward. In that way they'd still managed to practise their mental techniques daily.

After over two months of rehabilitation, they were eager to see some action. As two of the older, more experienced telepaths, they could not have been left out of the fight forever.

When Flo had asked for volunteers for the mission from her telepath family, Iris was the first to come forward. For her, it was personal. She believed that the enemy had targeted them because they were telepaths. The months in the hospital bed had nurtured her need for revenge. Foster had followed shortly after as he too had a vested interest in making the enemy pay for the devastation they had caused.

Their enlistment for the mission offered a double benefit. Not only were they two of the best telepaths, but their time in recovery had placed Iris and Foster outside of the regular shift rotation. As a result of their seclusion, their training for the mission didn't impact any of the sanctuary's other strategic resources.

It was making the best of a bad situation, which saw a continuing shortage of telepaths to cover critical assets. Sending two of their best on a potential suicide mission had not sat well with Flo. It was only after Frank and Pepper insisted that Foster and Iris were acting for the good of everybody that Flo agreed to them going.

The two telepaths were now showered and changed and had stowed their gear after being recovered from the sea.

As they followed Donald up to the bridge, Iris pondered about how she had ended up here, bobbing around on a boat in the middle of the ocean.

Although the boat as a whole seemed reasonably large to a land-based person like Iris, she found the bridge area decidedly small and crowded. On a visit to this former fishing boat before it embarked, she had learnt that the bridge was only designed for the captain and a few lookouts.

Now six people were present: Iris, Foster, Pepper, Will and two crew members who were piloting the boat.

Iris liked Pepper and trusted him. She hadn't had much to do with him personally, but he was widely respected.

On several visits to the Telepath School, he had always taken the time to smile and chat with the students. Pepper made her feel safe, partly because he towered over her.

"I understand you have some news for us?" Pepper said with a smile. He'd resisted the urge to interview them as soon as they landed, reasoning that five or ten minutes wouldn't make much difference after all his time at sea.

Iris handed over a package enclosed in a waterproof pouch. Foster offered an identical one as backup. With this arrangement, Pepper would still have received the vital information if one of the telepaths hadn't made it.

There would have been little point in giving further backup documents to the other parachutists as, without at least one telepath, the mission would certainly be suicide.

"We'll talk about the documents in a minute," Iris said, "but first Frank asked me to repeat something exactly as he said it: 'This is our old friend's handiwork'."

Pepper and Will stared at each other, confused.

"Could you repeat that?" Will said. It was not his briefing, but this revelation had sparked a quicker response from him than from Pepper.

"During the summit, Frank had a private meeting with Chancellor Chang. Chang told him that the real leader of Sanctuary Two is Harland Brand." Iris paused for questions but none came yet. "Brand fled there during the uprising. Over the last three years, he has not just survived but managed to take over as leader of the sanctuary."

"When did he take over?" Pepper asked. "When I attended the last summit on Frank's security detail, the leader of Sanctuary Two was Radka."

"Yes, he appeared to be leader then," Iris said. "And

he's the same person who turned up to this summit, still pretending to be the leader."

"Could you explain that again?" Pepper asked.

Iris continued. "This is the information that Chang provided, and Frank seems to think it's founded in truth. When Brand had arrived in Sanctuary Two, he went to stay with someone called Risslo Deripask. Risslo was a medium-ranking figure in their leadership; he naively thought that having the former leader of another sanctuary as a resource of vital information could enhance his career. He also believed that parading Brand around in public would raise his status, but he underestimated him. Brand used Risslo as a way to climb the social ladder quickly." Iris paused to take a breath and Pepper indicated for her to continue.

"The Kompaniya is like the previous leadership in our sanctuary – full of greedy psychopaths, always trying to gain more power. Brand sensed weakness in the leader Orlov and managed to align himself with Orlov's competitors. No one knows exactly what happened but it seems that, because Brand was an outsider, he was not seen as a threat. Once again he was underestimated and through whatever means, he rose to become their leader. He decided to stay in the shadows until he had consolidated his power, which is why he sent Radka to the summits in his place. I was told that Brand has been pulling the strings like a puppet master. The attacks were his revenge on us for overthrowing him."

"I expect his ego couldn't cope with losing," Will said. "He was always arrogant and believed that he deserved to be the ultimate leader. He used to say that only he could unite the three sanctuaries under one leader."

"Did Chancellor Chang provide us with any other support?" Pepper asked.

"It seems it is to his advantage to have the two sanctuaries fighting. He provided maps and plans for some areas of Sanctuary Two; those are in the document pack I've just given you. However, he refused to put his finger too much on the scales."

"That's nice of him," Pepper sneered

"He felt that just by telling us that Brand had survived, we would owe him a favour in the future," Iris said. "Chang's spies have stated that Brand lives in the capital buildings and has no holiday homes or residences elsewhere. He is even more paranoid than ever and sees the capital buildings as the safest place for him."

"We'll have to see how secure he really is," Will said forcefully.

"Did Frank say what the target was?" Pepper asked.

Iris was quite clear here. "The only mission is to kill Brand. At all costs."

"Well," Pepper said, "I suppose it's a simple mission: enter the sanctuary and try to kill a man who is paranoid and resides in the sanctuary's most secure inner sanctum. Essentially, we have no real maps or support, and we should also escape without dying. Is that basically the brief?"

Iris nodded meekly.

Will had never forgiven Brand for abandoning him.

He had guarded the staircase, trying to fight off the attackers so that he gave Brand time to prepare an escape that he expected would involve both of them.

When Pepper and the rest reached the roof, they found that Brand had already fled. Will realised now that it had always been Brand's plan to leave Will to his fate.

Will sought revenge against the man that he had served unconditionally for years. The man who he had risked his life to protect. Will had always known that Brand was selfish, but now he knew that he had no loyalty to anyone else.

"Was there any other information?" Pepper asked.

"He has a right-hand man called Nikolei," Iris said. "Frank said he was the new Will." She avoided looking in Will's direction.

"It seems that he has a new you," Pepper said mockingly to Will.

Iris hadn't known Will personally before the uprising, but she had certainly known of him in the capital. Before the rebellion, he was well-known for his brutality. Most of his time in imprisonment since the revolt had been in large part for his safety rather than just as punishment.

This had provided another reason for Will to volunteer to come on this mission. There was very little for him in the new regime. Perhaps if he died on the mission, it would give him some closure.

The news about Brand was a lot to take in. Pepper looked across at Will. He seemed to be keeping his anger under control, but the target of their mission could complicate things. Although Pepper had never been sure of Will's allegiances, one thing that did seem genuine was his hatred of Brand.

Pepper would have to consider carefully where he placed Will in any assault; he couldn't risk Will compromising the mission for his own agenda. At the same time, Will's strong motivation for taking out Brand was a reason why Pepper wanted to keep him on the assault team.

By now Pepper had opened the document pouches and was studying the information they had contained. "Did he suggest a strategy for this suicide mission?" Pepper asked. He hoped that as Frank wasn't risking just his men but also his best friend, he had a plan – but perhaps he was simply desperate.

"Although Chang didn't provide any contacts in the sanctuary, he has provided us fairly detailed maps and diagrams. This is as much information as he could gather on Brand's whereabouts," Foster said.

Pepper was nodding as he continued to look through the documents.

"That's great, but Brand's paranoid and any information we have is probably out of date now," Will pointed out.

Pepper always encouraged input from others. For many years he'd survived as a loner, but after meeting Frank and fighting side by side with the rebels to overthrow the previous regime, he recognised the strength of a team. He was smart enough to admit that someone else may know more than him.

"So let's get this right," Will said. "Our only source of information is maps that might be out of date. We have no contacts on the ground and we have only a small force that has to try to sneak into somewhere they don't know, without standing out. Oh and did I leave out the part where we have to take out a paranoid psychopath with heavy defences?"

"That seems to about sum things up," Pepper said, almost smiling. "Did you expect anything else? Would anybody else like to add anything before we try to plan for a potential suicide mission?"

After a short pause, Will began to talk to no one in particular. "I died on those steps when he abandoned me, over two years ago. As far as I'm concerned, I've been living on borrowed time ever since. If I have to die to take him out, I'm good with that."

"Well," Pepper said, "it seems that we have at least one volunteer. Perhaps I can persuade a few more. Let's look at the maps and throw some ideas around. We'll aim to present our initial plans to the crew in six hours."

GROWING PARANOIA

23 April 2206

Radka had been dreading being grilled by Brand after attending the summit with the brief of gathering information from the representatives of Sanctuary One.

The plan to check if they knew who'd attacked them was all well and good in theory. In practice, though, it was difficult to put discreet questions on the topic to someone who had been subject to the attack. With every representative from Sanctuary One on high alert, it was almost impossible to frame a question without raising suspicion.

He found plenty of suspicion back in his home sanctuary too, with Brand seeming to be permanently in a state of paranoia. As Radka waited outside Brand's office, Nikolei emerged and directed Radka to strip.

This procedure would have been humiliating enough for any member of the elite, all of whom like

Radka had a healthy ego, but it was made many times worse by the presence of Petra, Brand's personal telepath.

It wasn't just that he was taking off his clothes in front of a beautiful woman – this one could also read his mind. No matter how well he covered his genitalia, she would be finding out all of his insecurities and know that he was trying to hide himself, which would be even more embarrassing than her seeing him naked.

After the strip search, he was allowed to don a gown to guard his modesty. As an elite, he had previously undergone several medical procedures and recognised the robe as the type used for surgeries. It was designed to provide access for surgeons rather than to be something for comfort. On this occasion, Radka perceived it was chosen to keep him off balance.

As he entered the office, Radka was again struck by the starkness of the room. Brand had had the office designed to his specifications: the only furniture in the room was one large chair and one large desk at the far end of the room. The chair was occupied by Brand, leaving nowhere for any visitors to sit.

In the middle of the room was a dark line embedded in the wooden floor. It marked a distance of ten feet to the edge of the desk and was a demarcation line that no visitor was permitted to pass. No signs warned anyone against intruding past the line, but everyone who entered the office knew the rules.

Rumours were that once Brand had taken control and before the rule of the line was known, he had invited each of the surviving council members individually into his office. As soon as Councillor Melton West had stepped over the line to fawn over the new leader, he'd been subdued with electric prods and beaten close to death.

Before this episode, others had been suspicious of Brand's savagery; afterwards it was clear that he had been looking for a reason to make an example of somebody and had now shown everyone he wasn't to be messed with. West still walked with a limp today as a warning to any other councillors, should they consider stepping out of line.

"You've been back twelve hours. Why haven't I had your report yet?" Brand bellowed at Radka.

"I'm sorry, sir, I wanted to make sure I was presentable before I came to see you. I had to go home and get changed."

"Do you think I care about what you look like? You had two reasons to attend the summit. You were to maintain the façade that you're in charge and also to gather information for me. Did you achieve either?"

Radka started to stutter a reply but Brand interrupted, "Think carefully about your next words; they might be your last."

"I don't think they know who attacked them," Radka said slowly.

"You don't think? That's your problem: you don't think! You were supposed to confirm if they knew anything!"

"They're very guarded – they've recently been attacked, and that guy Frank was constantly questioning Chang and me. He said they didn't believe that it was a sanctioned attack from either of us. He asked if we could investigate whether it could have been someone from our sanctuary working without our permission."

"So he said that we aren't in control. Is that what he was implying?"

"No, I think he was just looking for our responses."

"Did you have an individual meeting with either Chang or Frank?

Radka looked confused. "No, we just had our daily meetings where the three of us discussed boring policies."

"You're a fool! If they'd suspected Chang, they would have approached you separately."

"No, I just don't think they had any idea who'd attacked them, and they were just fishing in the dark. Chang even suggested that the attack could have come from disgruntled individuals in Sanctuary One."

Brand paused momentarily. "I find it interesting that Chang raised this suggestion openly, with you all present. Did your spies learn of any meeting between Chang and Frank in private?"

"We monitored them both as best we could, but they were both protected by their security details so we couldn't monitor them every moment that they were at the summit."

"Did our telepaths pick up anything?"

"They tried, but other telepaths from Sanctuary One were there, and they blocked ours."

"What about Chang?"

"What about Chang?" Radka was getting confused. He also got the idea that he was angering Brand.

Brand spoke slowly as if addressing a child. "If the Sanctuary One telepaths were blocking us from reading Frank's thoughts, did our telepaths not pick up anything from Chang? You were in his presence for three days. Surely you used our telepaths to scan his thoughts?"

"They tried to read his mind, but they couldn't get through. They felt he'd been trained to resist them, as though he or someone else was putting up a mental wall."

"Which telepaths did you take?" Brand already knew the names of everyone that had been deployed, but he was looking for people to punish for what he perceived as lost opportunities. He'd given Radka simple tasks, and Radka had yet again failed him.

"I took Harper and Blossom."

"Harper and Blossom? You had your pick of any two telepaths from our pool, and you took a married couple! Did you not think that they might have been distracted?"

"I just asked for the best telepaths." As the words left his mouth, Radka became anxious, realising what Brand's next question would be.

"Who did you ask?"

Radka was starting to feel nauseous as he said quietly, "I asked Harper."

Brand motioned to Nikolei, "Take care of Harper and Blossom. It's time these telepaths realised that they might have some powers, but I have the real power! Ensure that Harper sees Blossom die but try not to kill him as we are short on telepaths at the moment."

Nikolei nodded and left the room.

Although Radka felt terrible about what would happen to the telepaths, he was more concerned about his own fate at the moment.

"I am starting to regret putting you forward as the face of this sanctuary," Brand said. "You need to prove to me that you still have value. Tell me why I should let you live."

"Have I not served you well?" Radka whimpered.

"Appealing to nostalgia may have worked with your mother, but you are not of my blood. I have provided you wealth and stature, and all you had to do was to look the part of a leader. What can you offer me going forward?"

"I will do whatever you ask, sir. What do you want me to do?"

Brand had picked up a knife from the desk and was twirling it around between his fingers. "Come here." He beckoned to Radka.

"What about the line?" Radka said, pointing to the line in the middle of the floor.

"I make the rules here; you have my permission to approach."

Radka eyed the two armed guards who stood against the walls and cautiously placed one foot over the line. Before his second foot could breach the line, the two guards had set upon him. He was shocked with stun batons and quickly collapsed to the floor.

They continued to shock him until he was a quivering wreck.

Brand waved the two guards back to their wall positions and stood over Radka. "I fear that our relationship has come to its natural conclusion. You may have been useful in the past, but you won't be attending another sanctuary leaders' summit." With that, Brand plunged the knife into Radka's left eye socket. The shock showed in Radka's face and he screamed, but he didn't die immediately.

Brand wiped the knife on Radka's shirt and then used it to slit his throat. He could have done that to begin with of course, but he knew that the guards would spread the news of his brutality, enhancing his reputation.

It was a testament to his level of skill and practice that not a drop of Radka's blood touched his own clothes. Now he'd tied up this loose end, he wanted the scene cleaned up. Nikolei had returned at just the right moment.

"Get Petra in here and get someone to clean up this mess," he instructed Nikolei.

Without stopping to acknowledge his orders, Nikolei opened the door and left again.

Once he'd motioned for Petra to go inside, he took the time to re-task Radka's security detail. It was fortunate that they had been more loyal to Nikolei than Radka, so all he had to do was brief their leader.

"Go back to Radka's villa, recover any personal items that you have there and then report to the barracks. You have been a loyal servant of the Kompaniya while you have guarded that idiot and if you were to take the odd valuable item from the villa, I don't think anyone would mind." Nikolei winked to the detail commander as he noticed Petra out of the corner of his eye.

As she entered the room, she could hear Brand's voice in her head. *Follow me.* He liked that he didn't have to spell things out to her. It seemed that telepaths could feel your intentions as well as hear your thoughts.

They left the office through a door behind the curtain at the back of the room. The staircase gave the option of a discreet escape to either the vehicles in the basement or Brand's private quarters above. As usual, the act of killing had aroused Brand, so this time they headed up to his chambers so he could take advantage of his telepath sexually.

24

TRANSIT ON THE BOAT

01 May 2206

The limited charts that they'd brought with them gave them only a general idea of the direction to head in. Pepper felt fortunate that they had access to any maps at all, but he was more grateful for Hook and Donald. Having spent most of their adult lives as fishermen, they knew the sea, the stars and the tides better than anyone he'd ever met.

Amazed that they not only had reached the Kompaniya kingdom despite all the challenges but also were close to the sanctuary, Pepper felt a sudden spark of optimism.

They had managed to dock the boat in a secluded cove, which they'd located using one of the only useful pieces of information that Chang had supplied.

If Chang's crude maps were correct, the capital was only sixty miles away from the sea. That meant that once they landed, they might just have a chance. Pepper hoped that a lack of a real resistance in this kingdom might have resulted in some complacency. He could only hope that things hadn't changed too much since Brand's arrival.

The group had crammed below decks for Pepper's final brief.

"I know we've been at sea for a while and I appreciate your patience."

"We appreciate your patience too," Iris piped up and the rest of the group murmured their agreement.

"That's kind of you to say. I'm sure that we are all keen to get off of this boat, but once we see what lies ahead of us, we may wish we'd stayed on-board," Pepper smiled.

"Enough of the sentimental stuff," Will interrupted. "Let's just get this over with."

Pepper ignored Will's outburst and continued, focusing on the maps on the boards more than the people present.

"We've got just the two vehicles. You've practised driving them and should now be comfortable that their steering wheels are on the opposite side to what you're used to back home. The first chance that we get, we'll attempt to obtain local transport and Kompaniya uniforms." He wished he could have brought Debs along but, apart from the need for her to stay behind to protect Sanctuary One and his personal concern for her survival, they had been concerned that women would stand out in enemy uniforms.

"I'm leading team one with Will, Dailey, Foster, Brown, Smith and Coosh. Angus is in charge of team two – Iris, Jones, Fred, Manning, Cenk and Nikki. Before we go any further, has anyone got any questions about the teams?"

"We know our teams and we're ready," Angus said in a calming voice.

"Good. The initial plan was to hit the infrastructure but now that we know Brand is still alive, we must try to take him out. While he is alive, he will never stop coming after us and our sanctuary will always be in danger." Pepper paused.

"We have the rough layout of the sanctuary and you have your briefs. I doubt we'll all be coming back but Hook will wait here for as long as he can. If anyone hasn't made it back by the time the boat leaves – and that includes me – I've ordered him to head back to the sanctuary. Any questions?"

"No questions, just a statement: no one kills Harland Brand but me," Will said.

"Although I like your commitment, there is every chance we'll all die before we get to Brand," Angus replied. "So I am countermanding that order to say: if anyone has the slightest chance of taking him out, do it."

Pepper was considering that the capital might not be hard to find. Blending in and staying there long enough to complete their mission was going to be the tricky bit.

The attackers on Sanctuary One had the advantage of having Brand's detailed knowledge of the capital layout. By contrast, Pepper and his teams were going in almost blind with just the rough maps and diagrams that Chang had supplied. Chang had promised that the information was accurate, but a paranoid narcissist like Brand would no doubt have plenty of surprises prepared for any would-be attackers.

Heading into the unknown and with limited

resources, they were susceptible to any traps, even those hidden in plain sight.

"One last thing," Pepper added. "Remember that the first chance you get, collect any enemy weapons and ammunition. From what we know, the kind of guns that you've trained with are close to the ones that the Kompaniya forces carry but not exactly the same. We will make do with what we have for now but replenishing our resources could make the difference between any of us surviving – or not. Does everybody understand?"

He glanced around the room to see many team members were nodding solemnly, as if it was dawning on them that this was about to get real.

Even with their telepaths, the chances were that some or all of them might not survive. But they had known the risks when they volunteered and they had to try to succeed.

25

HOW DO YOU SURPRISE A TELEPATH

23 April 2206

Glenn was waiting outside Brand's office. As head of Nikolei's Terror squad, he was usually waiting here for orders to inflict pain and terror on some unsuspecting target either in the capital or on some mission further afield. His squad was part of the shadow military, and although they didn't observe saluting and other military etiquette, they were professional and good at what they did.

Sitting observing the door wasn't the worst job in the world, but he hated having Petra here too. At times he had been lucky that Brand was using her for some other purpose while he was here, but a lot of the time she was just sitting in this waiting area, on call like him.

Certainly the telepaths were a useful weapon in the Kompaniya's arsenal, but it gave him the creeps being around someone who could read his mind.

Petra was tall and blonde with legs that seemed to go on forever. He tried to avoid her piercing blue eyes, but he was sure that she'd picked up his thoughts of lust on more than just this occasion.

Erotic thoughts weren't yet a crime in the Kompaniya, but he had to be careful as she had Brand's ear. Glenn knew that if he ever upset Petra, his life expectancy could be drastically reduced.

He noticed the large doors opening and rose to meet Nikolei. Glenn was a couple of inches taller than Nikolei but height didn't equate to power. Nikolei was feared for his brutality, and if Glenn was to prosper, he needed to serve him successfully. For the moment it suited Glenn to be a subordinate, but for a split second, he pondered that this might not always be so.

As always, small talk between them was minimal.

"I have a task for you."

"Yes, sir."

"The two telepaths Blossom and Harper have failed the leader, and they are to be punished. You are to take out Blossom in front of Harper. Telepaths are currently in short supply so, if possible, leave Harper able to operate, but feel free to injure him."

"Understood," Glenn answered. With no further delays, Nikolei turned around and went back to Brand.

A less experienced operator might have asked Nikolei for further information, but Glenn was kept in place for his expertise, and he was expected to carry out any task successfully. He had extensive files on any potential targets, including those in their own forces as a contingency.

Taking a radio from his belt loop, he called for his vehicles. "Bring the trucks round to the front steps. I'll be there in five minutes."

"En route," came the immediate reply.

Glenn liked being able to speak clearly on this secure network without having to use tactical speech or remember lots of coded terms. This frequency was set aside for his squad, who had grown to recognise his voice instantly.

Although he wasn't as ruthless as Nikolei, everyone knew he was not to be trifled with. His men both respected and feared him, and this was how he liked it. He treated them well if they did as he asked (however unconscionable the acts), but they also knew the consequences of not carrying out his orders.

Walking down the steps, he pondered how he could sneak up on a telepath – or in this case, two telepaths. Whatever tactics he used were going to be a gamble as there was a chance that they would know he was coming. He had to find a way to reduce the risk because failure was not an option in his position.

A plan was formulating in his mind as he stepped through the main doors. The two armoured trucks were parked up straight ahead, and he quickly climbed into the passenger seat of the front one.

"Take us to the armoury," he said while staring into space. He didn't need a reply as his orders were always followed, without question. He also needed time to muster his thoughts.

As they pulled away from the kerb, the second truck fell in behind them. Perhaps some of those in the trucks were privately wondering about their destination given the squad of ten, including Glenn, were already well equipped with side arms, assault rifles plus some heavy weapons in the back.

For the current task, though, Glenn had decided that

they needed some unique weaponry as taking out telepaths was going to require stealth and distance.

As they parked up at the armoury, he keyed the radio again. "Morgan and Kevin, get your sniper rifles out of the armoury." Releasing the radio button, he turned to the back seat of his own truck. "Alistair, come and get yours too."

Although all of his men were good shots, these three were the best snipers, and this was a job for the best. All the security guards at the armoury gates knew Glenn and didn't dare ask for identification. Once inside, the three squad members retrieved their weapons from one of the secure containers.

"You shouldn't need more than ten rounds but take a full box each," Glenn instructed them.

The vast majority of the Kompaniya forces would rarely fire their weapons, but his squad operated outside the standard rules and was well known for firing lots of ammunition. He wanted them to have plenty of rounds for the sniper rifles in case they were needed.

After they returned to the trucks, they drove off to the briefing sheds. The sheds were hangars where his squad could plan and practice tasks before they executed them. With the sheds situated close to the outskirts of the capital, the squad could use them to reach most places quickly and on more than one occasion had relied on them as a base for more extensive operations.

The men who opened the gates were more of Glenn's men; being paranoid was a prerequisite for someone in his position so he trusted no one else.

Leaving the vehicle, Glenn entered the first hangars and proceeded to the far corner that housed a secure container doubling as an office. He went through the filing cabinets and pulled out the files on Harper and Blossom. After reading them thoroughly, he went to a briefing room where his squad members were waiting for him.

"We have a challenging task ahead of us. We're to take out these two individuals." He passed around the photos of Harper and Blossom that he had taken from the files.

"The challenge is not that this man and woman are a physical threat but that they're telepaths. If we get too close, they will no doubt read our thoughts and try to escape. We cannot fail in this task, so I have a plan." Glenn was drawing on a chalkboard as he was talking.

"Our targets are a married couple who live together in a flat in sector five. You will see from the sketch that there is a cluster of four buildings. They live in building two, and we will position a sniper on the roof of each of the other three buildings: Kevin on building four, Morgan on building three and Alistair on building one with me. The rest of you will be positioned in the trucks in different directions approximately a kilometre away from the buildings." He looked around the room, noting each squad member was listening intently.

"Our targets' routine is to return home at five each evening and leave the building at seven each morning. We will be in place before they come home tonight and then take them out as they leave for work tomorrow morning. Take note of the insertion route."

He was drawing on the board and pointing to specific key points. "Once we've deployed to the rooftops, the mobile teams don't come back inside this perimeter until I say so. We will kill the woman in front of the man and then wound him. They are not authorised to carry weapons unless they are on operations, but if things go sideways and you have to approach them by vehicle, be prepared for anything. You all know what your tasks are and where you will be spending the night so equip yourself accordingly. We deploy in sixty minutes." With that, he headed back to the briefing room to prepare his own equipment.

26

TEAM ONE LEAVES THE BOAT

02 May 2206

"Our two teams will deploy at separate times as spreading out may increase our chances of success. I realise this means that each team is going to be alone and small, but in reality, the forces we're up against are so large, a few extra people will not make that much difference." Those were the last words Pepper said to the two teams while they were all together.

Pepper's team left thirty minutes before Angus's, taking a different route from the one Angus planned.

Iris and Foster had experience in communicating over moderate distances so it was hoped that they would be able to provide a way of communicating between the two teams. At the same time, because there was a good chance that the Kompaniya had its own telepaths, communication was to be kept to a minimum.

As his team drove through the outskirts of the docks, Pepper was reminded of a similar journey in his past.

On that journey, they'd approached a boat where Hook was on board, and now Hook was again on a boat as they were leaving it. On both occasions, they were on their way towards a sanctuary where they would face an enemy with superior numbers and firepower.

Other similarities struck Pepper: a feeling of deprivation in the area, lots of shipping containers, and an industrial area with poorly maintained roads. If this sanctuary mirrored their own before the takeover, the only people who travelled by vehicle would be the rich, the security forces and heavy trucks carrying stores.

The plan was to try to swap their vehicle at the first opportunity. Their truck was reasonably large to accommodate their whole team but taking it into the capital was a last resort. They were well armed and aimed to take any local security forces by surprise.

After driving for around ten minutes, Pepper saw a mobile checkpoint in the distance and asked one last time, "Is everybody ready?"

Coosh nodded from the driver's seat, and Will replied quietly from a rear passenger seat, "Let's get this over with."

Coosh slowed the vehicle slightly as they approached the checkpoint and Pepper gave a cursory glance at his silenced pistol, which was already cocked.

All four passengers of the sentry vehicle that waited ahead for them were outside, two hanging off either side.

Pepper mused that tactically it would've made sense to leave someone in the vehicle to radio for assistance, but clearly they didn't expect trouble. Perhaps the only people they were used to fighting were unarmed civilians.

His team wore the grey overalls previously worn by the Company guards but with no markings to make them less conspicuous. They had seen Kompaniya forces wearing similar overalls at the summits. As they were unsure what the locals wore in the Kompaniya sanctuary, they aimed to swap some clothes when they commandeered transport.

A sentry approached on either side of the team's vehicle. When the first one reached the passenger door, he motioned for Pepper to open the window. Their choice of semi-tinted windows was paying off as it was obvious that the windows were obscuring the sentry's view.

Maybe it was because the sentries didn't recognise the vehicle that they'd been slow to react. Pepper had hoped that coming from the docks would give them enough time to surprise their foes.

He pretended to struggle with the windows, and the delays prompted the sentry to beckon his comrades to approach. Meanwhile, Pepper had one hand on the inside door handle and the other tightly gripping his pistol.

Coosh had put the vehicle into neutral; he was holding a door handle with one hand and his pistol with the other. Will and Smith were concealed in the back seats.

"We go when I say 'three'," Pepper said before following up almost instantly with, "One – two – three."

As soon as they heard "three", Will and Smith threw open their doors. Will dived out of the vehicle to the right, while Smith went to the left. Then coming up to their knees, they both raised their automatic rifles to their shoulders.

The two sentries standing ahead of the vehicle were distracted by this abrupt exit, which took their focus away from the front doors. Pepper and Coosh quickly fired two rounds into each of their faces. As the sentries crumpled to the ground, Smith and Will each loosed off a three-round burst into the sentries furthest away.

The whole thing was over in less than sixty seconds, and the other three team members hadn't even needed to fire their weapons.

Then, within a few seconds, Pepper went from the passenger seat to launching himself forward. At a run, he reached the checkpoint vehicle, putting an extra round into the heads of the two far sentries in the process.

Yanking open the driver's door, he was relieved to see the keys in the ignition. The engine fired the first time and he put the truck in gear. Taking advantage of being the only ones at the checkpoint, the team manoeuvred both vehicles to the side of the road and quickly dragged the bodies to the rear. Smith pulled open the back door of their original truck, and they stripped the uniforms off the Kompaniya men before hurling the naked corpses inside.

With no one now blocking the road, Pepper hoped that if anyone appeared, they would just drive past.

The sentries' uniforms weren't in pristine condition even after the team applied the cleaning supplies that they had brought with them. But, as most of the blood came from headshots, from a distance it would be hard to notice the stains.

Although they were fortunate enough to find a uniform to fit Pepper, it had no rank markings so he would have to play the part of a junior should they encounter other Kompaniya soldiers. This was fine with Pepper as he would only need the uniform later as a temporary distraction. Once someone registered his skin tone, it wouldn't take long for any interaction to end up in an exchange of bullets.

Foster, Coosh and Will were likewise clothed in semi-clean uniforms. The other three missed out – but having four in uniform was better than none.

It was surprising to Pepper how well things were going to plan. He began to think they might actually survive this mission, but this was early days and complacency was the easiest way to end up dead.

Once they had transferred all of their own weapons and equipment to the sentry vehicle, they drove both vehicles for another ten minutes. When they came across some trees by the side of the road, Pepper motioned for Coosh to pull over. Dailey followed suit in the rear vehicle.

"We don't have much time. Dailey, take the vehicle over there and unload the bodies in the bushes. The rest of you try to cover them up as best you can," Pepper told them.

The foliage was in a dip lower than the road. Although this temporary camouflage wouldn't stand up to intense scrutiny, he hoped that anyone driving by wouldn't notice anything from the road. If the naked bodies weren't discovered immediately, it might give them a slight lead before the full might of the Kompaniya was unleashed on them.

In hostile territory, it was essential to preserve any resources that they could, including the rather shabby vehicle they had brought all the way from Sanctuary One. Once they had discarded the bodies, their little convoy continued down the road until they passed a burnt-out building at the side of the road.

Pepper let them drive for another five minutes before they circled back to the building to leave their own vehicle behind. The dirty van wasn't too conspicuous, but they needed to blend in where possible, and there was too much risk that it might be flagged as foreign.

After transferring most of its fuel to their new vehicle, they stashed the van behind the building and, within a short time, covered it with old sheets of steel and roof debris. A close examination would show that a serviceable vehicle had been abandoned, but from the road it was almost invisible.

They were in uncharted territory; they had no idea who owned this place or how often it was visited. Even if both the bodies and the vehicle were discovered, Pepper hoped that they would not be linked together.

In a short time, they had managed to acquire a new vehicle, enemy uniforms and weapons but Pepper didn't know how long their luck could hold out. He decided it was time for a quick pep talk.

"I'm not sure how long our luck will last, so don't get complacent. Leaving our truck here might give us a better chance of success, but we don't know what we're going to find once we hit the capital. The keys to the truck are in a magnetic key holder behind the front wheel on the driver's side. If any of us are fortunate enough to return this way and the truck is still here, it might mean the difference between reaching the docks or not. Take nothing for granted – none of us may get back home – but remember where the keys are as your life might depend on it. Let's mount up and be vigilant."

As Pepper stopped talking, everyone mounted the

new vehicle. No one said a word – except Will. "I don't care if we do escape. As long as I take out Brand, I'll have succeeded."

Pepper eyed Will cautiously, determining that he would need to take account of Will's mindset in future planning.

Pepper and Coosh consulted Chang's maps for the first time since leaving the boat. Now they'd experienced the ground, they needed to check the orientation. It took only a few minutes to confirm that they were heading in the right direction. Addressing everyone inside the truck, Pepper raised his voice. "Anyone not in uniform keeps back in the shadows. If we have to stop, try to conceal yourself as much as possible. Hopefully very few people will be around this early in the morning. We stick to the plan, recce the route and stop about a mile from the capital. Let's get moving."

The rest of the journey was uneventful. They passed no other vehicles and, when they came across a small side road, Pepper deemed it close enough to the capital for them to park up.

Dailey and Brown dismounted the vehicle in nondescript grey overalls, ready to depart on their scouting mission. Dailey was a few inches taller than Brown but with their tight-cropped brown hair, they could have been mistaken for brothers in a certain light.

Pepper took the chance for a final briefing. "Remember: don't be heroes, take your time. We intend to be here waiting for you. If you return and you can't see us, wait by that large tree over there. If we have to move, we will come back for you. I estimate that you should be back within two hours. I make it nine o'clock so set your watches. If you haven't returned within three hours, we will start driving down this road. If you return here and we're nowhere to be seen, wait until three o'clock, then head back to where we've hidden our vehicle and try to get back to the boat. We all know that this is a risky mission; I'm not asking anybody to go down this road and try to kill Brand single-handed. That wouldn't just be suicide; it would be a waste." He paused to let his words sink in.

"You are our first scouts, and if you are the only survivors from this mission, you may have some useful information that can be used on further missions.

"We don't even know if Brand's in the capital today but we have the element of surprise. We'll use Foster and Iris to coordinate the attack based on Chang's information, but if you two can provide any information, it may help us succeed. If all else fails, we might just hit the capital with all of our explosives and create chaos. Stay safe and get back to us." Pepper hoped that this final message would provide some added motivation.

"At least if you have to run for the docks, it should be getting dark and give you some cover to escape," Will added snarkily.

Pepper threw him a look that would have put fear into most people, but Will just shrugged it off.

With that, the scouts turned towards the capital. Dailey walked off immediately and Brown left fifteen minutes later.

27
———

WAITING ON THE ROOFTOPS

24 April 2206

Glenn's initial plan had changed on the way to the rooftops. He'd decided to post a second man with each of the other snipers. It was not so much that he was concerned that his men needed company – more that he couldn't chance anyone falling asleep and not being ready when the targets left the building.

As a consequence, only two men were left in each of the trucks, but they were far away and, as such, only a last-chance option.

He and his teams of snipers and spotters had been on the roof for hours, but they'd come prepared with warm gear and the night had passed without incident. It was five in the morning when Glenn decided to check on his teams.

"All teams confirm your status."

"Rooftop four, wide awake."

"Rooftop three, wide awake."

"Mobile one, wide awake."

"Mobile two, wide awake."

Glenn had ordered each pair on the rooftops and in the vehicles to deploy with a flask of hot coffee and of course he had brought along his own.

He'd avoided checking in regularly throughout the night as the point of the two-man teams was to allow them time to stagger their shifts and get some rest. He'd even allowed Alistair to grab a few hours' sleep while he kept watch.

Alistair was the best shot among the snipers. Glenn's ego wasn't so big that he would let the prospect of his own comfort jeopardise the mission.

Now was the time to get them up and moving about. He wanted them fully alert by the time the telepaths left the building. A groggy sniper might miss a critical shot and failure was not an option.

He had positioned himself on the highest building so he could monitor movement on the other rooftops, but he still required verbal acknowledgement from the whole team.

"Have you all had your snacks so you are now ready to go?"

Each location relayed in their turn, "Ready and able."

Glenn didn't usually micromanage, but this wasn't a routine mission so he had to be extra cautious. Their usual missions involved unsuspecting targets that they would go out and kill or terrorise. The type of challenge he usually dealt with included multiple targets and it was just a case of choosing the order in which to victimise them.

Glenn pondered that no matter how successful your

history was, you were only remembered for your last actions. The telepathic angle on this mission complicated things. At any stage, the telepaths could pick up on their thoughts and make a dash for it.

"Keep your eyes peeled. We're within the one-hour window and the targets could emerge at any time."

Time seemed to stand still. Every minute felt like an hour and each time Glenn checked his watch, it seemed not to have moved. Everyone in the team knew their tasks but tensions were high. Kevin and his spotter were focused on the fire escape, while Morgan and his spotter had been tasked to monitor the main entrance.

Each of the snipers was intermittently checking through his scope and then looking away to rest and keep his eyes sharp enough to take his shots. This left the spotters as the primary observers, each sporting a pair of strong, reliable binoculars.

Alistair and Glenn viewed the main entrance. At 6.30 Glenn looked through his binoculars and suddenly saw a man exit the building. Harper was known to have long dark hair but, as this subject was wearing a hat, it was hard to tell.

"Can anyone confirm if the man exiting the building is Harper? Kevin, keep your eyes on the fire escape in case this is a diversion." Glenn said, trying to prepare for all eventualities.

"This is Morgan; it's not the target."

"It's not him," Alistair said. The magnification on the sniper rifle was more intensive than the binoculars.

"Are you sure?" Glenn queried.

"One hundred percent," came Alistair's reply.

"We have confirmation; this is not the target. No one

is to shoot, stand down. Confirm this order; I repeat stand down!" Glenn shouted into the radio.

"Rooftop four, message received, stood down."

"Rooftop three, message received, stood down."

The unknown male continued down the steps and into the new day. Over the next ten minutes, several more false alarms followed. Most involved single individuals leaving the building but on each occasion, Glenn only stood the snipers down when he had confirmation from two sources.

The building plans showed no internal car parking, so the two exits were their only focus. He poured himself another mug of hot, sweet coffee. Only troops used to staking out a target, with the endless boredom of inaction paired with being continuously ready for action, knew the strain it took on your body.

"We're getting close to their scheduled departure. Everyone stay alert. Mobiles one and two, start your engines."

The drivers of both vehicles confirmed, "Engine running and ready to move on your orders."

"If we have a runner, I'll let you know. Until then, wait for my call to collect the bodies."

"Mobile one, understood,"

"Mobile two, understood."

Looking through his binoculars, Glenn saw movement at the building's front entrance and threw down his mug. Before he had the time to speak, Morgan came over the radio. "I can see them; they've just come out."

Looking through his binoculars, Glenn saw two figures in thick jackets and woolly hats; it was still difficult to know if they were the targets. "Confirm that's them?" he said to Alistair.

"That's them," Alistair replied.

"Everyone listen up. We have a positive identification; they've just exited the front door. We have limited time. Kevin and Morgan, get the woman in your sights and when I say shoot, let her have it. Three, two, one, shoot."

He had hardly got the words out of his mouth when he heard the distinct sound of two high-velocity shots. They were so close together that it was difficult to distinguish which direction the first shot came from.

Looking through his binoculars, he saw the woman falling backwards from the impact of the bullets. He couldn't see the expression on Harper's face, but he assumed it would be showing shock and horror.

"Take him in the legs," he said to Alistair, and he heard the rifle at the side of him before he saw the impact on Harper. Harper had been crouched over his wife so he should have been an easy target. The only problem was that, as he was already crouched down, it was hard to determine the effectiveness of the shot. "Hit him again in the legs."

Alistair had aimed the first round at the target's left thigh so this time he focused on the right. There was no doubt about his accuracy this time: as he fired again, Harper slid away from his wife's lifeless body.

Glenn was conscious of his orders to keep Harper alive, if possible. He also assumed that Harper would still be able to function as a telepath in a wheelchair. It gave him some sense of pleasure that this telepath wouldn't feel so superior in the future.

"Mobiles one and two, move in and recover the

targets." He liked that everything was going to plan. The two trucks would pull up outside building two with their first aid packs and administer medical attention to Harper, securing him to the stretcher to avoid any escape attempts. In the unlikely event that Blossom was still alive, his men wouldn't hesitate to finish her off.

Monitoring the situation from above, he saw the trucks arrive and his men quickly set to their tasks. In what seemed like only five minutes, the woman's body was tossed into the back of Mobile two, while Harper's stretcher was being carried to Mobile one.

"Kevin and Morgan, your teams can now leave the roofs and rendezvous with Mobile two. Mobile one, wait outside this building for myself and Alistair."

He didn't wait for a reply as he turned to gather his equipment. While Glenn collected his coffee mug from the roof, Alistair quickly stripped down his sniper rifle and stowed it in its case. Glenn watched while Alistair collected the two spent bullet cases – he assumed the sniper was just acting out of habit as part of his training as no one would be coming to investigate what had occurred here.

Glenn and Alistair took the elevator down to the ground and left the building to find Mobile one waiting with the engine running.

Climbing into the passenger seat, he waited for Alistair, who was stowing his sniper case and his other bag in the back of the truck. Glenn looked towards Harper still breathing on the stretcher. "How is he doing?" he said to no one in particular.

A voice from the back replied, "He's stable. Both rounds went straight through so he'll live, but if he walks again, he'll probably have a limp."

Glenn smiled at how smoothly everything seemed to have gone. He grabbed the radio for one last order before the mission debrief. "Take her body to the liquidation plants and then meet us at the briefing sheds. We'll drop our cargo at the hospital."

"See you at the sheds," came the reply from Mobile two.

With that, Glenn nodded to his driver, and they headed for the hospital. He was looking forward to telling Nikolei how well things had gone but would wait until after he'd debriefed his troops so he could be sure he had not missed any surprises.

28

TEAM TWO LEAVES THE BOAT

02 May 2206

Leaving around thirty minutes later, Angus's team took a slightly different route from Pepper's. Instead of heading directly north, they travelled northeast. Although this would take them longer, they hoped they could use the time to recce the area in more detail.

As Iris and Foster remained in telepathic communication, Angus was happy to learn that the other team had already managed to get uniforms and a vehicle. At times while on the boat, Angus had thought he was getting too old for this stuff. He'd always been a fighter, and he preferred the idea of dying fighting than peacefully in some bed.

The thirty-minute variance in departure times didn't seem to make much difference with traffic; there was still nobody on the roads. According to the map that Chang had provided, if they stayed on their current route, they would encounter a small town on the outskirts of the capital.

The plan was to drive around the town slowly, taking advantage of their tinted windows to help shield them from any cursory inspections. The dull colouring would also make the vehicle blend in. They had purposely painted one of the doors a different shade from the rest so that it would look more like a vehicle that had been cobbled together, a diversionary tactic to steer people away from noticing the vehicle had not been made in this kingdom. The absence of badges, insignia or numbers on display made it appear like any other nondescript vehicle.

When they arrived at the outskirts of the town, no one was on the streets. Angus wondered if an extended curfew was in place here. They'd tried to prepare for any situation, and every one of them kept their hands tightly on their weapons.

They slowly zigzagged in and out of the side streets, looking for anybody.

"Stop," Angus said.

"What is it?" Jones asked.

"Look straight ahead."

Amazingly, they'd appeared behind an enemy security vehicle; it seemed to be full of sleeping soldiers. Only the driver looked to be awake as he was moving his head slowly around. For the moment, it looked like he hadn't noticed them.

"Kill the engine quickly," Angus ordered. He couldn't believe their luck. "We don't know what this is yet."

"It looks like some badly trained soldiers are sleeping on the job," Fred said.

"Looks can be deceiving, but I'm not prepared to pass up on an opportunity like this," Angus said. "Jones, stay in the driver's seat, ready to pick us up if necessary but don't start the engine unless we signal you. Iris, I want you to stay in the truck too as we might need you to transmit what happens to the other team.

"The rest of you are going to exit the vehicle quietly. I'll take the right-hand side with Manning, and you other three take the left. We will use silenced pistols only, and I'd like to avoid shooting out their windows, but the key is speed and surprise. I will shoot the driver and if we manage to catch the rest unawares, open the doors and shoot them in the head. I say again, try not to shoot out the windows if you can as we need this vehicle."

Everyone nodded in confirmation. They opened the doors silently and got out of their vehicle slowly before walking up the street. Angus managed to get alongside the driver unseen, who it was clear from first glance was only young.

Barnes was in fact the youngest of his patrol and he didn't mind that the rest of his team were asleep. Every soldier in the area knew that nothing ever happened in this town, making it one of the easiest shifts around.

They were supposed to drive around looking for curfew breakers, but Slonk was small and insignificant. If it hadn't been so close to the capital, it was doubtful the town would even have had a patrol.

The inaction on this patrol was amplified by the laziness of their patrol leader. Aconex liked drinking and he liked women, and both took priority over any military duties. As the youngest, Barnes pulled most of the dirty jobs, but Aconex was a sadist so he was not about to question the order to stay awake while the rest of the team slept. It also made him determined not to wake anyone unless he truly had to.

He was considering what he was going to have for breakfast when he suddenly noticed a man staring in at him through his side window. The man had a scar down his face and only one good eye. The next few seconds seemed to happen very fast for Barnes. His mind was racing. "Why haven't I been watching my side mirror? Why is there anyone around at this time of the morning? Should I wake up Aconex?"

He noticed more people outside looking in through the side windows. Before he had time to open his mouth, his door was wrenched open by the scarred man and the last thing he saw was the flash of the gun as it was discharged into his face.

At the same time as Angus opened the driver's door, the rest of the team pulled open the other doors. The team all fired their silenced weapons simultaneously. None of the vehicle's inhabitants had managed to make a sound before they died, not even Barnes.

"Okay," Angus said. "Hopefully the silencers have done their job and no one has heard anything to alarm them, but we must move fast." He motioned to Jones to pull their vehicle alongside. "Get them all into the back of our vehicle quickly. Then I'll drive this one and we'll take both vehicles to the side street we just passed." In less than five minutes, both vehicles were parked up in a quiet alleyway.

Angus wasted no time. "Jones and Nikki, use some of our cleaning gear to remove as much of the blood from their vehicle as possible. We've been lucky that the windows are all intact but clean the blood off the windows. The rest of you strip their bodies and try to wipe off any blood stains from their clothes."

Now equipped with uniforms, enemy weapons and an enemy vehicle, Angus's team retraced their route back in the direction of the port. It was the only area that they knew of this new land, and as they'd been driving towards the town, they had been searching for places to hide a vehicle, bodies or anything.

Their route up to this point had been very flat with little in the way of landmarks. However, Angus had noted a river earlier that ran towards the docks and they returned there now. The river ran quite deep, and Angus had his team weigh down the bodies with stones before tossing them in.

He did not doubt that these bodies would be discovered at some stage, but if they stayed hidden for just a short time, it might allow him and his team to survive this mission. If they didn't complete their mission within a few days, the discovery of bodies wouldn't matter by then anyway.

Closer to the docks was what looked like an abandoned building. After dumping the bodies, they went back there to hide their vehicle.

At this point, Angus paused to focus his team.

"We've been over the plan on the boat, but now that you've had your first action, it is no doubt starting to feel more real. Keep your mind on the mission to take out our old leader, Brand. We have explosives to take care of infrastructure as our secondary target. If there are explosions before we get to Brand, his security is going to intensify so we'll try to use our explosives in the attack on Brand. You all know where the keys are hidden in this vehicle in case of emergencies. Remember it only has enough fuel to get you to the docks now we've siphoned off most of the fuel for our new wheels. If we get separated and we are being pursued, any of you that reach these wheels are to use them to head to the docks. Don't wait for anyone else as by then it will be everyone for himself and these wheels might get you back to the boat in time."

Angus never stopped being a trainer. In the pits he had trained his warriors to stay alive, and this team had become his warriors now. He'd trained them since before the boat left and, ever since the parachutes landed, he had been taking them through scenarios. Some of them had never killed before this mission and, as an accomplished killer himself, his goal was to give them their best chances of survival.

He understood that until anyone was faced with actually having to kill someone, there was no knowing how they'd react. The team had performed well up to now, shooting the vehicle inhabitants without hesitation, but in that case no one had been shooting back. If they were cornered, under fire, if they ran out of bullets or had to fight hand to hand, how would they do?

A big part of this team's survival depended on him, and the chances of this mission's success had just increased by a slither, now that both teams had security force vehicles and disguises.

29

THE BACKUP PLAN

03 May 2206

Brand's initial plan had been of limited success; the bombing of his old home sanctuary had been intended as a surprise attack that did not leave his fingerprints on the weapons. The attack should also have taken out the new leaders, but it hadn't been as effective as intended.

He'd always had a secondary attack as a backup plan. Although he'd still have some deniability, it wouldn't be as discreet as before. As that imbecile Radka had already raised suspicions that the attack had come from them, it was only a matter of time before they figured it out.

It had taken some time, but Brand had commissioned a batch of the communication drones to be weaponised and they were now ready to be deployed.

When Glenn and his men reached the docks, Narick and his crew of dockworkers had loaded half of the large crates. Igor, the first mate, was supervising the loading of the fuel, the food and everything else but Karcher, the engineer, was paying more attention to the drones and their components. It was Karcher's job to ensure that the drones were assembled and flight-ready when they got to their destination. He was worried that some fool with a fork loader would hit one of the boxes and the whole boat would be blown to smithereens.

"Be careful there, be careful there!" he was continuously shouting to no one in particular.

Luka, the ship's captain, had his own pressing activities to get on with: checking the charts and plotting the route, monitoring the ship's dials and attending to all the other duties involved in getting ready to sail.

Karcher was darting around everywhere. Whenever a net-load of components came too close to a crane, the side of the hold or anything else, Glenn saw him wincing.

Glenn had grave doubts as to whether the engineer's heart would survive long enough to complete his mission.

The mission was risky enough, and chances were high that they'd meet an enemy boat during the long voyage. The last thing they needed was a jumpy engineer so Glenn decided he'd need to have a quiet word with the captain. Perhaps if they lubricated him with enough alcohol to keep him calm, but within limits that left him sober enough to function, that would work. The engineer was critical to the mission so the captain would have to take responsibility for this.

Reaching the bridge, Glenn was pleased to see Luka calmly pondering over the charts. Although he knew little of nautical charts, Glenn pretended to take an interest in the maps and charts laid out on the table.

"Well captain, how are your preparations for departure going?"

Without taking his eyes from his work, Luka retorted, "We'll be fully loaded in two hours, leaving port in three."

Glenn thought that those three hours couldn't pass quickly enough. On land, he was a skilled soldier and fighter, but on the water, he wasn't as comfortable. Just standing on this bridge and feeling the boat roll, even though its movement was limited by the docks, was making him feel nauseous. Someone in his position couldn't show weakness, so he was determined to tough it out, while thankful that he could leave soon rather than deploying on this seafaring mission. Even someone of his fortitude would no doubt fail to keep his stomach contents in place on the high seas.

"Are you going to spend the next two hours just looking at that desk?" Glenn asked restlessly.

"There's a bottle of rum on the side over there. Take a drink, it will help with your sea legs."

Glenn was annoyed that Luka had seen through him but respected that the captain had no doubt seen plenty of sea virgins in his maritime career.

Glenn had drank slowly but was still on his third glass of rum when he heard the horn sound.

"What's that?"

"That means the loading is complete. I think you need to go below and meet up with your men," Luka said.

"I'll be back in a short while," Glenn said as he left the bridge.

Descending the steel ladder to the hold, he was a

little unsteady on his feet, but unsure whether it was the sea or the rum that was having the greatest effect.

When Glenn arrived, Narick was standing in front of the dockworkers, who had been ordered to line up in two rows. Not used to formations, they looked more like an unruly mob than some kind of soldiers on parade but having them assembled in this way served the required purpose.

Igor, standing alongside Narick, handed Glenn a bottle.

Some of Narick's crew rarely came on board the boats that they loaded. Today was a special occasion; they'd been told that they were to be honoured in a ceremony for their work loading the ship. Although they knew little about the full purpose of the mission, they recognised the warning labels on the crates and had been told that this was a critical mission.

Before he addressed the group, Glenn surveyed his men, who were standing against the walls of the hold. They looked more like a group of soldiers on parade than the dockworkers, even though they weren't dressed in smartly pressed uniforms.

Then he turned to the dockworkers. "I've been asked by the leaders of our government to reward you for your work on this operation. I realise that you may not know the full details of the mission ahead for this ship, but I can tell you that it's a matter that affects the safety and security of all of us. Your small contributions today will have more impact than you can imagine." He didn't know this for sure but it allowed him to play for time.

Glenn looked at Narick, a barrel of a man with calloused fat hands and clothes smeared with oil stains.

Although Glenn believed in leading by example, he was convinced that leadership was not about making yourself look like the lowest worker in your ranks. Everyone had their place in the order of things, but the dirt and grime on Narick's hands didn't sit well with Glenn.

"I'd like to call on your leader Narick to step forward."

Narick puffed up his chest, looking forward to his reward. His father had been a drunk and had told him that he would never amount to much. He wasn't a great reader, but he'd worked hard to get where he was. It had sometimes required smashing heads, but his men genuinely liked him.

As Narick stepped forward, Glenn's men discreetly unslung their weapons.

Holding the bottle out in his left hand, Glenn had his right hand behind his back. "This bottle is just a small token of the gratitude of our leaders and you will all receive your just rewards today."

Reaching out for the bottle, Narick didn't stand a chance. Glenn brought his right-hand round from behind his back to reveal the pistol he'd retrieved from his waist belt. He fired off two shots in succession, directly into Narick's head.

The next few seconds seemed to pass in slow motion for Igor. He watched in amazement as Glenn shot Narick. His shock grew when, before Narick's body hit the ground, Glenn's men levelled their assault rifles at the dockworkers and fired off numerous bursts into their group.

The whole episode lasted less than twenty seconds.

Now where a crowd of lively workers had once stood was a pile of bloody dead flesh.

Igor suddenly realised that the captain was absent. Even if the captain was aware of this, he was unsure of how safe his own position was now.

Glenn assumed Igor had been briefed by the captain but the look on his face soon told him that this cull had taken him by surprise.

Gripping Igor's lapels, he said quietly, "These bodies are now part of your cargo so I'll leave you to dispose of them." Igor seemed frozen in place, so Glenn grabbed him by his collar. "Do you understand?"

Coming back to life, Igor responded, "I'll have the crew ship them to the gel plants."

"No, you idiot, the whole point of today is to tie up loose ends. No one is to know about this ship. Wait until you are well out to sea and feed their bodies to the fishes."

As Glenn took his hands off Igor, the colour seemed to return to his face.

"I'll get this mess cleaned up," Igor agreed.

Glenn nodded and then headed towards his men. "I'm off upstairs to the bridge. Go back to the trucks and wait for me there. I'll be with you in about ten minutes." With that, he headed unsteadily back up the ladder to the bridge.

Arriving on the bridge, he found Luka with a mug of coffee poured from a pot on the side.

"Would you like some?"

Glenn was still feeling the effects of the rum, so he thought this was a great idea. "Thanks, I don't mind if I do."

"It's a shame about Narick and his team; they were

an efficient lot. Not once did I have a boat leave late because of them and they never banged one load into any of my holds or the side of any of my boats."

"That's all well and good, but we all know the details of this mission must remain secret. If word gets out what you are carting on this boat, you'll be a target as soon as you leave port. Only a limited number of people know about this mission, and most of them are on this boat."

"And do you know the full extent of the mission?"

Glenn thought carefully before he replied. Knowledge was power, but if people knew that you had that knowledge, it made you a target. "I have a rough idea, but if you want to fill in the gaps, I'm all ears."

"Are you sure that you want to know?" Luka smiled.

He didn't know the full story and, if Luka told him, no one would find out that he had. It was doubtful Luka and his crew would survive, let alone return home.

"Okay, tell me what I don't know.'

Luka was relieved to share the mission with someone. He hadn't even been able to share the mission with his family for fear of putting them in danger, although he still doubted that his family would be spared once he left port.

It had been a lonely few months since he'd been told of the mission. On that occasion, Glenn had delivered his written orders, sealed. He was ordered to go; there was no option of volunteering. He'd been tasked to put together a crew for this ship. He was a captain of his own boat, but the number in his original crew was not enough to work this ship.

"I assume that you know this ship has been refurbished, I'm guessing that it took over a year to fit it out," he told Glenn now. "It was designed to look like a large fishing boat, but anyone looking closer will see the modifications."

Glenn nodded, not to indicate he knew this information, but because he wanted to be off the boat as soon as possible so he didn't want to interrupt. He realised that Brand must have been planning this mission ever since he came to power, if not longer. That was an interesting fact but also a dangerous thing to know.

"We have a cargo of unmanned aircraft – you may know them as drones."

"I've been to the drone station and collected cargo from them."

"What you might not know is that the drones that land in this sanctuary come from another sanctuary like ours. A sanctuary that we are in conflict with. The drones we have on board are loaded with explosives. Once we reach a set point near the other sanctuary, we will launch these drones and rain down hell on our enemies."

Glenn recognised the magnitude of what he had just heard. Some rumours were that Brand came from outside of the kingdom but anyone who had raised such a question would be dead by now. If the supreme leader knew that Glenn had this information, his life would be worthless.

He hid his surprise from Luka well. This information conflicted with the history they'd been taught that they were the only survivors of the Water Wars, but that history was never to be questioned. Everyone just accepted that they had been the ones to triumph over their enemies. It would seem that nuclear annihilation may not have been as devastating as they had been told.

This information also raised more questions than it provided answers. He'd always wondered what the point of Councillor Radka was. He had all the benefits of the other councillors but never seemed to do anything. His security detail comprised solely of Kompaniya troops, which meant that they weren't loyal to him. And his recent execution seemed to be tied in to a trip he had just taken.

Glenn's thoughts returned to this mission. As a soldier, he reasoned that surely bombing someone would result in an all-out war. Unless they were weaklings or the bombs took out all of their leaders, they must mount some form of counter-attack.

He suddenly recalled a mission he'd been tasked with a few months ago. He had rounded up a group of seemingly unconnected families and executed them, before taking the bodies to the gel plants. It had seemed odd at the time as some of them were the families of Kompaniya soldiers or relatives of telepaths from the training facility.

If, like today, Glenn had been tying up loose ends, he wondered how long it would be before he was classed as a loose end too.

Fear for his own survival was useful to a point but, for today, he had completed his mission and it was time to head back to Nikolei and report on his success.

He had lost the taste for the coffee, and this news had just blown away any mental cobwebs left over from the rum. "I wish you a safe trip, captain, as well as a successful mission and a speedy return."

It was evident that Glenn was in a rush to leave the

boat, but Luka was glad to have shared his burden with someone.

"I doubt we'll meet again, but this ship holds enough alcohol to allow us to pass peacefully if we die at sea."

Glenn didn't like to dwell on his own mortality, so he just nodded and left Luka on the bridge as he went to meet up with his squad.

30

THE SCOUTS RETURN

02 May 2206

Brown was the first scout to return, and he was happy to see a truck waiting for him. All the same, he approached cautiously as he didn't know if enemy trucks each had their own distinguishing marks. If his team had left, he could be walking into the arms of the enemy. But as he got closer, he could see Coosh sitting in the driver's seat and he quickened his steps. He was pleased to see that the rest of the team were all sitting safely in the back. Pepper had always been concerned that his dark skin would make him stand out, which seemed to be the reason why he'd also taken cover in the back of the truck.

In the beginning, the three companies on Earth had been multicultural. Back then they'd run the world through governments that represented a variety of ethnicities, but even then that had included an undercurrent of racism.

Since the Water Wars, the companies had become

more blatant in their racial attitudes, treating minority groups once again as second-class citizens. It was well known that Chang was a believer in the purity of Asian skin. Centuries ago some Asians had been called yellow skins, even though their skin was more pink than yellow. The previous leaders of Sanctuary One had seen themselves as white, despite their obvious pinkness as well, and in becoming Sanctuary Two leader, Brand brought with him biases to reinforce any existing belief in white superiority.

Pepper might have been accepted as a soldier by the Company, but the Kompaniya could well be less tolerant. Their headquarters based in the cold north of Europe had a climate that tolerated paler skin more than other areas, plus few people anywhere were as tall as Pepper.

One reason Frank had been against Pepper going on this mission was that he saw Pepper's conspicuousness as adding just another risk of failure in an enterprise most people saw as a one-way mission.

Their different views on whether Pepper should join the mission had led to one of the few arguments they'd ever had. Frank had been adamant that this was crazy, but Pepper pointed out that he had been a similar height for most of his adult life and had always had the same skin colour. After surviving a lifetime of being hunted by the Company, he believed that his chances hadn't changed. He was adaptable and knew how to react when a situation turned bad.

As a compromise, Pepper had proposed that if Frank could offer an alternative commander for the mission, he would consider not going. Frank had been forced to admit that, given they were heading into the unknown,

Pepper was one of the best suited for the task and they had made peace with this decision.

"Okay Brown, what did you find out?" Pepper asked impatiently.

"The capital is not walled. The main road shown on Chang's map has a patrol on it, but there's a side road not far away that we should be able to use to avoid the checkpoints. The enemy vehicles all look similar to the truck we're using, and their uniforms are also the same. If anyone inspects us too closely, they may notice some differences, but we should pass a casual glance enough to get close to the capital and the government buildings. I was trying not to draw attention to myself so couldn't get too close to the government buildings, but even from a distance, I could see that they're well-fortified. Several enemy trucks are stationed and crewed around the government buildings."

"So we can get into the capital, but the government buildings are going to be the challenge," Pepper affirmed.

"Yes, that about sums things up."

"We can use our explosives as a distraction," Pepper said as he started to think through their options. "By the way, did you see anyone of my complexion?"

"Quite a few workers were around even early in the day and they looked to be a variety of ethnicities, but none matched the darkness of your skin."

Pepper was already formulating a plan in his head. Explosions linked with the view of someone of his complexion might draw the guards away from the government buildings. It was risky, and he wasn't sure he'd survive, but there were no safe options here.

Whatever plan they enacted, it would have to take

place quickly so, while he was waiting for Dailey to return, he looked over the charts with Will and Coosh.

Once Dailey turned up, Pepper had a quick debrief with him to confirm Brown's information and then addressed the whole team.

"Angus's team has already entered the capital. They will communicate the results of their recce through Iris and Foster, but unless they find something remarkably different from what we know already, I've come up with a plan. Will and I are going to create a diversion with a number of our explosives. The plan is for me to be widely seen and it's hoped that both the explosions and the sight of a dark-skinned warrior will draw the security away from the government buildings. Our escape plan is currently a work in progress, but I'm sure two survivors like Will and I can figure something out."

"No way!" Will exclaimed. "I am going to kill Brand myself, and I can't do that if I'm elsewhere creating a distraction."

"We're all aware of your history of being a master strategist in the former regime; it's time you lived up to your reputation. All you've got to do is to formulate an escape plan by the time the explosions begin. The plan needs to result in our safe escape and reaching the government buildings in time to join the attack on Brand. Can you do that?"

Will threw a cold glance at Pepper, but for once he was lost for words.

"Have you anything else to offer?" Pepper asked. He was again met with Will's silence.

Pepper went back to addressing the whole team. "Looking at the map and comparing that with the intelligence we've gathered so far, there seems to be a stand-alone building close enough to the government buildings to cause a distraction but far enough away to create a hole in their defences. We'll drop the rest of you off closer to the government buildings and then you will advance on foot with the rest of the explosives in your rucksacks.

"The element of surprise and the fact that some of you are dressed in company uniforms will hopefully allow you to blend in during the confusion. Angus's plan is to gain access to the garage below and take out Brand as he tries to escape. Most of you will be part of the backup team to provide support outside the government buildings. Coosh, you'll take charge of the team until you link up with Angus and he allocates roles."

Coosh nodded.

"Do you see any chance of escape?" Cenk asked.

"Once the attack's complete, the plan if we're captured is to align ourselves with the enemies of Brand and to say that we've been sent here to support them in overthrowing him. It is well known that Brand is not popular as he was an outsider who rose to power over the heads of other elites in the sanctuary. The other leaders will be happy to see him go, even if they grumble a little."

"So you're relying on the mercy of our enemies?" Will spat.

"If Radka or someone else chooses to fill Brand's vacancy, it is highly likely that they'll be thankful for our help. Our first option will be to try to escape, but we need contingencies as we are far from home with no available support. Nobody's going to rescue us," Pepper said.

Their entire mission had been building up to this point. By now they were all just impatient to proceed.

"If anyone wants to stretch their legs or have a final check of your kit, do it now. We leave in ten minutes." With that, Pepper got out of the truck to have one last stretch of his legs.

31

ASSAULT ON THE KOMPANIYA GOVERNMENT BUILDINGS

03 May 2206

A shattering of glass, the vibrations in the air and the smell of cordite – for Brand, the experience of a bomb blast was nothing new. The sound of this explosion burst through the bustle of the early evening, as most of the general public were trying to get home to the safety of their hovels even in the absence of a curfew.

Although three years ago Brand had arrived here with little in the way of physical goods from Sanctuary One, he had brought years of experience and strategy with him. It was now time to take advantage of the emergency escape route that he'd replicated from his former office

The explosions initiated the emergency protocol: at the first sign of trouble, Brand and his security detail would take the hidden staircase to the garage.

The security team headed down the staircase in front of Brand. He was following them out into the car park when he was blasted off his feet by an explosion. The explosion had decimated the men in front of him. Looking up, his first images were of their bodies, scattered around the garage.

As the dust temporarily cleared, he saw the face of a man looking back at him, a face he thought he'd never see again. The face was partially obscured, one of the eyes was framed in a rifle scope, but it was unmistakably William.

Before Brand could react, Nikolei came out of nowhere. He threw himself in front of Brand and received a three-round burst that Will had intended for Brand.

As Brand pushed Nikolei's corpse to one side, he was aware of more explosions and gunfire. Petra staggered into view, trying to stem the flow of blood gushing through her fingers from a neck wound.

"Why had she not seen this coming? She was a telepath, it was her job!" Brand cursed.

Even though he'd used her on multiple occasions to satisfy his physical urges, he felt no sorrow in seeing her fall. She had failed in her duties to protect him. If she'd survived this debacle, he would've arranged for her punishment afterwards.

Seeing Will approaching, Brand drew a pistol from a shoulder holster. He had security to protect him, but he'd never been shy in inflicting violence on others. Before he could identify his target, though, he felt a pain in his right shoulder as he was thrown backwards.

His clothing was constructed with inbuilt body armour designed to stop a pistol bullet but whatever had hit him was more powerful than that. The jacket had reduced the impact, but the pain was excruciating, and he could feel his right arm flopping as though his collarbone was broken. His own pistol made a metallic sound as it clattered to the ground.

Like a cornered animal, Brand went into survival mode. Ignoring the pain, he tried to pick up the gun with his left hand but before he could reach the handle, a shadow loomed over him.

"William, how pleasant to see you." Brand tried to muster a smirk.

"You left me to die!" Will exclaimed.

"Yes, that was unfortunate, but I'm sure you understand that there just wasn't enough room in the helicopter for you. As you've seen, I had a long way to travel, and I needed bargaining power. Turning up with you instead of your weight in valuables just wouldn't have cut it. But that's all in the past, let's look to the future. I have power again here. I can make you rich if you want or give you your old position, now it seems you've just created a vacancy on my security detail."

Brand had barely finished his sentence when Will fired a round into his left kneecap. He screamed out in agony but fought to stay in control. The pain seemed to bring a tear to his eye, but he tried to remain in control until the end.

"What are you doing, William?" he grimaced.

Without hesitation, Will fired off another round into Brand's right knee. Brand was now making whimpering noises instead of speaking in sentences.

"They tortured me; I almost died!" Will shouted. "At times I wished I had died. They thought they'd broken me like some wild animal. The thing that kept me going was my chance to wipe out your legacy. Being on the inside of the sanctuary allowed me to obliterate you from history. I removed every statue and defaced any plaques or signage with your name on it. I never expected a chance to repay you in person for leaving me behind, but here we are."

"Stop what you're doing!" Angus shouted as he ran towards them. "I told you before we came in here, for now, he's more useful to us alive. He might get us out of this city and then he's all yours."

But Angus was too late. A smile came across Will's face as he fired a three-round burst and Brand's head exploded. Will felt some extra satisfaction as some of Brand's blood and brains splattered on his boots.

Angus was angry. "You fool, I hope your revenge was worth our lives. If we don't survive this, it's on you."

"I never expected to get out of here," Will replied. "As soon as I found out Brand was here, my only goal was to take him out. Anything else would just be a bonus."

"Well, you've taken him out, but now we need a plan to help us survive. We've got what seems to be his personal convoy, and although it would have been easier to have him with us as a hostage, the tinted windows might just get us out of this."

Angus gestured towards two almost identical large black cars in the car park – along with their tinted windows, it looked like they had reinforced doors and bodywork. The assault team had disposed of the drivers before Brand and his security detail had arrived and luckily the vehicles hadn't been damaged in the ambush. The location of the garage and the access stairway had been one of the most useful pieces of information supplied by Chang. No one knew how Chang came by this information, but Angus was still thankful for it.

If Brand had used an alternative escape route such as the roof, there would have been nothing that they could do, as reaching the roof in a fortress like this would've been impossible, especially for such a small strike force. Luckily by heading for the car park after the first explosions, Brand had walked straight into their trap.

In truth, Angus wasn't sure if their odds of escape had become better or worse with Brand's death. Either way, it was time to initiate an escape plan.

32

EXPLOSIONS AND MAYHEM

03 May 2206

Their plans had to remain fluid. One initial plan had been for Pepper and Will to cause a distraction and then remain at a distance from the government buildings as backup. After considering the small size of the strike force, however, Pepper figured that they needed to join the assault team as everyone had to do as much as possible.

While they were planting their explosives, Will blended in with his Kompaniya uniform, while Pepper – trying to keep a low profile until after the explosions – was wearing a scarf around his head, dark glasses and a cap pulled down over his ears. The plan for him to be more conspicuous after the explosions had seemed fine in concept but, in practice, Pepper wondered if his dark skin would have been less noticeable than the disguise.

Now he sat in the truck next to Will, who was in the driving seat.

"Ready?" Pepper asked.

"I know the plan," Will said with some condescension. "You're going to walk around outside, and I'm going to wait ninety seconds and detonate the explosives. I then wait for five minutes for you to be noticed, you jump in the back and we head away from here."

"Okay, start the clock," Pepper said as he took off his disguise and got out of the truck.

Pepper tried to make eye contact with as many people as possible. He wasn't sure if it was his height or his skin colour, but most people tried to look away. He'd walked briskly for just over a minute, careful not to go too close to the bombs they'd placed next to the columns of the building.

When the first bomb exploded, the sound was deafening, and the smoke and flames that it created spread confusion around Pepper. The next three bombs went off almost simultaneously, producing noise, fire, smoke and debris that were disorientating even for Pepper.

Quickly he ran and dived into the back seat of the truck. "Get us out of here."

Will didn't need to be told twice. He drove off towards the government buildings as fast as he could manage without drawing attention to themselves.

As they drove around the second corner, they passed another security truck speeding in the opposite direction.

"Take the side streets," Pepper shouted from the back.

"I thought we needed to get to the government buildings."

"We won't get anywhere if we encounter any more

security forces. Drive carefully but avoid the main street."

Will reluctantly took his advice and, after about twenty minutes, he parked up not far from the main square. With a nod at Pepper, he left the truck and made his way quickly towards the government buildings and, he hoped, Brand.

Staying with the vehicle now seemed to Pepper to be his best option, so that he could keep out of sight and still be available as backup. After reapplying the scarf and dark glasses, Pepper sat in the driver's seat trying to look casual.

At first the explosions had drawn all of the security vehicles in their direction, but now some of the vehicles seemed to be patrolling erratically.

One of the Kompaniya trucks cruised by Pepper before doing a U-turn and pulling to a stop six feet behind him. The two troopers in the front of the vehicle climbed out of their seats and began approaching Pepper, one on each side of his truck.

His disguise might be okay from a distance, but Pepper knew it would not hold out under closer inspection. He lowered the windows and watched in his side mirrors as they approached.

They reached the front of the vehicle almost at the same time, both stopping next to the open windows. Maybe it was because they were approaching another Kompaniya vehicle or perhaps it was due to their lack of combat experience, but neither of them had bothered to draw their weapons. Seizing the element of surprise Pepper opened fire, quickly firing two rounds into the trooper closest to him.

Before the first body had even begun to fall, Pepper

fired three rounds through the open passenger window into the second man. Both had received at least one round square in the face, and neither of them managed a final death twitch.

Without waiting for any further company, Pepper sped off, being careful to avoid drawing more forces towards the government buildings. He was fortunate that the patrol vehicle had only been crewed by two people, but they must have radioed ahead as within minutes he noticed two other security vehicles behind him.

Accelerating as much as he could, he rounded the bend to find two more security trucks blocking the road ahead. He slammed his truck in reverse, catching his pursuers off guard. Unprepared for the sight of Pepper speeding towards them, the driver of the first truck swerved to avoid him but the camber of the bend combined with his speed made the truck skid off the road and slam into a barrier.

The driver of the second vehicle had heard the noise of the first crash and came round the bend a little slower. He seemed more skilled as he brought his truck to a halt side on, blocking Pepper's escape.

Unfortunately, while the driver was busy avoiding Pepper and turning his vehicle into a barricade, he failed to notice that Pepper had thrown two grenades out of his window. The one aimed at his truck fell short so its power was limited, making broken glass and steel fragments the primary damage to the occupants.

The crashed truck wasn't as lucky, as the second grenade rolled directly underneath and exploded just as it reached the fuel tank.

Limited in his options now, Pepper drove for a point

halfway between the two barricades. Skidding to a halt by the side of the road, he deliberately parked front on to the two remaining vehicles while the carnage he had inflicted on the others spread out at the rear.

Short on bullets, he doubted he could fight his way out of this situation. His only hope was to try to escape into the woods at the side of the road. His chances of escaping were low, but if he could delay his capture, he might give the others long enough to get away or die in the firefight. His main goal was not to give up any information that could damage the mission or his sanctuary.

He fired off three rounds and saw one of the enemy fall, but suddenly his vehicle was taking fire from all directions. He crouched under the engine block as he was showered with glass from all of the vehicle windows.

Whenever the onslaught paused, he fired off a couple of rounds as a way of dissuading a full-on assault.

He still had a few rounds left when he heard, "Hello there in the truck. My name's Glenn and I'm in charge here now. I've told my men to stop firing, and I'd appreciate it if you did the same."

Pepper almost laughed out loud at the notion that after trying to kill him, they were now trying to negotiate. He was at least grateful for the language training before their arrival here. Once they had known their destination, he had been able to focus on learning only one new language.

He manoeuvred around to try to get in a better firing position while keeping the engine block as his primary protection, as the voice continued.

"I don't know who you are, but there have been

some explosions in the capital, and if you have any information that could help, I'd really appreciate it. If you throw your weapons out of the windows and step out with your hands up, you will not be harmed."

Pepper didn't wait to hear any more. He pointed the barrel of his pistol in the direction of the voice and fired off two more rounds.

33

THE RIGHT PLACE AT THE RIGHT TIME

03 May 2206

Glenn and his team had only just left the docks when he saw smoke rising in the distance.

The radio chirped abruptly, "Hello all stations, this is Call Sign Five Alpha. There have been explosions in sector Bravo. I think it's the gel plants or the power plants. We can also hear gunfire."

Instantly Glenn turned to his driver Czarzeb. "Put your foot down and get us to the government buildings." It sounded like someone was panicking on the radio. He needed to get a better idea of what was occurring, but also to check in with Nikolei as soon as possible.

He went back to the main radio. "This is Glenn. Who's guarding the government buildings? Have any attacks occurred there?"

"Glenn, this is Call Sign One Delta. We have a squad in front of the government buildings, but we have experienced no issues so far."

"This is Glenn. Do not leave your current location.

I'm heading to you." He couldn't believe that he had just been thinking about their sanctuary being attacked, and now it had happened.

Grabbing the squad radio off his belt, he prepped his squad. "You'll have heard over the main radio that there have been explosions and gunfire in the capital. We are heading to the government buildings, but the situation is fluid. Stay alert and nobody sleeps." To an outsider, it might have seemed odd for him to instruct his team not to sleep during the day, but they were a team that was used to deploying for indefinite periods, so sleeping in transit had become the norm. Today the transit was as dangerous as the destination.

"Understood," came Morgan's reply from the second vehicle.

The main radio crackled to life again. "Hello all stations, this is Five Alpha. We are chasing a stolen Kompaniya vehicle, and the driver is a tall black male. He's definitely not one of our troops as he's already fired rounds at us. We're pursuing him down route seventy-three, and we are currently ten minutes north of junction twenty, over."

"Hello Five Alpha, this is Five Delta. We're heading down route seventy-three from the opposite direction. We'll cut him off at junction twenty, over.

"Five Alpha. Message understood, we'll drive them towards you, out."

Glenn quickly calculated where they were in relation to the ongoing pursuit and determined that they weren't far away. Most of the Kompaniya forces rarely took part in weapons exchange with people who wanted to kill them. They used training ammunition on mission drills and fired into the odd crowd of unarmed protestors. As a result, they weren't prepared to handle this pursuit, but his men were.

"Take us to junction twenty," he said to Czarzeb.

Picking up his radio, he quickly briefed the rest of this squad. "Listen up. We're off to assist the troops in pursuit of an enemy of unknown origin. The person they are chasing may or may not be linked to the bombs that have just gone off. We're going in hot so if we arrive in the middle of a gunfight, be careful." Glenn's men would know that the inexperienced troops on their side could be just as much of a threat as the enemy, but it didn't hurt to remind them.

As they rounded the bend, Glenn observed two Kompaniya vehicles ahead. One had crashed into a barrier and was on fire, and the other had broken windows. Several uniformed men could be seen using the vehicles for cover as they seemed to be exchanging gunfire with someone in the distance.

Grabbing his handheld radio, he shouted, loud enough for Czarzeb to follow the instructions too, "There's a gun battle ahead. Take up our standard barricade position, we are going left."

Glenn's modified vehicles had bulletproof sides and windows, and the hatches in the tops opened up into armoured turrets with firing holes in the steel protection welded above.

In the time it had taken for the trucks to be parked nose to nose, at least one more Kompaniya trooper had fallen.

He grabbed the main radio. "Hello all Five Alpha and Five Bravo personnel. This is Glenn and I am now in charge of this assault. I want everybody to get behind cover and stop firing."

Looking through his binoculars, he could see two trucks parked in the distance, which he assumed was Five Bravo and, in the middle of these two barricades, a single vehicle was stationary.

The single-vehicle had numerous bullet holes in the sides and, even from here, he could make out that the driver's window was open. With the blacked-out back of the truck facing primarily towards Glenn and the front towards the far barrier, it provided only a limited view of the man inside.

"Alistair and Morgan, get in your sniper's nests." They'd already been preparing, and within a minute of the order the roof hatches were opened and the snipers perched behind their steel turrets. On one occasion they caught a glimpse of a hand that looked to be dark-skinned, but it only appeared for a split second to fire off a round and then disappeared.

Like most Kompaniya trucks, Glenn's vehicle had a loudspeaker system, he grabbed the handset and addressed the man ahead. "Hello there in the truck. My name's Glenn and I'm in charge here now. I've told my men to stop firing, and I'd appreciate it if you did the same."

Pressing the switch on his hand radio, he addressed Morgan and Alistair. "I want him alive if possible. He might be injured already but try not to shoot him in the head." He would avoid giving too much away over the main vehicle radio as he'd decided not to use the other Kompaniya men.

For the moment, the shooting had stopped, so he tried to engage the driver some more. "I don't know who you are, but there have been some explosions in the capital, and if you have any information that could help,

I'd really appreciate it. If you throw your weapons out of the windows and step out with your hands up, you will not be harmed."

It wasn't definite that this man was involved in any attack, but this was too much of a coincidence for Glenn to believe that he was innocent and at the moment any information could help.

Before anyone could say another word, a hand appeared partly through the driver's window and fired two rounds in Glenn's direction. He assumed that the shots weren't meant to be aimed at any particular target but instead were a message that whoever was firing wasn't coming out without a fight.

34

ESCAPING WITH A BODY

03 May 2206

As Angus looked at the carnage in the car park, he realised he didn't have any time to waste.

"Will, get Brand's body in the trunk of the first black car. We need to keep up the pretence that he's still alive. We are taking the two convoy vehicles so everyone else needs to pile up the rest of the bodies over in the corner behind the other cars. We haven't got time to do a proper clean-up as the battle noises will bring out some scrutiny pretty quickly."

"Why am I the one loading the body in the trunk?" Will protested.

"He's your mess, so you can clean him up," Angus growled.

The external shutter doors were closed, but once they opened them, they would no doubt encounter more of the Kompaniya forces.

"Manning, Nikki, Coosh and Fred, get in the rear vehicle with Will. Nikki, you're driving. Cenk, you are the driver of the front vehicle, joining Jones, Iris and me. Our aim is to head for the docks. Leaving the capital, we shall stay in convoy as long as possible and be as conspicuous as possible. Keep your headlights on and if anyone tries to stop us, press your horn and power through. Brand wouldn't stop for a checkpoint, and we shall play on the fear his convoy instils. Don't open the windows in the back vehicle. We intended to have him in the back vehicle to produce in an emergency but at least hiding his body in the boot should disguise the fact that he's already dead."

Once they were loaded into the vehicles, Angus checked the communications between their shortwave radios. "Hello, are you receiving me?"

"Yes, loud and clear," Will replied.

"We all know the route we took here and the rendezvous point. Stay close and be vigilant as I'm opening the door." Angus pressed the door opener labelled on the dashboard of the car and then watched as the door rose.

As soon as daylight began to flood through the doorway, Kompaniya security forces moved forward with their guns at the ready.

"Floor it," Angus said to Cenk, who accelerated while keeping pressure on the vehicle horn. Recognising Brand's convoy, the troops immediately jumped out of the way, and at least one of them raised his hand in a salute. Assuming that their leader was in one of these vehicles, they were not about to endanger their lives by slowing down his convoy.

As the two cars sped across the square, they veered left, retracing their entry route and avoiding the site of the diversion. Angus didn't know how long their subterfuge would last. With the battle scene they had left behind in the garage, it wouldn't be long before the bodies of Brand's team were discovered.

To reduce radio chatter, Angus had held off communicating with the backup team until the vehicles had broken out but now that they were in full flight he tried to make contact. "Hello backup team and Pepper, this is the assault team. Sitrep, over."

The backup team and Pepper had stayed with the vehicles to provide escape options; thankfully, they now had Brand's convoy as well.

"Assault team, this is backup team. We have been under intense fire and have lost the vehicle, emergency protocols being initiated."

Angus knew that this meant that they were trying to make it to the port by whatever means possible and he didn't rate their chances on foot. He quickly spoke to Cenk, "Keep your eyes peeled for the others. If any of them survive, we may encounter them soon. Slow down slightly so we can watch for them. If I say 'stop', hit the brakes." Turning around to Dailey and Iris, he continued, "Be ready to throw the back doors open."

He still had no reply from Pepper, so tried again. "Hello Pepper, this is the assault team. Sitrep, over."

"Foster's up ahead. I can hear him in my head, but he's muffled," Iris shouted.

When they turned the corner, they found Dailey leaning against a wall with one hand on a pistol and another trying to support Foster. Foster had something wrapped around his leg, and even though daylight was fading, the streetlights showed that the cloth was stained dark red.

"Stop," Angus said. Immediately Cenk pulled up

beside Dailey and Iris threw open the back door. Between the two of them, Dailey and Iris bundled Foster quickly into the rear of the car and closed the door. Then they were again on their way.

"Where are the others?" Angus asked.

"I have no idea, it was chaos," Dailey answered. "The diversion only drew the security forces away temporarily and when they headed back, it didn't take them long to identify that we weren't on their side. We tried to delay them and take them away from the government buildings. During the firefight, Foster got wounded, Smith got killed, and we got separated from Brown. Without the vehicle, we have the only working radio."

Angus keyed the radio again. "Hello Pepper, this is the assault team. Sitrep, over." He waited a couple of minutes and then tried again. After several further attempts, it was clear Pepper was in no position to reply.

As they neared the outskirts of the capital, Angus radioed the rear vehicle. "Put your foot on the accelerator but keep a safe distance between our vehicles in case we encounter heavy artillery. Take no chances. Even if someone looks innocent, be on your guard, shoot first. I'd rather you survived with a guilty conscience than be dead. If either of our vehicles is disabled, head for the ports and remember where we stashed the other vehicles. Good luck."

As fights went, Angus perceived this one as a partial success. They had assassinated Brand and, up till now, some of them had survived. On the downside, they had no idea where Pepper or Brown were or if they'd survived.

The mission wasn't over yet; they were behind

enemy lines and had only one escape route. As a long-time fighter, he had never feared death as hope had always kept him alive. Now he drew on that hope to push on.

Once they reached the end of the city limits, Angus was concerned about how conspicuous the convoy would be. After weighing up his options, he decided it wasn't worth the risk of staying together until they reached the docks.

He assumed that the security around the capital would be more intense than at the docks, but the last thing he wanted was to lead any pursuers to their escape boat. Thinking fast, he picked up the radio. "We're pulling over, park up behind us."

He looked at Cenk, who was already steering their vehicle to the kerb. There was no need for a reply from the other car as it pulled in behind.

Angus jumped out of the passenger seat and ran back to the other car. He didn't want to give this information over the radio in case someone else was listening in.

As soon as Will wound down the window, Angus began briefing them.

"At the next junction, we are going to split up. We'll head to where I left our vehicle, and you can head to where team one left theirs. If you can make it there, then switch vehicles and head for the port. If the vehicle is not there, get as close to the port as you feel safe but ditch this car as soon as you can."

"How long do you intend to wait for us – or, if we get there first, how long do you expect us to wait for you?" Will asked.

Angus expected this kind of question from Will.

"Whoever arrives first is to wait a maximum of four hours for the others. If Hook decides it's too dangerous to wait, he can override that. It's better for someone to escape than no one."

"Understood. Hopefully, we'll all get out of here. Good luck," Will said.

"Good luck to you too," Angus replied and headed back to his vehicle.

Back in his seat, he turned to the others. "At the next junction, we are splitting up from the others. We'll aim to recover the vehicle I came in. Whoever gets back to the boat is going to wait a maximum of four hours for the others, so we aren't waiting around. Let's go, Cenk."

There was no need for a big speech as they were in flight mode. Cenk accelerated away and Nikki followed.

Angus knew that once the cars split, the perceived strength of their convoy was lost. Anyone seeing one of the vehicles on its own might consider it suspicious, and they were in enough danger as it was.

Soon they reached the crossroads, as Cenk acknowledged by hitting the car horn. Looking in his rear view mirror, he saw Nikki flashing his lights. Then suddenly both cars were alone.

35

—————

CAPTURE

03 May 2026

Expecting the enemy to return fire, Pepper was surprised when what he heard next were words rather than bullets.

Glenn had grabbed the loudspeaker again. "Hello, all troops who can hear me – do not shoot. I repeat, do not shoot, stand down." The last thing he wanted was poorly trained troops firing in his direction.

It seemed to Pepper that whoever was now in charge was determined to take him alive, and that wasn't part of his plan.

Glenn switched to his team's internal frequency. "Alistair, Morgan, have you got a shot?"

"I can take out his hand next time it appears," said Alistair.

"Okay, you have a green light. Let's see if we can disarm him. If he can't fire back, we may be able to take him alive. Alistair is the only one with permission to shoot. As soon as he shows his hand again, take the shot."

Picking up the mike, he continued the dialogue with the enemy. "Hello again. That wasn't very friendly, was it?"

Pepper was wondering if this guy would ever shut up, as he positioned his pistol outside of the window. Before he had a chance to pull the trigger, he felt a searing pain in his wrist, and he dropped the pistol through the window.

Observing through his binoculars, Glenn had seen the barrel of the gun poking out of the window and then heard the crack of Alistair's rifle.

He watched as the pistol clattered to the ground and the hand disappeared from sight. At this distance, it was hard to see whether they'd hit the gun or the man, but at least this was one less weapon for the man to fire at them.

"Alistair, what did you hit?"

"I had a perfect shot of his wrist when I fired. From this distance I can't be one hundred percent sure but it looks like that's what I hit. I doubt he'll be firing with that hand anytime soon."

Pepper was in a lot of pain, but his priority was to stem the flow of blood. Being right-handed made it challenging to apply the dressing, but the thought of bleeding to death provided him with the impetus to figure it out. Once he stopped the bleeding, he used the morphine in the emergency medical bag. He knew that this would slow him down, but now that he couldn't shoot back, he was running out of options.

Glenn pushed his men to proceed. "Kevin, you and Pavlo go down the left-hand side of the vehicle. Vlad, you and Tang take the driver's side. Everyone keeps in formation; we don't know how badly injured he is so if you get a chance, take him alive but the priority is that you stay alive. Morgan and Alistair, cover the squad from above and do whatever you can to avoid shooting him in the head. I want him alive."

His men were kitted out in their usual tactical gear of black body armour, helmets and chest rigs, while they leapfrogged forward in pairs. Always one man on one knee covering a door while his partner ran ahead to the next position.

Glenn knew this could give the enemy warning, but he used the loudspeaker anyway to communicate with the Kompaniya troops. "Those are my men advancing, no one else is to fire. They're just going to have a chat. I repeat, don't shoot my men! Stand down all other teams."

That voice was starting to annoy Pepper, but it did tell him that they were close. It was now or never. He wedged a smoke grenade in the crook of his right arm and pulled the safety pin out with his left hand while holding the lever closed. Using his left foot, he managed to lift the lever on the passenger door and kick it open while rolling the smoke grenade out of the door with his left hand.

Through the binoculars, Glenn saw the first smoke grenade roll out of the passenger doorway.

"Stay sharp; it looks like he's making a run for it. Alistair and Morgan, keep an eye out for anyone exiting the vehicle and remember, I want him alive."

The second smoke grenade was a little easier now that Pepper had figured out what he was doing. This time he just threw it through the shattered driver's side window.

Again Glenn grabbed the microphone. "Don't let the smoke worry anyone. My men are still in charge, and you are still not to shoot. Stand down all other troops; I repeat stand down."

He had to maintain control, concerned that one of the other troopers would panic and shoot his men by mistake. Glenn was willing to risk the deaths of a few Kompaniya men if the enemy soldier got out of the vehicle and started to shoot. His men were more valuable to him as a well-trained trooper was a limited resource.

He knew that his decision to take charge would please the other teams. After all, his men were taking all the risks, and he was taking all the responsibility. If anything went wrong, the blame would fall on him, but he was prepared to accept that. Nikolei held him in high regard so he could get away with most things.

All the other troops knew his high standing. The walls at the military academy were decorated with photos not only of all the council members, but also of Nikolei and Glenn together.

Knowing who was in charge or could cause your premature death was a survival instinct that most Kompaniya troops learnt.

Alistair's voice came over the radio. "I haven't got a target yet."

"Nothing on my side," Morgan added.

"Keep me informed," Glenn said.

The smoke was starting to swirl around the truck. As Pepper was getting ready to leave, he stuffed the last of the fragmentation grenades into his left pocket. He'd already been struggling from an earlier wound in his shoulder, and now the bullet through his wrist was making things worse. He had lost some blood and that, together with the morphine, was clouding his head.

He was running short on energy and his planned exit from the vehicle turned from a tactical roll to a tumble to the ground. The smoke was starting to thin in places but, as he couldn't see the troops approaching, he hoped that they couldn't see him. He began crawling towards the hedge, cradling the grenade in his left hand.

As the smoke began to wash over the four assaulting troops, Morgan came over the team radio. "I can see under the smoke. He's crawling for the woods. I can just make out a figure crawling under the smoke."

Glenn quickly grabbed his radio, "Kevin, Pavlo, Vlad and Tang, confirm that Morgan isn't about to shoot any of you?"

"This is Kevin. It's not me crawling."

"This is Pavlo. Not me either."

"Tang. Not me."

"Vlad. Not me."

"Take the shot," Glenn said.

A second later there was the unmistakable crack and thump of a high-velocity bullet being fired.

Pepper had heard the troops approaching, but before he could do anything else, he heard a noise in the distance and felt the impact of the bullet in his thigh. The morphine helped, but it didn't prevent the excruciating pain. Instinctively he let out a guttural cry and immediately realised that the men approaching him would have heard it.

Glenn's men were close enough to hear the groan that followed too, and this spurred them on.

The smoke grenades that Pepper had thrown out of the vehicle to provide cover were also disguising their approach. All four men were now walking slowly towards the truck. Their limited vision heightened their use of their other senses, and they were all listening intently for anything out of the ordinary.

Finally reaching the first hedges of the woods, Pepper managed to pull the previously loosened grenade pin out with his teeth. With all of his remaining strength, he tossed the grenade behind him as he crawled over into the woods and fell into a drainage ditch.

With that last act of defiance, Pepper collapsed into unconsciousness.

Kevin and Pavlo were close enough that they could almost touch the rear of the vehicle when suddenly there was the thud of something hitting the ground in front of them.

"Grenade!" Kevin shouted loud enough for all of them to hear. "Passenger side of the vehicle, take cover."

Kevin and Pavlo were close enough to the vehicle that they hurled themselves onto the platforms mounted at the rear. The platforms were typically used to allow extra troops to travel in emergencies, and this was definitely an emergency.

At the same time, Vlad and Tang dived for the driver's side of the vehicle, trying to shrink behind the truck wheels for protection.

Instantly there was a huge bang, and a flash as the shrapnel and the shock wave emanated from the grenade. The heavy truck took most of the blast, but not everyone came through it unscathed.

All four of them were suffering from ringing in their

ears and Vlad had been hit by several pieces of shrapnel, in both the back and leg. Tang was doing his best to administer first aid, but he was also dealing with a couple of minor shrapnel wounds of his own.

"Medic, medic," he was shouting at what he thought was the top of his voice, although the ringing in his ears made it hard for him to hear his own voice.

Kevin and Pavlo had been luckier as the platforms had kept them off the ground, so they had avoided all of the shrapnel.

"What's happening?" Glenn was shouting over the squad radio. He had heard Kevin's warning about the grenade, but the smoke was still obscuring his view.

"Alistair, Morgan, what can you see?"

"Tang looks to be administering first aid to Vlad," said Morgan.

"I can see Kevin and Pavlo walking around," said Alistair.

Just then, the wind changed, and the smoke started to blow away from the vehicle, unveiling the scene ahead.

"Did you get him, is he still alive?" Glenn was shouting over the squad radio, but no one was replying. He himself had been close to a grenade that had gone off during a previous mission and remembered vividly that it had taken ages for the ringing in his ears to subside.

Not wanting to lose the sniper support, he knew he had to go forward himself. "Czarzeb, grab your kit and first aid gear. We are going forward."

Before he left the loudspeaker on the truck, he made one last broadcast to the surrounding troops. "Listen up all troops. This is Glenn. I am approaching the truck. Do not shoot, I say again, do not shoot."

The explosion and the smoke had created enough chaos. Before he went forward, he wanted to avoid being shot by his own side if possible.

As Glenn and Czarzeb went forward, he gave one last order to Alistair. "Alistair, you're in charge here. Keep an eye through your scope. If you need to shoot one of the Kompaniya troops to protect us, do so."

The smoke had cleared enough for Glenn and Czarzeb to run towards the vehicle. When they reached it, they observed the damage. All of the tyres were shredded, and the side was covered with pieces of shrapnel embedded in the truck's protective skin.

Glenn shouted to Tang, "How's Vlad?"

Tang couldn't hear the words, but it was clear what the question was so he just raised his thumb in the air.

Knowing that his two wounded men would survive, Glenn turned his attention to the others. Kevin and Pavlo were facing the hedge and aiming their weapons in that general direction.

Glenn approached Kevin and tapped him on the shoulder to get his attention. "Where did he go?"

Still struggling to hear Glenn, Kevin pointed towards the foliage at the side of the road. Glenn motioned to his men by lifting his arms out in a straight line. They understood and fanned out, heading into the bushes.

It wasn't long before Glenn saw the body in the ditch. It was fortunate that the prisoner hadn't escaped, but he looked in bad shape. "Czarzeb, see what you can do to keep him alive. Kevin, go back to the trucks and get Alistair and Morgan to bring them forward."

Kevin nodded and ran off towards the trucks.

It didn't take long for the trucks to arrive. After checking that both Vlad and the prisoner were stable, Glenn had them loaded into the truck. Then he drove towards Five Bravo's position and instructed their commander to work with Five Alpha and give first aid to anyone who needed it. They were also to call for assistance to recover the vehicles and any fallen comrades.

His priority now was to get medical attention for the two injured men with him.

He could have gone to the hospital and claimed priority status, but the interrogation compound was well furnished with medical staff and equipment.

That was their ultimate destination, so that was where they headed.

36

WHO'S IN CHARGE

04 May 2206

Vadim Boyko had been a long-time survivor on the Kompaniya council. Surviving this long was primarily achieved by blending into the background so that he was not seen as a threat to anyone with ambitions of power, nor as an easy target whose resources others could consume. Striking this balance required a strategic mind.

When Risslo started parading Brand around, Vadim was wary of the former Sanctuary One leader's potential threat but kept his suspicions to himself. After Brand had disposed of Orlov, a few of the old guard had tried to challenge him, but they had been no match. Vadim had decided then and there to play the long game.

Vadim had gambled that a paranoid narcissist such as Brand would accrue many enemies and so he had continued to bide his time and let someone else weaken Brand.

Now the time had arrived. With the attack on the capital, Brand's disappearance and rumours of his death, someone had to take the helm. It was still a gamble as Brand could have set this as a trap to see who the most significant threat was, but countering that was the discovery of the bodies of Nikolei, Petra and Brand's other guards in his own garage.

Vadim doubted even Brand would sacrifice his bodyguards just to flush out potential rivals. He wasn't getting any younger, and he knew that if he didn't act now, one of the other council members would make a play for the throne. It would be easier to garner support once he'd taken power, so he decided it was now or never.

Vadim's head of security Sergey had been gathering information as the attacks unfolded and it was his sources that had notified them of the bodies of the security detail.

"Get the men, the cars and all the weapons. We are going to the government buildings."

Vadim didn't have to be more specific. Sergey had been part of the audit for the last day, checking on their resources, their network of spies and who the potential threats were. Sergey knew this meant identifying all the men they could spare and all the weapons they had at hand. They would only get one chance at this, so there was no point in trying to keep reserves available.

As his convoy drove through the city, Vadim saw Kompaniya armoured vehicles everywhere and checkpoints on every main road.

Vadim's official car was the second vehicle in his convoy and made for rapid movement along their route.

They were stopped at only one barrier where, after a cursory glance, they were allowed to proceed.

As the convoy reached the main square, Vadim observed a long line of vehicles parked ominously in front of the government buildings. Needing no instructions, Sergey parked the front vehicle and dismounted as the rest of the convoy parked up in a line alongside.

Sergey got out of the vehicle with four of his men at the cordon. He recognised Morgan as one of the Terror squad and, as he seemed to be in charge, headed directly for him.

"What's all this about?" Morgan asked. He held his rifle tightly and had over a dozen armed men ready to back him up if the situation got violent.

"Councillor Boyko needs access to the government buildings," Sergey said, pausing for the expected response.

"We are on lockdown!"

"And does this lockdown contain orders to stop a council member from entering the government buildings? If so, who gave those orders?"

Before Morgan could answer, Vadim had appeared behind Sergey with another four of his men.

"Get out of the way!" he ordered.

Morgan had not expected to deal with this kind of situation. Even though he was scared of what Glenn's response might be, he didn't think it was wise to start a gun battle with a member of the council and his men. He gestured to the others at the cordon to move, and they parted to create a corridor for Vadim and his men.

A skeleton crew of Sergey's team stayed with the

vehicles, while the rest followed him through the main doors into the lobby.

Vadim, Sergey and as many of the men that they could fit into the elevator filed in. The remainder of the men split into two detachments: the first headed up the stairs to meet their comrades in the elevator when it stopped and the second stayed in the lobby to guard the steps.

When the elevator doors opened, they met Glenn and two other armed men.

"What's going on?" Glenn asked nervously.

"Where is Leader Brand?" Vadim countered.

"We don't know," he replied hesitantly.

"You don't know where the leader is? Then who is in charge? Who's giving you your orders?"

"Nobody at the moment," Glenn answered solemnly.

"As the first council member here, I'm taking charge. Notify your men," Vadim said.

Walking into Brand's office, Vadim realised he had almost forgotten how sparse it was. Like most people, he had avoided entering this office at all costs. Now, though, it was easier, with Sergey and four other men flanking him and Sergey had stationed sentries at the front door.

Glenn had been on the radio to his men when Vadim had made his way into the building and he approached the office now. Sergey motioned to the sentries to let him enter as he knew Vadim wanted to question him.

"What do we know so far?" Vadim asked.

"Some explosions occurred but they seem to have been intended as a distraction only and they didn't damage any key assets. There was an attack on Leader Brand's protection unit, which may have been the main target. Leader Brand is missing and we don't know who the attackers were. We have managed to kill some of the enemy forces and we have also captured one of their leaders. Mr Sebastian is currently interrogating him."

"You've captured one of them?" Vadim was surprised that his sources hadn't leaked this information already.

"Yes, he is a tall black specimen, which indicates that he's an outsider."

Vadim was intrigued by this piece of information. He had thought that finally someone had gathered the spine to challenge Brand. Yet if the threat was from outside the sanctuary, the situation could be more serious than his first impressions had led him to believe. "Continue to maintain the lockdown around the government buildings and my men will supplement your guards. Send a team to each of the other eleven council members' homes and have them escorted here."

"Under whose authority?" Glenn asked cautiously.

"Under my authority, in the absence of the leader. If we are under attack, someone has to take charge. We cannot waste time on bureaucracy so, as the only council member here, I will take charge until the rest of the council arrives and we formulate a plan." Vadim wasn't giving Glenn any time to question him.

"Also get a message to Mr Sebastian: if he hasn't already killed the prisoner, he is to stop the interrogation immediately. He is to administer medical attention if necessary, as I want the prisoner alive and well. He may be the only answer we have to who is attacking us."

Glenn offered no more questions but left the office immediately, talking constantly into his radio as he went.

"What do you think, Sergey?" Vadim asked.

"If the Kompaniya troops continue to support you, and with the addition of our men, we will probably outnumber the combined forces of any bodyguards that the council brings with them. This gives you leverage."

"My thoughts exactly."

Vadim employed Sergey not just as his head of security but also as a sounding board for his strategies. To survive this long, he'd relied heavily on Sergey.

The other paranoid council members would never trust a subordinate for fear of betrayal, but Vadim's collaborative approach was his strength. He knew that trusting no one was the route to madness, and if the risk of trusting Sergey cost him his life, so be it. With someone like Brand in charge, on any given day you were never sure if you would live to see the next sunrise anyway.

Vadim took great pleasure in sitting in Brand's high-sided chair. He found it darkly amusing that, even in Brand's absence, when he stepped over the line in the floor, he'd expected to hear shots or an explosion – as if the line was actually booby-trapped rather than just a mentally implanted barrier.

It was crazy that the line was so synonymous with brutality that, even in the empty room, breaching it gave one pause for thought.

"Make sure that when the other council members arrive they're escorted to the council chambers, but I want advance warning before the first one arrives. I will be waiting for them to avoid giving anyone the time to decide to take on my new position."

"I'll brief the men downstairs," Sergey replied.

"One last thing: once I leave this office, nobody else is to enter on pain of death. I want our men, not the Kompaniya men, guarding this door. If another council member enters this room before I have solidified my power, they might get the idea that they should be in charge. If the men have to kill a council member, we will come up with a story later, but unless Brand returns, I plan to stay in control."

With that, Sergey nodded and left Vadim alone with his thoughts.

37

PEPPER'S TORTURE

03 May 2206

As the bumping of the truck jolted him back to consciousness, Pepper found himself aching all over. His head was throbbing, and he was tied tightly around his ankles and wrists. Lying on the floor between the feet of several troopers, he could feel dried blood caked on the side of his face.

This hadn't been the first time in his life that he'd been thirsty, but his knowledge that shock was classed as the loss of circulating body fluids didn't help him deal with it. The trauma of the explosion had produced unforeseen symptoms. He felt weak and his throat was parched as though he'd been drinking gasoline. What wouldn't he give for a glass of fresh, cold water? Pepper knew now why they'd been called the Water Wars instead of the Coal Wars.

When the troopers came to unload his body, they seemed unimpressed to find him alive. As they lifted him by the plastic ties that bound him, the ties cut into his skin. Dragging him to his feet, two large troopers jostled him into a building and down several corridors.

In a short time, he was bundled into a small, sparse room. He saw a mirror on the wall, a single chair and a table with a tray full of spikes and other sinister-looking items spread over it.

The man who seemed to be in charge of the interrogation was already in the room. He motioned to the others to secure Pepper but did not speak at all. The man was dressed smartly in a white shirt and red tie, which to Pepper didn't seem like the clothes of a torturer.

Yet the man was playing with a selection of sharp objects from a steel tray on a table. Picking up spikes and other items that looked capable of breaking skin and bone, it seemed that the man was doing his best to instil fear without any conversation.

After supervising Pepper's confinement and ensuring he was securely restrained to the chair, his interrogator left him on his own for what seemed like aeons but was probably only around thirty minutes. The man had seemingly done this before and knew that leaving someone with their thoughts was part of the process of breaking them down. The anticipation of pain could be as effective as inflicting it.

Over the years, Pepper had seen interrogations from both sides of the practice and tried to use his experiences to his advantage. He knew that the beatings would begin at some stage. Then the sleep deprivation and the other methods would eventually take their toll on his mind.

The person being interrogated would eventually realise that their only chance of survival would be in giving some answers. On the plus side, anything he gave away at that stage would be unreliable.

One of his previous experiences of interrogation had been during his service for the Company. Suspicious of a spy in their midst, his commander Strong had singled Pepper out for the treatment. The mainstay of their interrogation involved a few days of beatings, which eventually stopped not because Pepper had given them any useful information but because one of Strong's subordinates had spoken up for him, thinking that Strong's dislike of Pepper was the real reason behind the beatings. In the absence of any evidence of a spy, it was easy for Strong to stop the interrogation – and the personal nature of it seemed to be borne out when no one else had been questioned.

Pepper expected that this time he was dealing with more dedicated professionals.

When the chief interrogator returned, he came with an entourage of two taller men, both bald and with multiple scars on their faces. They were dressed in black fatigues with rubber aprons over the top. Pepper began to brace himself for the blows that he expected to follow but was surprised when the interrogator started to speak.

"Hello. My name's Mr Sebastian. I have been tasked with gathering some information from you and I would appreciate it if you would cooperate. If you haven't gathered by now, you are a prisoner who is now at my mercy. You have been involved in the death of some of our security forces and some of their colleagues would like to see you have the same fate."

Sebastian paused to let this information sink in before continuing. "I am not an unreasonable man. I can't guarantee what ultimate fate the leaders will determine for you, but I can assure you that if you don't answer my questions, you will feel lots of pain in the interim. Let's start with something simple. You know my name, but I am at a disadvantage. What shall I call you?"

"Aren't you going to buy me dinner before you try to violate me?" Pepper said. He knew that pretty soon he might not be in the position to crack jokes, so he took advantage of the situation.

"Ha, ha, ha, excellent, we have a comedian. I'm so glad that you aren't going to make this easy." Sebastian nodded to the attendees. One punched Pepper in the face while the other beat him around the thighs with a baton.

For the next six or seven hours, Pepper had endured what Sebastian called "softening up techniques".

Intermittent beatings, questions and then more beatings.

On more than one occasion he heard the same speech from Sebastian. "You're not telling me the truth. I can tell you're lying."

The periods of unconsciousness seemed longer and longer. During one of his lucid moments, he noted that utensils were not in use today. It appeared that Sebastian was in this for the long haul.

He'd hoped to hold out for twenty-four hours, by which time he deemed the mission would have succeeded, or the information he divulged would be too late to do his people any harm. With no clocks or windows and infrequent periods of consciousness it was difficult for Pepper to track the time accurately.

Even when he capitulated, he told Sebastian only enough to satisfy his curiosity.

Pepper confessed that they'd been sent to disrupt Sanctuary Two as revenge for the attack on his homeland. He had divulged that they had been deployed in groups of four and that there were four separate teams – an exaggeration he made in the hope that, if their mission failed, the enemy would waste time hunting for people who didn't exist.

The numbers were close enough to the truth to make it plausible, but he hoped a search for extra teams would make the Kompaniya spread its net wider.

He further divulged that they had swum in from a boat offshore, after which they had no communication between the teams. Initially, Sebastian hadn't accepted his full story as the squad had caught him with a radio. After more beatings, he had spun a yarn that the radios were only for communication within a team and that they would stop using them if a team member was lost.

His sanctuary's protocols before deployment had involved more sophisticated uses of encrypted frequencies, but after Sebastian's men had beaten him with increasing brutality, he had sold his story.

They were again alternating between beating him into unconsciousness and reviving him.

Sebastian was insulting him as he had earlier. "It's amazing that someone so big everywhere else has such a small worm between his legs. Perhaps it only looks small because the constant kicking has swollen your testicles so much," Sebastian said with a wry grin. Pepper was happy for the insults as they created a pause in the beatings and other forms of physical abuse. "I'm impressed with how much you have endured so far, but I think it's time we stopped playing around and got serious with this interrogation."

Suddenly there was a knock on other side of the window into the next room. "Go away, you fool, can't you see I'm busy?" Sebastian paused when he saw a telephone being held up through the glass. "You must excuse the interruption in our little chat. Apparently, I have an important call but don't worry; I won't be away long enough for you to miss me."

It was only a few minutes before Sebastian returned. "This is rather embarrassing, but we've misplaced the leader. I don't suppose you know where he is?" he asked in a far-too-friendly tone.

Pepper's eyes were so swollen he couldn't see out of them. He could only just make out the direction of the questioner, and through dry swollen lips he managed to gasp, "It wasn't me, I've been here."

The thought that somehow the mission had succeeded wasn't lost on him, but he was in no condition to show pleasure. He needed to play for time to help his team escape. Deciding to feign unconsciousness, he let himself go limp. In fairness, it wasn't such an act as within seconds he slipped into unconsciousness for real.

His response seemed to frustrate Sebastian more. "I know you've been here all this time, but this was something to do with your mission. I will ask you again, what do you know about the disappearance of the leader?"

Not caring if this was a tactic or genuine exhaustion, Sebastian motioned to one of his assistants, who threw a bucket of ice-cold water over Pepper. In his current state, the water had minimal effect, but Sebastian noticed a small movement, and that was enough.

"You inbreeds attacked our capital, and you have

kidnapped our glorious leader. Where have you taken him? What is your plan?" Sebastian shouted.

Pepper had made the decision. His team seemed to have achieved the impossible and against all the odds had managed to get to Brand. This news could be just a trick from his interrogators, but he had to believe in his team. He would hold out for as long as possible and hope that it gave enough time or they'd overdo the torture so he could give his life for the cause. Pepper gave an inaudible croak to get their attention.

Sebastian came closer. "Where have you taken him? What have you done with him?"

Gathering all of his strength, when he could feel Sebastian's breath on his face, he groaned, "Go to hell."

This had the desired effect. Momentarily losing control, Sebastian punched him in the mouth and blood splattered over his nice white shirt.

Pepper took a little pleasure in the hope that Sebastian had bruised his soft, tender hands. Even though his bruises prevented Pepper from looking at him now, he remembered the first time they'd met he had quickly sized up the interrogator as a coward. Someone who gave orders rather than carry out the physical torture himself. He almost smiled at the thought that the man asking the questions would have given up any information with very little pressure applied.

Gathering himself, Sebastian addressed two large attendants. "Get him out of that chair and don't stop kicking him until he isn't in a fit state to sit back down."

The two thugs didn't need to be asked twice; he was punched in the face over a dozen times before his restraints were released and he was thrown to the floor.

Next came the real assaults. For the next hour they

took it in turns to kick him with heavy steel-toed boots. They knew their trade and avoided too many kicks to the head, but the rest of him seemed fair game. At times the pain from his body became too much, and he passed into the bliss of unconsciousness. He lost count of the number of times he had blacked out and then been aroused by a blow so painful that it overcame the previous numbness.

The last assault he remembered was a barrage of kicks to his genitals and, eventually, the excruciating pain had been just too much to bear.

He had no way of knowing how long they had left him to sleep, but he was suddenly revived by the shock of a large bucket of fluid being poured over his head.

He didn't know what the liquid was and he could barely open his eyes to discern its source. He could taste his blood running down the back of his throat, but this was not the first time that Pepper had awoken bleeding and bruised.

This time Pepper was dragged from the floor and secured to a steel chair. His back was on fire and his spine alternated between shooting pains and numb paralysis. All he could think was that the beatings never got any easier in his life.

He wished he was more mobile although he doubted if mobility would provide any benefit at the moment. The plastic straps on his wrists and ankles barely held him to the chair, but he appreciated the pain as they cut into his skin because it confirmed that he still maintained some feeling.

He was unsure how much damage the beatings had inflicted but, whenever the numbness abated, he felt pain like fire burning inside. It was a fair assumption that he had sustained internal bleeding. He'd tried to protect his main organs by crouching in a ball, but eventually his strength had given out and they had continued to assault his kidneys and his genitals.

Pepper had seen the results of sustained assaults on a man's lower regions. The traumas, infections and complications had ultimately been the cause of the death of such a victim. When they had gone to work on Pepper's spine, he had been concerned he may never walk again.

Always the optimist, even willing to give himself for the cause, he thought that he was still going to survive this ordeal.

He assumed that by this time his teammates would have already either succeeded or failed and wondered why the Kompaniya was still keeping him alive.

It seemed like he had been fighting death for most of his life. Given that in his past he had been pursued by the security forces of one sanctuary, which he was now working for, being captured by the security forces of another seemed ironic. After all of these years of surviving, he felt tired and wondered when he would reach the time to embrace death.

38

THE KOMPANIYA COUNCIL MEETING

04 May 2206

Councillor Zuzu Green was the first one to enter the council chambers and observe Vadim sitting at the head of the table. Sergey was positioned behind his chair with over a dozen security guards stationed around the walls.

"Ah Zuzu, welcome."

"When the troops turned up, I thought it was Brand who had summoned me."

"It appears our leader has disappeared," Vadim countered.

"So you've called me? Under what authority?"

"I've called the whole council here. It seems that we are under attack and have no leader. We are vulnerable and need to come up with a plan to protect ourselves."

Vadim knew that Green had been a friend of Risslo but, when Brand had finally disposed of Risslo, he had dived for cover to protect himself. Like most of the current council members, he was a coward. They were only interested in protecting their positions and, even though they had vast resources, they pushed to gather more, always operating close to the edge of the rules without raising their profiles enough that Brand needed to take action.

It took only thirty minutes for the other ten council members to assemble. Each arrival had initiated similar conversations. "Why has one of my equals summoned me? Where is Brand? Who is in charge?"

Each time Vadim repeated the same story: he was formulating a plan, they were all in danger and somebody had to take charge temporarily to provide them cover.

He had arranged for some refreshments, and each of them was now seated and holding some form of alcoholic drink.

Hoping that the drinks would help smooth the situation, Vadim began. "We know that we're under attack, but we don't know by who. I'm prepared to stay here in the government buildings, while the rest of you take refuge behind your villa walls with your security details."

"Who died and put you in charge?" Gretzky asked

"Although it isn't confirmed yet, it might be that Leader Brand has died. As for me being in charge, if anyone else wants to step up and put themselves in harm's way, I'd like to hear your suggestions. And before anyone decides to volunteer, I'd just like to add something for you to consider. At the moment, all we know is that Brand's missing – not that he's dead but that he's missing. What do you think Brand's reaction would be if he came back and found somebody else thinking that they are in charge?"

He paused to let this point sink home. "I agree with what you're all thinking. Brand may see that person as a threat, and we all know what happens to anyone who threatens him. I'm prepared to take this risk for the good of the sanctuary. Does anyone else want to take that risk instead of me?"

Looking around the room, his confidence grew, as not one of them dared to make eye contact with him.

The council members fell into two categories. The sheep would be happy to hide behind their villa walls while somebody else took charge and faced the risks that came with that. The others saw the leader's absence as an opportunity to seek power for themselves but were not yet prepared to risk making a move in case Brand returned. Until Brand's death was confirmed, they would bide their time.

Surprised as he was, it seemed to Vadim as though his gamble had paid off.

"So what is your plan?" Gretzky demanded. "While the rest of us are cowering behind our walls, waiting for the next attack, what are you going to be doing? Hiding in Brand's office?"

"On the contrary, I'll be coordinating with our troops to search for the enemy and any other threats. I'll authorise patrols to search the whole sanctuary. If we can take any of them alive, we will interrogate them. Otherwise we will kill them without mercy."

Vadim waited for a moment, as though he was allowing time for the others to speak, and then continued, "It's been over twenty-four hours since the explosions and the masses will be starting to get restless.

If they think for one minute that we're not in charge, they may start to think we're vulnerable. I suggest we move the curfew from ten o'clock to seven for a few days. We'll catch a few curfew breakers and, rather than send them to the gel plants, we'll execute them and display their bodies on stakes in the main square."

"What's the purpose of that?" Green asked.

"It will be part of our strategy to scare the masses. We also need to spread the word that the sanctuary is under attack and that we must all stick together against a common enemy. Giving the masses an enemy will deflect their focus away from us and they will fall into line. Is everyone happy with these actions?"

Again he looked around the room as if searching for their approval. There was a little murmuring, but most of them nodded. Their agreement simply removed the need for conflict, however, as Vadim had already made his decisions.

"Just to confirm the plan," Gretzky said. "We are going to send out some patrols and we will kill a few curfew breakers. And that's going to solve all of our problems?"

Vadim knew that Gretzky was just posturing and decided to give him a little leeway as long as he didn't go too far. "No, this will not solve our problems, but it will buy us some time. We need to find out who attacked us. Does anyone have any information on who attacked us or on the location of Brand?"

As he expected, no one had any information to offer. Yet this little bit of theatre encouraged them to believe he wanted their input.

"Assuming that something has happened to Brand and everyone around this table is telling the truth, the risk is not from within and that puts us all in danger. Give me three days. In those three days I'll gather as much information as possible, and I will get word to all of you individually as to what's happening. After today it would seem cautious to avoid being all in one place at the same time. I suggest we do not have a full council meeting until we know where the threat is coming from and can take precautions to mitigate it."

As the number of murmurs around the room grew, he used their fear against them. "This is for your safety. We know that they've attacked the government buildings already and, as only a few roads lead here, a council meeting would be an ideal target for any enemy. You are safer spread out in your villas. I only called you here today so that we could all decide together on our next steps. Once I can guarantee it is safe, I will get word to you all about a full council meeting where we can discuss the way forward."

Vadim knew that some councillors would be unhappy with his actions, but no one was prepared to say anything. "We've stayed here long enough as a combined target, so if no one has any immediate business, I suggest you return home."

The moment he stopped talking, Vadim nodded to Sergey's men, who opened the large wooden doors.

Vadim would have liked to leave first to avoid questions, but he waited behind to stop any other councillors lingering and taking the time to talk among themselves. The last thing he needed was someone to stay behind and try to vote in another leader. His men had their orders and started shepherding the council members out.

As soon as the others had returned to their villas, his

leadership would be more secure. By suggesting that he would decide when it was safe for the next council meeting, he'd provided himself with an excuse to maintain power without the council.

His men had done their job. As soon as Sergey was sure that all the council had left with their security details, he met Vadim in Brand's office.

"Get me the three most senior leaders of the Kompaniya forces and have them meet me here," Vadim said before adding, "Also, get me Glenn. He might be useful and I want you to keep an eye on him."

There were too many Kompaniya troops for anyone to know them all, but specific individuals were well known to the council members. Nikolei was known for his brutality, and all the councillors were wary of him. If any of them was called for an audience with Brand, they tried to keep a cautious eye on Nikolei for signs that he was ready to pounce. The worry was always with them that they had inadvertently carried out some action that had been misconstrued and would seal their fate.

They also knew Glenn and the Terror squad. Their duties didn't just involve terrorising the masses; they also provided escort functions when Brand summoned council members to his office and they'd even executed council members for the leader. As a consequence, their arrival at a councillor's villa was cause for confusion and fear.

Vadim was mindful that they still didn't have much information on who had attacked them. His only hope was that their prisoner was not dead yet. Sebastian was known for keeping people on the cusp of death for a long time, but sometimes he got carried away.

Like all the council members, Vadim was a proud

white man. Naturally, he saw himself as superior to the masses, but had been raised to see people of darker skins as less than human. The possibility that his fate might now rely on one of these sub-humans appalled him.

He needed an update on the status of the prisoner and he needed it now.

39

WAITING ON A BOAT

03 May 2206

As soon as Angus and his team were on board, Hook started up the engines.

He'd delayed starting up the engines earlier, both to save on fuel and to avoid drawing attention to the boat. Now that prep for departure was underway, there was no turning back.

Standing on the deck, Angus asked, "How long do you intend to wait before we cast off?"

"We'll be ready to leave in two hours. I'm willing to wait around for another two hours beyond that, but that's the maximum," Hook replied.

"Can't we wait a little longer?"

"I didn't expect anyone to make it back here. Now that you have, there's no telling if you've been followed. Chances are we won't even make it out of port, but the longer we stay here, the lower our probability of escape. It would be nice if someone made it home to tell them what happened. How likely do you think it is that the others will make it?"

"We barely made it through, just lucky that our vehicle was still where we left it. I've no idea why we didn't encounter more Kompaniya forces, but both our teams had already lost people in the capital. After the explosions and Brand's disappearance, the odds on both teams getting back without any contact with the enemy are almost zero. If the others met any sizeable opposition, it could finish them."

"If we're going to stay in harm's way for a few more hours, I'd like to think we're doing it because some of the team could still get back here."

"I'd like to be able to give you more reassurance, but from what we encountered out there, I'd say the odds are fifty-fifty."

"I've gambled on worse odds so we'll stick around for a little while. Just remember that this isn't a speedboat. When we do leave the dock, we'll be pulling away at a steady pace to avoid drawing attention to ourselves. If anyone reaches the boat with the enemy in pursuit, we might all be lost."

"I'll get the guys ready to lower a boarding plank if any of our team returns. They've replenished their gear and are ready to take out any opposition quietly. Keeping the plank on the boat for now might avoid unwanted attention."

"I'm going to grab a coffee. Do you want one?"

"I'll catch you up on the bridge once I've checked on the team's readiness."

The two of them separated as the tension continued to grow.

Foster was down below having his wounds tended to

while three more of the crew sat against the boat side. They were below the rails out of sight, while Cenk stood next to them leaning on the gunwale as a lookout.

It was not long before Angus joined Hook for coffee on the bridge. Time passed slowly, and they both began intermittently pacing around. Every time they exchanged glances, they tried to feign indifference, but they were both seasoned fighters and waiting for comrades to return from a mission was never easy.

"It's already been two hours," Hook said to Angus.

"Didn't we agree on four?"

"That was the maximum limit. We are now prepped, all the systems have been run up and we are ready to leave."

"We knew that we would get to this point. We just need to give the others a bit longer."

"Okay but just as long as you know, the longer we stay here with our engines running, the more suspicious we look. We've got enough fuel reserves to idle here for a while, but any boat wasting fuel is going to draw some attention."

Angus knew that, like him, Hook wanted to wait for the others. This was a tough balancing act between saving the lives of the people already on this boat and remaining as a lifeline to anyone left to return.

"Once we agree it's time to go, how long will it take us to get underway?"

"Ten to fifteen minutes. We've pulled up the main anchors and have minimum fenders and moorings attached."

"Let's try to give them another hour. If nobody's back by then and our circumstances haven't changed, we should cut our losses."

"Okay, an hour and no more, as long as we haven't been approached by any port officials or come under attack," Hook agreed.

Just then, something exploded in the distance.

"Was that one or two explosions?" Angus asked quickly.

"It sounded like two very close together but either way we're done. Get the plank lowered for ten minutes, while we cast off all the moorings. Once we're down to the last two ropes, we pull it up and leave," Hook replied.

Angus nodded and headed for the steps.

40

THE DASH FOR THE DOCKS

03 May 2206

The escape plan had been straightforward: head for the docks and get on the boat. If they could swap Brand's cars for the ones they'd arrived in, it might increase their chances of success but, if it came to it, it could be every man for himself on foot.

Nikki did a slow drive-by of the place where they'd left their initial vehicle and no one could tell if it was still there.

"I can't see it," Will said nervously.

"Wasn't the whole point of camouflaging it to stop people seeing it from the road?" Fred said innocently.

"Thanks for stating the obvious," Nikki replied. He went only about half a mile further on from the hiding place before pulling over to the side of the road.

"Someone is going to have to go back and check if it's still there. The sooner we find out, the sooner we can head for the port and hopefully escape the Kompaniya.

Give me one of those handheld radios and let's get this over with," Will said.

Without any hesitation, Nikki handed him the radio.

"If the vehicle's there, I'll pull in behind you and we can swap. If a trap is waiting back there and you haven't heard from me in thirty minutes, I'm probably not coming, so don't wait for me," Will said before quickly leaving the vehicle and disappearing into the undergrowth at the side of the road.

Without any need for orders, Coosh and Fred got out and knelt at either end of the car. Their positions would look natural enough to a casual passer-by, who might not be willing to check a government vehicle any closer, but they were conscious of being behind enemy lines and both of them covered interlocking arcs of fire, looking out for potential threats.

As Will navigated his way through the overgrown field, he had his rifle slung over his neck and his right hand on his pistol grip. Staying low, he skirted round to the back of the trees where he and the rest of Pepper's team had left their vehicle.

He moved stealthily, listening for any out-of-the-ordinary noise. It was getting a little darker than when he'd first been here, but the place still felt familiar. Even in the low light, he noticed the outline of the truck before he reached it.

He couldn't believe his luck and mused that back home it would have been stripped for parts by now. He had to remind himself that this sanctuary had had no rebellion and in an authoritarian system, it was easier to keep the masses submissive.

When he reached the front of the vehicle, he took one last look around before bending down and retrieving the keys. Wasting no more time, he unlocked the driver's door and was pleased to hear the engine burst into life. He was starting to believe that they might survive this suicide mission. As he drove onto the road, he was steering with one hand while keying the radio mike with the other. "Hello Nikki, this is Will. I've got the truck, and I'll be passing you shortly. Follow me down the road and the first chance we get, we can transfer you all into here."

"We've got bulletproof windows – are you sure that you want to take point?" Nikki asked.

"Yes I'm sure. I think I've got more ramming power, but I hope it won't come to that."

"Understood, we'll wait for you to pass." After Will drove past, Nikki pulled on to the road behind him, also starting to like their odds of surviving more and more.

On their steady drive towards the port, the roads became more winding. Every time Nikki came round a bend, he expected to find Will's vehicle in flames and a Kompaniya ambush waiting for them.

Everyone in the car had their guns ready, and their nerves were stretched tight.

They still had Brand's flag flying on the front of the car, hoping that this would delay enemy gunfire long enough to give them the element of surprise.

"Trouble ahead," came Will's voice over the radio.

"What kind of trouble?" Nikki asked.

"A two-vehicle roadblock. I'm going to ram it, so speed up and follow me through."

Nikki came round the bend just in time to see Will approaching two Kompaniya trucks parked up at angles, nose to nose. Will was driving at full speed and barged through, forcing a path for Nikki's car to follow.

The sentries at the roadblock were focused on Will driving away and didn't have time to react to Nikki's car before it reached them. As Nikki drove through the gap that Will had created, Fred and Coosh lowered the bulletproof windows in the back slightly and each tossed out a grenade before quickly raising the windows back up.

They hadn't gone far when they heard the two explosions.

Nikki called Will on the radio. "Any damage to the truck?"

"A bit of panel damage but nothing that will affect its performance. What about the car?"

"This thing's built to last. It hasn't got a dent on it, even though the guards managed to get off a few shots."

"What were the explosions about?"

"We left them a couple of grenades as a present. It looks like they have incapacitated either the Kompaniya vehicles or the troops staffing them."

"You can go faster in the car so head for the docks and I'll stay to the rear to block anyone following. Pull over about ten minutes before the port."

Surprised that Will was being such a team player, Nikki simply replied, "Okay."

Will was finding the road had more bends than he remembered so he tried to balance checking his mirror with keeping his eyes on the road ahead.

Ten minutes after they'd encountered the checkpoint, his belief that they'd evaded pursuit was growing and for a moment he lost his concentration. Before he had a chance to check his mirrors again, he heard the crack of rifle bullets and simultaneously felt the pain in his left shoulder.

Fighting to ignore the pain, he tried to make himself a harder target by trying to swerve the vehicle with only one hand on the steering wheel. He could feel the blood soaking through his shirt but, if he didn't stop his pursuers quickly, the wound would be the least of his problems.

The Kompaniya vehicle behind was fairly beaten up, with a shattered windshield and panels hanging off the front, and steam was coming from its engine. Despite all that, it was still keeping pace with him.

Will had to think fast. His chances of escape diminished the longer this went on and the more blood he lost.

Looking at the floor of the truck, he managed a smile as he caught sight of the hatch. The Company trucks had initially been fitted with these hatches so that they could dispense tear gas during riots back home. Today he had a better idea. Flipping the hatch open, he could see the road below speeding past. Unsure if it was the loss of blood or staring at the road that was making him dizzy, he switched his focus to the task at hand.

Bullets were still coming through the shattered rear windows, so he crouched as low as he possibly could while maintaining control of his truck.

With one hand on the steering wheel and the pain in his shoulder making it hard to move his left arm, he had to switch to steering with his right elbow. Then, with his right hand, he unhooked a grenade from his belt rig.

Continuing to steer with his right elbow, he managed to hold the grenade in his right hand while removing the pin with his left. He could feel the pressure of the safety arm increasing as he prevented the grenade from going off immediately.

The next phase of the manoeuvre was critical. He passed the grenade to his left hand while slowing down slightly to reduce the distance between the two vehicles. With the bullets still coming, over the shorter distance it wouldn't be long before one of them connected.

He released the safety arm and counted, "One thousand and one, one thousand and …" Before he got to "two", he rolled the grenade through the hatch below and accelerated away as fast as he could.

The Kompaniya vehicle had almost touched the rear of his truck just before he accelerated. As he sped away, it seemed only a split second before he heard the explosion.

Looking in the mirror, he saw the front of the vehicle behind him lift slightly. Immediately the bullets stopped and his pursuers veered off of the road until the vehicle came to a halt. It had been a risky move as the fuse on any grenade didn't last exactly three seconds. Yet it had paid off. Without going back to check, he could only assume that the fragments had ripped through the soft floor of the Kompaniya vehicle and shredded its occupants.

"What's going on?" Nikki asked over the radio.

"Nothing to worry about. I had some unwelcome admirers, but they've decided not to follow us after all."

"Are you okay?"

"I'm fine. Keep going and I'll meet you at the agreed point." Will lied because he thought his survival chances were better alone.

Pulling over to the side of the road, he struggled with the first aid kit and managed a haphazard patch-up job of his wounds. Not only was the first bullet still in his left shoulder but he had caught a ricochet after it.

At first, he hadn't noticed the second bullet as it was smaller, but it was adding to his blood loss. With only one good arm, it was no easy task, but he eventually managed to stem the flow of blood. It was too dangerous to linger so, with his left arm in an improvised sling, he got back on the road and rushed to catch up with the others.

Their journey from the port seemed to have taken a lot longer than following the same route in the opposite direction had. Eventually, he reached the others, who were parked up a mile or so from the port, and he pulled in behind them.

A large patch of bushes at the edge of the road disguised a deep ditch. Will contemplated that the ditch seemed the ideal home for the car.

He stayed in the driver's seat as Nikki approached from the front.

"What happened to you?" Nikki said with an air of disbelief.

"Stop fussing." Will was trying to maintain a brave face, but his blood-soaked shirt told another story.

"You've been shot – get out and let us give you some first aid."

"I've been shot before and we haven't got time for this. Head round the back of the port and in about twenty minutes, go through the fence," Will told him.

"Do you think you'll last twenty minutes?" Nikki was trying to lighten the mood, but Will looked terrible. "Aren't you coming with us?"

"I prefer the truck to walking. I'm going to take my chances with the main gates. If I don't succeed, at least it'll create a little diversion for you."

"When did you become such a hero?" Nikki asked in disbelief. "You'll never get through the gates!"

"I fancy my chances better in this beast than with the rest of you on foot."

It was evident to Nikki that Will was trying to divert the conversation. If he really thought the vehicle was the best option for getting into the port, he'd take them all with him.

"Come on, let us help you. It's not that far now."

"If I get to the boat, I'll see you there but don't wait for me."

"How will we know if your diversion's worked?"

"You'll hear it. Just be ready to get through the fence," Will replied.

Will stayed with the truck while the rest of the team pushed the car into the ditch and set fire to it. It was important that once Brand's body was discovered, it wasn't immediately identified. Nikki briefed them all on the plan before they headed off on foot. It was becoming darker, providing them with some cover from any prying eyes.

It was true Will had been shot before, but this time it was different. The blood had soaked through his temporary bandages, and he could feel it starting to pool in his lap. Even if he'd wanted to go with the others, he doubted he could get out of his seat. Unsure of how long he had left, he could at least go out on his terms.

Will sat at the side of the road, allowing the rest of the team a head start. He was feeling ever weaker, but he took some comfort in knowing that Brand was dead. However today ended, he had achieved his goal of ensuring Brand's death and, as a bonus, he was the one who'd pulled the trigger.

After around twenty minutes, he pulled back onto the road and slowly drove towards the port.

By now the rest of the team had skirted around the port. While some of them began cutting a hole in the chain-link fence, Nikki called Will on the radio. "Are you still alive?"

"Yes, but driving and operating the radio at the same time is a bit of a challenge. Are you at the fence?"

"We are almost through it."

"Wait for my signal and then rush for the boat," Will said, discarding the handset.

"What's your signal?" Nikki asked but received no reply.

Ahead Will could now see the main gates of the docks. He was still driving slowly, and the sentries reacted straight away. "Here comes the party," Will exclaimed as he accelerated towards the gates.

One of the men raised his rifle and managed to get off a shot as Will crushed him against the gates before they sprang open. Several other guards had jumped for cover, but the gates had damaged the front of Will's truck, which was now stationary and under fire.

Will was incapable of putting up much of a fight. The impact of the gates had opened his wounds further, and the volume of bullets from the guards was increasing as they approached.

He fired off his last magazine in the direction of the approaching men just long enough to make them pause their firepower. Looking around his cab, he saw two cans of gasoline in the back and grabbed the last two grenades on his belt.

With no time to think, he pulled both pins out and

threw one grenade towards the fuel cans and kept hold of the other while releasing the handle.

At the back of the docks, Nikki and the others heard the explosions. "Go now, get through the fence," he shouted.

As they squeezed through the holes in the fence, they were all thinking the same thing. "Please let the boat be there still."

Running to where they had last seen the boat, Nikki was the first to speak. "Where is it? It was here."

"Have they left without us?" Fred asked in desperation.

Nikki still held the radio and flicked to channel sixteen. "Hello Dolphin, hello Dolphin, where are you?" He was working hard to maintain his composure. "It's team one. We're at the rendezvous point." In effect, Nikki was only part of team one but he didn't know if the rest had survived.

"Hello team one, this is Dolphin. Keep walking around the dockside in the opposite direction from the drop-off point."

Abandoning the idea of walking, they gathered the last of their energy to break into a run. Coming around the corner, they saw the boat in the distance, which spurred them on to run even faster.

A plank was being extended from the boat to the docks. For a second, Nikki thought that this could be some elaborate ambush, but by now he was past caring. This was their last chance to leave here alive.

They didn't slow down and began racing up the plank as soon as it touched the docks. Cenk was standing above them, peering down from the boat.

Reaching the top of the plank, Nikki threw his arms around Cenk in relief.

Behind Cenk, Nikki saw Angus. "We didn't know if you'd make it. Is this everyone?" Angus asked.

Nikki took a deep breath before he answered. "I'm not sure about Will. Those explosions were courtesy of him. He said not to wait, and by the sound of those explosions, things are going to get a lot busier around the port very soon."

"Are you sure he's not coming?" Angus pressed him.

"He was wounded when I last saw him. He was trying to hide how seriously he was injured but was doing a bad job of it."

"Okay, pull up the plank. Everyone who doesn't need to be above decks, get down below. Nikki, you and your guys go below and restock with ammunition and anything else you need. We can relax when we're out of the port, but until then we might still have a fight ahead of us."

As everyone tended to their tasks, Angus rushed back to the bridge.

"We've got most of the survivors back, but it looks like we lost Will."

"Doesn't sound like a great loss to me," Hook observed.

"I wouldn't be so quick to judge him. It sounds like his last action was to sacrifice himself so the others could get to the boat."

Hook knew that there was more grey than black-and-white when it came to combat. "If he did that, well maybe he wasn't all bad, but you'll have to excuse me, at the moment, my priority is to try to get us out of here."

While Angus had been talking, Hook had pushed

two levers forwards, and the engines suddenly got a lot noisier. As they pulled away from the docks, they could see trucks moving around the port. He steered the boat between two large tankers and began to weave in and out of the collection of buoys and mooring points. Their boat was small enough that it didn't need a pilot tug to move it in and out of port, but it was still big enough to draw second glances as they headed out.

Scanning the docks through the binoculars, Angus almost forgot to breathe. He could see squads of troops running around and vehicles heading in all directions.

Hook and the other two crew on the deck were feverishly moving dials and pressing buttons. Angus didn't want to distract anyone, but he felt he needed to break the tension. "Who knew it would be this simple?" he said to no one in particular.

Hook gave him a warning look. "We slipped into this port in the dead of night, but we don't know if there are specific protocols for leaving. We've been flicking between the different radio channels since we arrived and believe that we've identified the main communications channel. We still have no idea what to say if we get challenged by water or land."

"I never realised you were so optimistic," Angus countered.

They skirted dangerously close to a large cargo ship, which seemed to be taking all of Hook's concentration and he didn't reply.

The next twenty minutes passed in a blur as Hook used the cover of the larger anchored ships to disguise their departure.

The engine seemed to be the only source of noise on

their boat, as though everyone was holding their breath to avoid giving away their location.

As they passed the last lit buoy, they were suddenly out into the open sea.

Angus and Hook let out a deep breath at almost exactly the same time. If they'd been with everyone else on the boat, they'd have felt the level of tension drop among them at that moment too.

"How long before we launch the message drone?" Angus asked.

"Let's give it another thirty minutes or so. It should be too small to show up on their radar, but I'd rather err on the side of caution."

"We can always wait until tomorrow," Angus suggested.

"We could do, but I'd like to send a message back home ASAP. The enemy could still send something after us so we aren't in the clear yet. At least this way, even if we don't make it home, we've provided a sitrep for Frank and the others."

"If I ever feel depressed or down, remind me not to come to you to raise my spirits," Angus said, smiling.

"Pepper was the optimist, and he doesn't look to have made it." Hook said and regretted it immediately. That was the end of the conversation for a while as they both pondered Pepper's fate.

EPILOGUE – CELEBRATING SUCCESS

8 July 2206

Although the emergency drone had arrived weeks ago, the coded message had been relatively short on information.

Zap had worked with Professor Hawkins to produce the miniature drones, and they were both ecstatic that this prototype had managed to make it all the way home.

Weight was an issue, so the payload was a simple capsule containing a predetermined coded message.

"Mission Success" would mean that Brand was dead and that everyone in both teams was safe and on the way home.

"Mission Failure" would mean that Brand had survived, and the team was trying to escape. This message was the worst-case scenario as once the message had been sent, they were still at risk of capture.

But "Hopeful Return" was the message that they'd received. It meant that Brand was dead. It also indicated that they'd lost some of their people. As a plus, the survivors were trying to make it home.

Now the remaining heroes were returning.

Hook found it hard to believe that he'd managed to keep the boat clear of anyone who might have been chasing them. It seemed destiny now that he was bringing them in to precisely the same berth as they'd departed from months ago.

He'd radioed ahead once they were close to home, giving a welcoming committee time to be quickly assembled.

Frank was waiting at the harbour with Flo, Eric and Debs. After the boat was berthed, he spoke to Hook over the radio. "I've got the medics ready to take off your injured. Are you prepared to receive them?"

The council members had decided that they wanted the masses to know how the heroes had dealt with the threat and to celebrate them.

Over a month after the survivors had returned from their mission, on the eve of the celebrations, the council was meeting to ensure everything was on track.

"It seems like we have got the word out, and everything is prepared for tomorrow. Has there been any chatter about potential trouble, Spider?" Frank asked.

"I've been tapping my sources for weeks. Apart from the usual issue of petty crime in a crowd of this size, there is no talk on the street of any serious threats."

"We've had no spikes in crime. In fact, the patrols have noted bad behaviour has slowed down a bit since we made our announcement," added Debs.

"Everyone likes a bit of good news," said Hubert.

"It doesn't hurt that we identified a threat for them and provided the solution," Karla chipped in.

"This is a great time to remind people of how much better they have it today after all the brutality of the elites," said CT.

"What about threats from outside? Is there any sense of retribution? Have we had any news at all of our missing team members?" Hook still felt guilty for leaving people behind.

Frank addressed this. "Zap's working on our external defences and we've detected nothing yet. We've received only one trade drone since the assault, and there was no mention of the attack in the correspondence from the Kompaniya. Has anyone heard anything from Chang?"

Everyone around the room shook their heads.

"I doubt we'll hear from him until he thinks that things have calmed down. He set us against the Kompaniya with his information about Brand, and now he's probably waiting to see how it plays out," Spider said.

"I'd have thought that the Kompaniya would be glad to see the back of Brand," Hook said.

"Maybe so, but it would be hard for the new leader to keep power if they were perceived as weak," Spider smirked.

"Let's try to focus on the positives instead of worrying about retribution. Give me a rundown on the ceremony," Frank said firmly.

"The main ceremony is due to start at noon," Karla said, having organised most of the ceremony. "Frank, you're going to give a speech honouring the combatants for dealing with the dangers they faced, and the fallen for the sacrifices that they made. After the speeches and the presentations, you will attach stars to a large plaque – one star for each of those who didn't return. The plaque will be attached to a wall in the lobby."

"What about the team members whose fate we don't know?" It was clear to everyone that Frank was referring to Pepper.

Angus, who was attending this meeting because of his integral part in the assault, spoke up. "As much as I'd like to believe that Pepper and Brown evaded capture, we have to face facts. Whether they died fighting, were tortured or are still prisoners, I feel the pain of leaving them behind. We have to move on and honour them as the heroes that they were. Even Will gave himself for the benefit of others."

"I respect that you saw Will's actions first hand, but he has tried to kill some of us in the past," Frank noted.

"You'll remember from the debrief that my initial plan was to capture Brand and use him as a shield. When Will killed him, I was angry and I let him know that. Looking back, it was a fluid situation. If we'd tried to take Brand alive, it would have made the situation even more dangerous for us. Once Will found out that Brand was alive, he made it clear that his only goal was to kill him. After he'd killed him, he did as he was told. In the end, he sacrificed himself so that his teammates could escape. As soldiers, we've all done as we've been ordered in the past. I believe that Will changed, and he was on our side in the end."

"I'll take Angus at his word," said Hook. "If he believes Will deserves to be honoured with the rest, I support that decision. I challenge anyone else in this room to contest that." He looked defiantly around the room for any disagreement.

"It's not just us who need to forgive him. Too many people out there suffered because of Will," Karla pointed out. "He's still viewed as a narcissistic psychopath, and I think people would rather have him fade into the past than celebrate his bravery." As Karla always had her ears to the ground, her words carried a lot of sway in this matter.

"Have you got a better proposal?" Hook asked Karla directly.

"Can I offer a suggestion?" Flo cut in quietly.

"I think you've earned that right after all you've done for the sanctuary. Go ahead," Frank said.

"When you put the plaque on the wall, have named stars but add another one with no name to represent Will, as one who has made a sacrifice but can't be named for some reason."

"As always for someone so young, you show great maturity," Spider said. "I'd like to adjust that idea a little and have no names on any of the stars."

"Are you suggesting that we don't honour the people I lost?" Angus asked.

"No. I'm suggesting we honour them all as heroes. I have people in harm's way who could never be acknowledged if they were lost. They are risking themselves for our intelligence."

"You mean your spies?" CT said with some disdain.

"Hold on, we all know how valuable Spider's sources are. If it weren't for their intelligence, we wouldn't have seized most of the weapons being smuggled throughout the sanctuary, and we could have an active rebellion against us," Frank pointed out. "I'm happy to go with this as long as the majority agree. Hands up all those for."

He looked around the room. After an initial delay, Hook raised his hand, followed by Spider and then everyone else.

"Well, that was easier than I thought," Frank said. "If no one has any objections, I'd also like to suggest that after today anyone else who is honoured on this wall needs to be proposed by at least two council members and agreed by the majority."

Again the proposal was passed unanimously.

To allow all the council members to attend, the meeting had begun late in the day and it was now almost midnight. The thought of the ceremony tomorrow was bringing up all sorts of emotions for Frank.

It was hard to believe that only a few months ago, they'd had a relative peace, which was then broken by the bombings and their counterattack. He thought of the way that they'd fought back and how they'd succeeded in taking out Brand against all the odds. Most of all, he thought about how much he missed his friend Pepper.

"You all have the programme in front of you for tomorrow, so may I suggest that everyone goes home and gets some rest. It's going to be a big day tomorrow. The speakers are due to start early, broadcasting the good news and celebrating how safe we are now. Let's make it a day to remember."

"Don't stay around too late yourself," added Karla. She was used to treating her fighters like children. Even though she was younger than some of the other council members, she was often viewed as their mother figure.

"There being no further business, let's get out of here." Frank didn't need to tell them twice; the people in the room dispersed like a group of cars racing in every direction. Eric escorted Flo away.

Eventually, only Debs and Frank remained. Frank could see that Debs was a bit low.

"Are you okay?" he asked.

"I just wish he'd come back."

"I know, but the big lump is a survivor. I haven't given up hope yet."

"I haven't either," Debs said as she mustered a smile before walking out of the room.

Frank considered following her, but he knew that they both needed to grieve in their own way. He headed up to his apartment with his security detail, looking forward to a nightcap to help dull his feelings before bed.

SANCTUARY SERIES BOOK THREE PREVIEW

09 July 2206 – Attack of The Drones

Zap stood nervously in the control room of the government buildings, monitoring the screens on the walls. The screens showing the sky around the sanctuary had been installed as part of his new security plans, mirroring the ones installed at the drone farm. One large screen showed an overview of the entire sanctuary while three smaller screens allowed him to zoom in on specific areas.

Outside, the final preparations for the ceremony were underway, with the crowds quickly filling the square. Zap had been working on a response for any potential attack from the sky.

On the large screen, he noticed a large dot heading inland that suddenly split into three smaller dots on separate trajectories. The other system at the drone farm had been set up to monitor the incoming trade and communication drones from the other sanctuaries.

These drones tended not to keep to a specific timetable as their limited fuel supplies relied on good weather.

Zap had been concerned about the risk of retribution after they had taken out Brand, so he had proposed setting up this control room to provide real-time monitoring for Frank and the other council members.

When he'd spotted the first dot, he was unsure if this was a standard delivery or something more ominous. Finding it had turned into three dots had initially caught him off balance, but he had quickly determined that three drones at once was not a good sign.

A drone attack had been one option that he'd prepared for but planning for something was totally different from having to execute it. Ironically, today the leaders were planning to tell the masses about how they'd taken out the perpetrator of the attack on their capital and how this would make everyone safer.

He immediately picked up the phone and called the drone farm.

Lee answered the phone on the second ring. "Hello."

"Lee, this is Zap. Are you seeing what I'm seeing on the monitors?"

"I'm seeing three unidentified objects heading this way if that's what you mean? Do you think they're delivery drones?"

"We won't know until they get here and that will be too late. We have to assume that those incoming dots are hostile. They're heading on different trajectories so only one would reach the usual drop-off point anyway. Prep the countermeasures. I'm off downstairs to tell Frank."

"I'll have them up and ready in ten minutes."

"Make it five. I'll call you back shortly and I want the mini drones ready to fly."

"Understood."

Zap bounded out of the control room and down the stairs to Frank's office. Debs was waiting outside.

"I've got to speak to Frank."

The security guards at the door knew Zap but still felt uneasy letting him in alone.

"He's busy prepping his speech."

"This can't wait!"

She could see the anguish on Zap's face. "What's wrong?"

"We're under attack. Something is heading towards us in the sky."

Debs didn't need any further persuasion. Throwing the door open, she herded Zap through.

Frank looked up from his desk. Flo, who was sitting in a large comfy armchair, also turned towards them.

With no time to waste on a lengthy explanation, Zap launched straight into the briefing. "We're under attack. I was monitoring the screens upstairs, and I saw one large dot split into three smaller ones. If it had just remained one dot, I'd think it was a delivery drone, but with three dots it looks like this is the drone attack we feared."

"Let's get upstairs. Can we stop them?" Frank asked as he headed for the door.

"Lee is prepping the mini-drones at the farm. I'm hoping that we can take them out, but they've never been tested in a real attack."

Reaching the control room, they all rushed inside.

Looking at the screens, it was clear to Zap that the

dots were closer and their separate trajectories had become more distinctive.

"Where are they heading?" Frank asked.

"If each one continues in the direction it's heading in, one will hit the drone farm and another either the power or gel plants." Zap paused.

"What about the third one?" Frank asked frantically. "Where's that heading?"

"It's heading straight for us here," Zap said quietly.

"Can we get them all?"

"We will try, but we need to take them one at a time. What's your priority?" Zap asked.

Frank quickly began to process this information. The government buildings could always be rebuilt; the drone farm was a key asset, and so were the plants. "Take out the one heading for the drone farm first, then the one heading for the plants and last, the one heading for us."

Frank then looked to Debs, "The square is full of people. We need to get them away,"

"I'll get the word out, I'll tell them all to go home, whatever it takes," Debs said.

"We've just been playing recordings over the speakers telling everyone how safe they are. How's this going to look?" Zap asked.

"It's going to look a lot worse if we allow thousands of people to be killed when we could have stopped it," Frank turned back to Debs. "Go do what you can."

As Debs headed out, Flo took a second to inspect her surroundings. The control room was just an office with a few digital monitors on the walls, a bank of telephones and a few radios. It had been fitted out for functionality rather than luxury. Feeling a little useless, she went and looked out of the window at the crowds below.

Zap had called Lee as soon as they got back into the control room. "I'm going to put you on speakerphone."

"Are we ready to launch?" Frank asked.

"Remember it will be just one target at a time. Do you still want them taken out in the same order?" Zap asked.

"Yes, protect the drone farm first," Frank confirmed.

"Okay Lee, launch Zephyr one and target the one heading for you, then the one for the plants and finally the one heading for us. Let's try to take them all out."

Before Zap had time to speak, Hook walked into the control room. He'd been waiting downstairs for the ceremony to start but, once Debs had briefed him, he'd headed straight up. Before he could say anything, Frank raised his hand to stop him.

"Zephyr one is launched," Lee replied.

On the large monitor, a smaller dot could now be seen heading towards the furthest of the three dots.

Over the speaker, they could hear Lee's muffled voice as he used another phone to instruct the team at the launch pad.

"What's the plan?" Hook finally asked.

"It looks like three drones are heading for critical targets," Zap told him. "Ideally, we are going to take them out over the sea by exploding our small drones next to them. We've packed the small drones with explosives. As long as they get close enough, we stand a good chance."

"A good chance?" Hook questioned.

"They are a bit of a blunt instrument. We've tested them against stationary targets, but with our current technology it's difficult to make them explode at just the right time. Unfortunately here we aren't dealing with stationary objects – they are very fast-moving," Zap said with some anxiety in his voice.

Zap would have preferred something more precise, but he knew that they were lucky to have advanced this much in such a short time. Looking at the screens, he was glad that he had insisted on such long-range capacity, which might just have given them enough advanced warning.

"I don't like that this is our only defence. Is there anything else we can do?" Hook asked.

Frank looked to Zap, who just shook his head. "We could have mounted heavy machine guns all along the coast if we had the resources and manpower, but we didn't know what the threat would be so I did the best I could."

"That wasn't a criticism," Hook added.

"I know, I also wish we had other options."

"Why would they have travelled together?" Frank asked. "You said that there was initially only one dot and then it split. Why would they have come all the way from another sanctuary together?"

"My initial thought was that they might have stuck together for fuel efficiency – the two rear drones would have flown through the thinner air that the front drone moved in its path. That would make sense over a short distance, but for a longer trip, the risk is too great that one of them could hit another and destroy all three. It's more likely that they were all launched relatively close together, and they split up shortly after launch."

"Are you suggesting that they were launched at sea?" Hook asked.

"It seems the most viable option at the moment," Zap answered.

Hook and Frank exchanged glances. Before Frank could give the order, Hook was already voicing their shared concern. "We need to get an attack boat out there right now."

"Send two," Frank said.

"But we've only got three in total," Hook replied.

"I don't care. If something is out there big enough to launch three drones at the same time, dealing with it might take more than one attack boat."

Without a further response, Hook picked up a phone attached to the wall. "Hello, sea command, this is Hook."

"What can we do for you, sir?"

"We've got a potential target. We're not sure, but a large boat may be off the coast launching drones filled with who knows what. Scramble Attack boats one and two." He turned to Zap. "Can you extrapolate a bearing based on the initial direction of the dots?"

"Give me five minutes, and I'll have a rough set of coordinates and a bearing for you."

Hook was still cradling the phone's receiver. "Let me know as soon as the boats are launched and I'll have a target location for them."

"Will do," came the quick reply.

"Oh and get the crew of Attack boat three ready as a backup."

"The third crew are all off duty. Are you sure we need them as well?" a stunned voice checked.

"Yes," Hook shouted into the phone. "Get them recalled now. We don't know what we're up against."

"Of course, sir," stammered his subordinate.

"Call me when the two boats are launched." Hook said, hanging up the phone without waiting for a reply.

By the time Hook had got off the phone, Zap had a printout ready to hand him. "That's my best guess of the direction based on their initial appearance."

"Thanks." Hook was always impressed by the way that Zap seemed to be thinking of several complex things at once. Within a second of handing him the printout, Zap had turned back to monitor the screens.

Zap was usually calm, but his recent work on the defences had put a lot of pressure on him, and Frank could tell he was getting anxious – but so were all of them.

On the screen in front of them, the three incoming dots had maintained their courses. A new smaller dot had appeared, heading on an intercept course for the closest one.

"Isn't that close enough?" Hook asked.

Zap shook his head as he spoke into the phone to the drone farm. "Lee, detonate Zephyr one on my count of three: one, two, three."

All eyes were on the screen. Just when it looked like the smaller dot was about to shoot past the larger one, both of them disappeared off the screen.

"Did we get it?" Frank asked.

"It's not showing on the screen, so it has either been blown to pieces or crashed. Judging by the monitor, I'd say either way it was still over the sea."

"Fantastic," Hook shouted.

"With two more of them still incoming, it's too early to celebrate yet," Frank said.

This cooled Hook's enthusiasm slightly, but he still seemed fired up.

On the screen, two dots were heading inland, but another smaller dot was racing out to meet the one on the left of the screen.

To the three of them in the control room, the dots seemed to be moving in slow motion. Yet the distance between them was getting steadily smaller until, at the last minute, Zap said, "Detonate Zephyr two."

For a second they all held their breath as the smaller dot disappeared. But this time the larger dot continued to be visible.

"What happened?" Hook shouted. "Did we miss it?"

Before anyone could answer, the larger dot changed direction, seemingly no longer moving in a straight line. Then it slowed for a few seconds before it also disappeared.

"Did we get it?" It was Frank's turn to ask.

"I think so," Zap replied. "My best guess is that the explosion didn't destroy this one but damaged it enough that it couldn't stay in the air. I estimate it was only just inland and away from any heavily populated area but we'll have to check that later. We've still got one left, and it's getting closer to us."

Their eyes were now transfixed on the screen as the last dot got closer and closer to their location. The smaller dot was visible but it seemed to be too far away.

"Can't you speed it up?" Frank asked Zap. He was usually calm and unshakeable, but the stakes today were very high.

"It has only got one speed. They are pretty fast, but I can't make it go any faster."

For a few seconds nobody spoke. They could actually hear the drone outside in the distance, and the gap between the dots on the screen still seemed too wide.

"Take it out," Frank shouted.

The dots were almost touching, and Zap waited as long as he dared before shouting into the phone, "Detonate Zephyr three."

This time, the experience was quite different from witnessing dots converge on a screen. At the same split second that the dots disappeared, a loud booming explosion came from outside. The windows in the control room shook, and a couple of them even cracked.

Looking out of the windows, they all remained still for a second as they watched burning debris falling from the sky.

Frank picked up a radio handset. "Debs, what's happening down there?"

It was difficult to hear her over the screaming and moaning in the background, "It's chaos down here," she said. "We managed to get a lot of the people away but not enough. There were so many of them and we couldn't move them all in time." Frank could hear the despair in her voice. He wasn't looking forward to seeing the carnage below. "I just saw an explosion in the sky; somebody just blew something up above us."

"That was our doing," Frank replied. "We tried to take out the enemy drone before it was close enough to do any damage, but we ran out of time and we may just have made things worse."

"We had no choice. We had to do something," Hook said. "It looks like we got two out of three, that's better than none out of three."

"I doubt that will comfort the people who have

suffered today," Frank replied before speaking into the radio again. "Do you need any help down there?"

"We've got troops setting up an outer cordon to stop any more people heading to this location and anyone who doesn't need medical attention is getting evacuated. I've enlisted all the military medics and doctors and some civilian ones too. This is going to be a long day. Do you think more bombs are coming?"

"We think the drones were launched from a ship and we are sending out a welcoming party," Frank said into the radio. "Keep me informed of the progress."

Turning to Hook, he didn't need to say anything.

"If there's a boat out there, I'll find it," Hook said as he reached for the phone on the wall.

ACKNOWLEDGEMENTS

I've thoroughly enjoyed the time I've spent creating the latest installment in the Sanctuary Series. I've written the words, but its publication was only possible with the support of others. I'd like to thank:

My amazing siblings; Pete, Teresa & Trish for always providing positive support.

My Mum and Dad for all of their support in my life.

My fantastic editor Tanya for helping me remove the chaff from the wheat.

My cover designer Sara for once again creating a brilliant cover.

Most of all, I'd like to thank you the reader for taking the time to read my words and allowing my characters to come to life.

ABOUT THE AUTHOR

Ged was raised in Yorkshire, a child of the sixties, an avid reader with a passion for life and learning.

He served for over twenty years as a British Army Royal Engineer, moving to New Zealand after completing his last tour of Iraq in 2004.

Since leaving the military he has embraced entrepreneurship. From trading foreign exchange currencies on international markets, to building Amazon businesses and writing non-fiction. He was able to use his military experience to lead a team rebuilding houses after a major earthquake.

Ged finds inspiration living in the stunning countryside of the South Island of New Zealand, where he enjoys breath-taking views of the Southern Alps.

ALSO BY THE AUTHOR

Fiction

Sanctuary Series - Book One

The Hunger Rebellion: A Dystopian Tale

Non - Fiction

Find the author's full range of non-fiction books under the
name Ged Cusack.